Praise for *A Marriage in Middlebury*

"Nothing makes for a ~~good story~~ ... ~~second~~ ~~chances, misunderstandin~~... ~~ning,~~ and that's exactly what te... Hill experiences in Anita Higm.... ~~lovely~~ new novel, *A Marriage in Middlebury*. When Charlotte's old beau returns to the quaint town, fiancée in tow, you'd think the old sparks would be snuffed out. Think again. Higman has created an ensemble of characters both romantic and quirky, and the greatest pleasure in reading the book is that all of their stories matter."

—Trish Perry, author of *The Perfect Blend* and *Tea for Two*

"An exquisite love story! *Marriage in Middlebury* offers readers the perfect blend of sweet and savory with a variety of humorous twists and intriguing turns throughout. This beautifully written tale touched me in deep places while lifting my spirits every step of the way. Highly recommended!"

—Janice Thompson, author of the Weddings by Bella series

"Anita Higman is an up-and-comer in Christian fiction. Her storytelling has an appealing light touch that blends beautifully with interesting and quirky backgrounds and all the drama good romance should have. In *A Marriage in Middlebury*, you'll almost see the flickering candles, taste the tearoom delicacies, and sway to the rhythmic music that pleasantly transports you along Sam and Charlotte's star-crossed road toward the happy ending Charlotte's been dreaming about her whole life."

—Sandra D. Bricker, award-winning and best-selling author of Laugh-Out-Loud fiction, including the Another Emma Rae Creation series

"What a delightful story! From the first page of *A Marriage in Middlebury*, I cared about the characters, and I felt right at home in this charming setting. I would love to join her heroine, Charlotte, for an afternoon tea and chat about her past and current feelings for Sam. I've been a longtime Anita Higman fan, and this book delivered everything I've come to expect."

—Debby Mayne, author of the Class Reunion series—*Pretty Is as Pretty Does*, *Bless Her Heart*, and *Tickled Pink*

"Delightful characters, a setting that draws you in and holds you in a hug, and the perfect Higman plot all add up to a most satisfying read. I hope this is a series! Novel Rocket and I give it our highest recommendation."

—Ane Mulligan, President, Novel Rocket, www.novelrocket.com

Other books by Anita Higman

Love Finds You in Humble, Texas
A Merry Little Christmas
Winter in Full Bloom

A MARRIAGE IN MIDDLEBURY

Anita Higman

Abingdon Press fiction
a novel approach to faith

Nashville, Tennessee

A Marriage in Middlebury

ISBN-13: 978-1-4267-3387-1

Published by Abingdon Press, P.O. Box 801, Nashville, TN 37202

www.abingdonpress.com

Published in association with the MacGregor Literary Agency.

Library of Congress Cataloging-in-Publication Data

Higman, Anita.
    A marriage in Middlebury / Anita Higman.
    pages cm
    ISBN 978-1-4267-3387-1 (book - pbk. / trade pbk. : alk. paper) 1. Marriage—Fiction.
I. Title.
    PS3558.I374M37 2013
    813'.54—dc23

                                                                2013014478

Printed in the United States of America

1 2 3 4 5 6 7 8 9 10 / 18 17 16 15 14 13

To Betty McDonald—a beloved cousin
who lit up our family and our
world with Christ's love
and who now resides in heaven

Acknowledgments

Much gratitude goes to my editor, Ramona Richards, at Abingdon Press, for her excellent editorial work on this manuscript.

Many thanks go to Sandra Bishop, my agent at MacGregor Literary, for all the time she spends working on my behalf. You are appreciated.

Happy cheers go to my friend, Martha Marks, who offered her help and encouragement.

And a big hurray goes to my beloved husband, Peter Higman, who has been taking care of the dishes for decades so I can go back to my office in the evenings for another round of play with my characters.

Homecoming means coming home
to what is in your heart.
—Author Unknown

1

Charlotte Rose Hill always said that a good tearoom should be a gathering place where customers were like family, troubles melted like butter on hot scones, and homemade was a given. Of course, it was also the place where the local grapevine got its bloom. As well as its blush.

Charlotte yoo-hooed to her cook, "Remember, use a light touch folding those capers into the chicken salad, Lil. Think of them like lovers whose hearts you can't bear to break."

One of the younger waitresses, Eliza, pulled Charlotte to the side and said in a blustery whisper, "Got two problems already. Our jolly old elf, Mr. LaGrange, is hiding by the fireplace again, and he's packing a flask of something that he keeps pouring into his tea. Man, you could fuel a flame with that breath of his."

"Yeah, he's been spiking the tea with schnapps for years."

Eliza's facial muscles, which usually got a workout, went deadpan. "You mean you knew about LaGrange and his drinking?"

"Someday when I find the right words I'll say something to him. Hmm. It's a good thing it's springtime and there's no blaze in the fireplace. Otherwise he might blow himself up. What's the other problem?"

"Oh, it's not a problem, but I saw a guy on the street earlier when I set out the tearoom sign for today's specials."

"Yeah, well that happens a lot in Middlebury. You know, men and women milling around, living their lives."

"Cute. But this guy . . . well, he looks just like Jude Law. Didn't you say one time you had an old sweetheart that looked a lot like him?"

Charlotte leaned against the doorframe to steady herself.

"Wow, you've gone as pale as those daisies on the tables," Eliza said. "You okay?"

"I'm fine." Was it Sam? After all these years, could it be *her* Sam?

"So you think it could be this mystery guy you refuse to talk about? I want details."

Charlotte gave Eliza's cheek a pat. "Thanks for the heads-up."

Eliza tugged on a loose thread on Charlotte's sweater. "That's all the juice you're going to give me? Hey, I'm the one who spotted him."

"And I appreciate it. Really. But we have guests." Charlotte grinned and then made her way over to one of her regulars, a retired teacher named Edith Mosley. "How's that tea?"

Edith's iron gray eyes softened a little. "Hits the spot on a nippy spring morning, but you can't keep giving me free pots of fancy tea. You'll come to ruin if you're not careful."

"Whatever you say." Charlotte let the comment wash over her. Eliza knew the routine. She'd slip the money back into Edith's purse later, since she needed the money for her electric bill. "How's your daughter?"

Edith's fingers tightened around the handle of the china cup like knotted roots.

Charlotte could always tell a person's frame of mind by the way he or she held the teacup.

"Mmm. My daughter's the same . . . fit as a fiddleback and just as poisonous." Edith chuckled.

"Oh?" Charlotte hoped Edith wouldn't rehash the list of her daughter's insufficiencies. She had them memorized.

"My daughter and I strain for love like two asthmatics trying to take in air." Her laughter turned into a rattling cough. "I guess we need one of those refresh buttons. Isn't that what you young people call it? Something we can push so we can wipe away the past. Start over." Edith took a long swig of her tea. "Oh, that apricot ginger tea is good today."

"Thanks," Charlotte said. "We all need a refresh button, Edith." She reached into her apron pocket to feel the river stone, something she'd kept from her past. It was a reminder of the smooth things in life that brought delight and in the hard things—those potentially sanctifying moments that tumbled off the rough edges and turned humans into real people. Poor Edith was being tumbled.

"Go on now. Get." Edith shooed her with both hands. "You've got paying customers to tend to. And don't forget to eat one of those Darcy Scones for me. You're looking thin-ish."

"First time I've ever heard that a size 10 was thin-ish." Charlotte poured the older woman another cup of tea from the little pot. Then she busied herself with chores here and there as her thoughts wandered back to the man Eliza had seen on the street. Could it be Sam and would he stop by the tearoom? Every time the bell jingled on the front door, she jumped and then looked. She would need to keep her wits about her, so she deliberately calmed herself and strolled over to one of the high schoolers who frequented her tearoom. "Hey, Mindy. How's it going?"

Mindy—who was a real drama queen if there ever was one—handed Charlotte a note. Her fingers trembled as if the piece of paper were a newly discovered fragment of the Dead Sea Scrolls. "This guy I like," Mindy said, "named Brenner, well, he's been texting me a lot, but this is an e-mail he sent me today. I want you to tell me if you think Brenner is like, you know, enraptured."

Charlotte unfolded the note and read Brenner's e-mail.

Saw you across a crowded cafeteria yesterday. As your new lab partner, I thought you should hear the truth. Your clothes, well, they look like rejects from a secondhand store. And what's up with your hair? It looks scared like it's seen a slasher movie. You're welcome to thank me for my candidness by bringing me some of your home-made cookies. Brenner.

Charlotte wanted to throttle Brenner. Who did he think he was? "Mindy, why do you care about this guy?" She handed the note back. "It's obvious he's nothing but a royal—"

"But didn't Shakespeare say 'methinks you protest too much'?" Mindy jerked on her jacket zipper, making it ride up and down. "I mean, Brenner is going to so much trouble to be mean, well, maybe he really likes me."

Charlotte sat down across from Mindy. "Look, Brenner doesn't need your attention. He's needs *detention*."

Mindy tugged on her long braid. "That's clever, Char."

"Well, you asked my opinion. Brenner is infantile and rude."

"But he makes me laugh and forget that sometimes life can be like this total chasm of misery. Nobody else can do it. And Brenner does know how to be all that genteel stuff when he wants to be." For a moment, Mindy traded her cocky expression for a more vulnerable one. "You really don't see any covert signals of interest?"

"No, I don't. But listen, someone in the tearoom asked about you the other day."

"Oh, yeah? Who? No. Come on. Please don't tell me it was Raymond 'the sniffer' Kolowsky." Mindy rolled her eyes. "He sniffs everything. He tries to hide it, but he's got some kind of OCD thing about odors."

"Well, I told him I'd pass his greetings on to you."

"Great. Now he'll think he's got some kind of cosmic connection to me, so I'll have this pet following me around everywhere." Mindy tossed the last bite of the strawberry cake in her mouth and said through chews, "Actually, Raymond is worse than a pet. He's kind of a brain-freak. You know, all grey matter and no social skills. He can't stop talking about star clusters and celestial dust."

"Well, that sounds romantic . . . if you looked at it from a certain vantage point."

"Yeah, all the way from the moon."

Charlotte laughed. "But you should keep an open mind. Didn't you say a lot of the guys at school were mimes who just copy what everybody else is doing?"

"Yeah, I said that." Mindy licked her fingers one by one, flicking each one in the air as if she could make them fly. "Best frosting goo ever, Char. It's like sweet pink lava." She wiped her palms off on her raggedy jeans, slipped her shoes back on, and grimaced.

Charlotte rose from the table and looked at Mindy's feet. "Shoes too tight?"

"They're the coolest stilettos ever, and I can't stop wearing them, but they're like smooshing and molding my feet into these angry little gargoyles."

Charlotte chuckled. "Guess it's hard to let go, even when something or someone is pinching the life out of us."

Mindy stroked her peacock-feathered earrings as she stared at her. "I get it. You thirty-something women love coming up with those double entendres."

"Yeah, it's what we old ladies live for." Charlotte gave Mindy's sleeve a tug and then tidied the shelves of stuffed animals that she kept around for the wee ones.

She glanced around her world, and once again, felt a wave of gratitude. The old Riley house really had become a good place to create a tea cottage. It had been marvelous fun decorating each room with murals, depicting all the faraway lands she hoped to visit one day. And just like all the countless times when she played tea growing up, running The Rose Hill Cottage Tearoom was all she imagined it to be. It was a sanctuary for her and for all of Middlebury. She just wished her parents had been alive to see it.

Charlotte smiled, thinking of her various customers. They reminded her of the teacups they drank from—precious finds in spite of an occasional chip or two. She couldn't imagine changing her life, except to have someone to share her joy with. As that thought rolled itself around like a silver tea ball on the counter, she let her fingers rest on the pearl necklace Sam had given her before he left, before their world fell apart.

Some new arrivals caught Charlotte's attention, and then the bell jangled again. When she glanced over to the door, this time the man Eliza had seen was standing in the entry. It was Sam Wilder—her Sam. She would have recognized him anywhere. In that moment the years distilled into pure memory. That Wilder boy—oh, how he had wrapped her in his love, and how he had melted his heart to hers like they were two chocolates left out in a warm sun. It was so long ago, and yet it felt as if no time had passed.

Charlotte tightened her fingers around her necklace—enough to burst the strand apart. Pearls spilled from her neck and onto the wooden floor. A mania of bouncing beads ensued, and several of the children made a game of chasing after the runaway pearls.

Sam glanced around at the children, but he seemed to be searching for something—someone. Her. When he found her face, he lit up like a sunburst.

"Hi, Charlotte. It's been a long time." Sam started to pick up some of the beads along with the children.

"Yes, it has. Much too long." Charlotte chuckled. "Apparently, I've come undone." She scooped up the last two pearls.

"I see that." One of the kids filled Sam's palm with the beads. He ruffled the boy's hair. "Thanks." He took a few steps over to Charlotte and gingerly poured the pearls into her cupped hands. "I hear your tearoom is becoming quite the place to be in Middlebury."

"That was my intention. I want people to feel good here . . . like a second home."

Sam stuffed his hands into the pockets of his jacket. "I guess I've waited a long time to ask you this."

"Ask me . . . what?" Goodness. Had she forgotten how to breathe?

"Got tea?"

2

*T*ea? Oh. I do, of course. Your favorite." Charlotte glanced away, embarrassed that she had thought he might have meant more than tea. She wished she'd had time to color the gray out of that mousey blonde hair of hers. Or put something else on besides her casual clothes. Or at least freshen her makeup? Too late. She poured the pearls into her pocket and gave him her best welcoming smile, one she hoped would compensate for the deficiencies in an older face and figure.

"It's good to be back in Middlebury," he said. "Good to be *here* too."

Oh, my. Sam Wilder. There he was, standing before her and heaven, dressed in jeans and tweed and looking like the Sam she'd always loved. Of course, at thirty-seven, he was seasoned: a bit beefier around the middle; a sprinkling of wrinkles here and there, and yet his eyes were still as blue, and he was just as striking as ever—in an earthy kind of way. The intensity in his expression, though, looked new. The boyish twinkle was replaced by an assessing tilt of his head. "I'm so glad to see you, Sam."

He pulled her into a hug. "I hated living in the city. Too much hurry and noise and fumes. I missed everything about this town."

"You did?" Sam's embrace pulled a thousand tiny strings, and they were all attached to her heart. Oh, if they could only go back in time. If only she'd had more courage in her youth, perhaps things would have worked out differently. By now, they would have had a couple of children together; they would have been a family.

If only.

"You smell like mint leaves." Sam let her go without ceremony, but as he moved away there was mist in his eyes. "I hear you blend your own teas."

"Yes. Just like I did in high school. The mint comes from my herb garden out back." Charlotte clasped her hands together to keep them from flailing around. "Would you like some tea? I know your favorite was always China white with a sprinkling of rose petals."

Sam chuckled. "Guess we'd better not let that news out on any social media sites."

Charlotte grinned and touched her cheek, the warm spot where his jacket had tickled her skin.

"By the way, that was the tea I loved back then, but I guess my tastes have changed over the years. I love a different kind of tea now."

"Oh? You do?" Why did that tiny confession sound so forlorn? "What is it?"

"Sweet tea . . . lots of ice." Sam gazed at her. "You know, except for the shorter hair, you seem just the same to me, Lotty. Even the way you rest your hand over your cheek."

Sam had been the only one to call her by that endearment. Lotty. How she had missed it.

"This is an incredible place." His hand lighted across the antique table and the framed needlepoint design. "It's so you. Homey. Welcoming. Like those cinnamon rolls you used to bake me."

Charlotte fingered the pearls that tumbled around in her apron pocket. Someday she'd have her necklace mended. Someday. "It means a lot to me to hear you say that."

"I wished I'd stopped by through the years," he said, "but as I'm sure you remember, my dad and I weren't close, so I've never really come home much. I just thought it was easier if I—"

"Sam, I understand. There's no need to explain."

Sam looked toward the front door.

Was he expecting to meet someone? The customers munched and chatted, but some of them stole glances at him.

Sam shifted his weight from one foot to another. "I guess you heard about my father."

"Yes. I'm so sorry." She reached out to his hand but didn't touch him. "Is his heart any better?"

"I'm afraid not. Nelly called me and told me I'd better come home to see him." Sam stroked his chin. "I want to talk to you about that but first there's something else I need to tell you."

The bell on the front door rang and Sam looked back again. "I have someone I want you to meet."

"Meet?" While Sam was occupied looking toward the doorway, Charlotte fluffed her short bob, but then feeling silly, she scooped her hair behind her ears.

Sam gestured behind him, motioning for a woman to join him. "Audrey?"

A petite, young woman with bouncy chestnut hair, walked through the tearoom and over to her. "It's good to finally meet you." The woman stuck out her hand. "I'm Audrey Anderson."

Charlotte gave Audrey's hand a friendly shake. She seemed pleasant enough, and with her amethyst-colored suit and her violet eyes, she looked as pretty as wisteria blossoms in full bloom. It was only natural for Sam to have a girlfriend. Even a pretty one.

Sam patted Audrey's hand. "Charlotte, what I've wanted to tell you is . . . Audrey is my, well, she's my fiancée."

Forks clanked, and some of the customers stopped eating. Edith may have coughed. Curiosity was a palatable thing in Middlebury—as potent and heady as her black current tea. But for Charlotte, this was one curiosity that she wished would not have come to visit. "What a surprise. You're getting married." Charlotte took a step back, wondering if he noticed the flush on her face. "Congratulations. You should both stay for lunch. It'll be on the house. To celebrate." Her beloved Sam was engaged. There would be no going back now.

Sam's fiancée wiggled her engagement ring in front of Charlotte. The diamond, large and domelike, could have outshined the Enchanted Rock of Texas.

Charlotte remembered to breathe. "Your ring is lovely."

Audrey circled her arm though Sam's. "That's sweet of you to offer us lunch to celebrate. He said you were like this, you know."

"Like what?" Charlotte drew up her brows, wanting desperately to understand. And wanting desperately to crawl under a table.

"Sam said you were kind and generous to everyone you meet." Audrey smiled, but there was a flash of some other emotion too vague to recognize. "I hope we can be close. You and me."

Charlotte sputtered unintelligibly.

"I don't have many friends in the city," she said. "And living way out here, well, I'm bound to get lonely."

You'll never be lonely with Sam by your side. Charlotte remembered the stone in her pocket and panicked, thinking that God might ask her to befriend Audrey. It would certainly be one of the hard things in life, one of those sanctifying things God might use to make His imprint on her clearer and brighter. If it were up for a vote, though, she would still decline such a generous opportunity from the Divine. Charlotte recovered her voice. "I never miss an opportunity to have a friend. But for now, let me seat you both, and I'll get you some menus."

Audrey rubbed her arms. "It's kind of chilly out there for spring."

Sam slipped his jacket off and set it around her shoulders.

"I'll put you where it's extra warm." Charlotte seated Sam and his fiancée in the coziest spot and handed them some luncheon menus.

Audrey whipped out an iPhone from her Prada bag. "You know, Sam has been raving about your cooking. He calls you Julia Child with Southern roots."

Charlotte smiled but didn't dare look at Sam.

"Sooo, would you cater the reception for our wedding? It'll be in June." Audrey held up her iPhone as if she were already keying in some information.

Charlotte tried to smile, but she feared it came off lame. Never had she been so lacking in words, and never had the stone in her pocket felt so heavy.

3

If life were a hotel, Charlotte thought this would have been a great time to check out. She sifted through a few reasons to refuse Audrey's request to do her wedding reception, but this time her vocal cords refused to *engage*. Apparently, though, Sam hadn't had a problem using that word in his vocabulary *or* his life—since he was fully *engaged*! "I don't have anything booked for June," Charlotte heard her mouth utter against all good horse sense. "I'll do the food for your wedding."

Audrey popped up from her seat and wrapped her arms around her. "Thanks, Charlotte. Now I know it'll be wonderful."

Charlotte patted Audrey's back as if she were burping a baby. Her scent was elegant and expensive. Guess she lived a Chanel kind of life.

Over Audrey's shoulder, Sam smiled and mouthed the word, "Thanks." But he suddenly looked itchy rather than delighted. It reminded her of an incident in the twelfth grade when they'd traipsed through a creek full of deep grass to go fishing. Later he'd broken out with the worst case of poison ivy the doctor had ever seen. And now, minus the calamine lotion, Sam squirmed just as he had back then. Perhaps he'd realized that Audrey's request was preposterously thorny and problematic and quite a few other flamboyant adjectives come to think of it.

"Now," Audrey whispered in her ear, "We've got another favor to ask of you."

Charlotte swallowed a sigh. Another favor? What was it now? They probably wanted her to bear their children for them too. *God help me.* She was a much finer Christian woman when she wasn't being emotionally ravaged. Charlotte eased out of Audrey's hug and looked at Sam. "What do you need?"

"It's about my father." Sam set the menu down. "To be honest, Charlotte, he's dying. In fact, I've taken a leave of absence from work. I don't think he has much longer to live. We've been at the house since yesterday. And now, well, he's been asking for *you.*"

Charlotte choked on her saliva.

Audrey patted her on the back.

"Asking for me?" Charlotte gave her head a shake to try to process his news. "But why? I don't understand." She had to be the last person on earth Percy Wilder would ever want to see.

"He never told me why. I guess you two didn't really get along, but the details have always been a mystery to me." Sam laced his fingers together, and his thumbs wrangled with each other as if they were in a skirmish. "My guess is he wants to make peace with the people he's slighted over the years. It's something he needs to do. Something he *should* do. I hope you'll give him one last chance to make things right."

When worded that way, what decent human being could refuse? Charlotte rummaged around in her spirit, hoping for a nugget of courage, but none was found. In the end, she nodded. "Of course, I'll go and see him."

Sam tilted his head, gazing at her with his old affection. "I knew you would. In fact, if it's all right, since Audrey and I ate two hours ago, do you mind if we go now? Can you take a little time off?"

"Right now?" Charlotte slipped her hand into her pocket and squeezed the stone until she could feel her heart pulsing in her fingers.

Audrey grasped her arm. "Sam, look at her. She's gone all pale. Maybe we should suggest another time. I don't think this is—"

"No, it's all right." Charlotte wiped her sweaty palms on her apron. "I have enough staff today. It shouldn't be a problem."

Audrey bobbed on her toes. "Maybe we could chat about the wedding plans as we drive you over."

Charlotte smiled. After giving Eliza and the rest of the staff instructions, she buttoned up her sweater and headed out with Audrey and Sam toward the Wilder house. The drive was wearisome, watching Audrey fawn all over Sam as if he were a little boy who'd just fallen down and scraped his knee, and it became equally mind-numbing listening to Audrey chatter on about the upcoming wedding. Somehow she survived the trip, though, and soon they were parked in front of the Wilder house. It was more of a stone monstrosity than a home, but it rested on two hundred acres of the loveliest property she'd ever seen. Hard to believe, though, except for the hired help, Mr. Wilder was the only person living there.

As they walked the path up to the front door, their shoes chewed their way across the crushed granite—Sam's loafers, Audrey's knee-high boots, and Charlotte's China doll shoes—all of them together creating some kind of erratic beat.

Charlotte hadn't been on the Wilder estate in almost two decades, and she'd only seen the older man a few times over the years. She'd gotten glimpses of him at the local cemetery where he stopped to feed the birds. He'd never really acknowledged her existence during those years, let alone had a friendly conversation with her. To be summoned to his deathbed was no less than a shock. But Charlotte was the last one to discount God's interference into the affairs of men.

Sam pulled out a key from his pocket and slipped it into the lock. He looked back at them both, but Charlotte wasn't sure why. Perhaps he was giving her one last chance to run.

A plane flew overhead, taking out the sun as if the earth's bulb had lost power for a second. It was a good thing Charlotte didn't believe in omens.

Sam turned the key and let the three of them in through one of the heavy oak doors. Charlotte glanced around in the dimly lit entry hall. The house was just how she'd remembered it. Dark. Dusty. And foreboding. Mr. Wilder had not filled his home with elegant furnishings as would most people with his wealth; instead he had spent his fortune on relics. If memory served her, the house possessed artifacts from the Titanic, display tables full of old coins, military pieces, tables and chairs adorned with the horns of animals, mineral collections, and art and antiques from all over the world. In other words, Mr. Wilder's home was a museum.

But rarely was anyone ever invited into his world.

A birdcage filled one corner of the room, and while Audrey held Sam's attention over a statue, Charlotte leaned toward the bars of the cage for a closer look inside. No living bird squawked or fluttered its feathers, but a stuffed parrot sat lopsided on an inner branch. How odd.

When Mrs. Wilder was alive, had she no input in the furnishings and décor? Guess not. Mr. Wilder did tend to control life around him with such a military grip that it would make the government look slack. To say the least, Mr. Wilder was an eccentric man. The only other certainty about Mr. Wilder was that for some reason unknown to Charlotte—he had grown to hate her. She wiped the perspiration off her forehead with the back of her hand.

Audrey coughed, startling Charlotte. The three of them disengaged from their curiosities and without much falderal, they moved as one down a long corridor as if they were about to face a firing squad. Neither the house nor the circumstances seemed conducive to chatter.

Audrey touched an item here or there as they walked along. Perhaps she'd resigned herself to living in the house and was making an effort to find her place among the relics. Somehow Audrey Anderson must have found a fissure in the old man's heart.

Charlotte didn't feel resentment toward Audrey. Well, maybe a little, but the bulk of her emotion was confusion—even after all these years. Usually when two people fell in love in Middlebury, they got married. People were joyous. Good things happened to them. They had a family and carried on with life. *But not for me.* Percy Wilder had destroyed her flight of happiness as easily as the swatting of a fly.

Charlotte squelched the urge to cough. Particles of dust, which were lit by the gas flames along the passageway, swirled in the air. Sam opened a set of doors, which apparently led to Mr. Wilder's bedchamber. Antiseptic odors mixed with a fusty smell prickled her nostrils. Mr. Wilder's bedroom could boast of very little furniture, but what caught her attention was the incessant ticking of clocks, including the large mahogany grandfather's clock. The only wall décor was a framed Confederate flag, which hung on the north wall. A nurse sat in a chair on the other side of Mr. Wilder's four-poster bed, reading a book.

Charlotte recognized the woman—Lucy Loman—a tall woman with a kindhearted air and enough bobbing red curls and freckles to put anyone at ease. Lucy was also the nurse at her doctor's office, and she liked to drop into the tearoom from time to time to order her unique brew.

Lucy closed the book and rose from her chair. "Mr. Wilder's just dozed off." She glanced at Charlotte, a look of perplexity flickering on her brow. There was a lot of that going around. They nodded to each other but didn't say anything.

Charlotte had been avoiding looking at Mr. Wilder, but now she let her gaze drift over to his long, thin frame, which lay deathly still in the bed. He'd been a robust man in his prime, but now after succumbing to age and illness he was no more than a thin leaf of a man, and from the look of his ashen color he would not last beyond the night.

4

*L*ucy stepped out of the room.

Mist clouded Charlotte's sight until she had to blink back the tears. In spite of the past, in spite of everything, compassion flooded her and washed away any remnant of anger. *Lord, I forgive this man for what he did.* She would say whatever it would take to help Mr. Wilder find a peaceful end.

As if the man could read her thoughts, Mr. Wilder's eyes fluttered opened, and he looked straight at Charlotte. He lifted the oxygen mask off his face and in a raspy voice, murmured, "Miss Hill. You've . . . come."

"Yes, sir." Charlotte stepped up next to the bed.

Mr. Wilder paused, trying to catch his breath. "Please . . . let me have a moment of your time . . . alone."

Charlotte would have liked for Sam and Audrey to stay in the room for moral support, but it was not meant to be.

Audrey and Sam backed away, leaving Charlotte standing by the bed. "We'll be just outside the room if you need us." Then Sam smiled at Charlotte and mouthed the words, "Thank you." That was twice he'd thanked her for something she'd done, and yet in both cases she felt no bravery. Mostly fear. Probably a clear sign of a weedy moral fiber on her part.

When they were alone, Mr. Wilder whispered, "Come closer."

Charlotte sat down in the chair next to the bed. She could see Mr. Wilder fully now and the ravages left by time and sickness—the blue serpentine veins on his hands, his once clear eyes, now watery and deeply set, but most of all, one couldn't miss the way torment clung to the man like a foul spirit. The look of Mr. Wilder was how she always imagined King David at the end of his reign when he was dying in his imperial bed. Only Mr. Wilder had never known God.

He lifted his head briefly and then fell back. "Are we alone?"

"Yes, sir."

"I didn't think . . . you'd come."

"I was sorry to hear you've been ill."

"You haven't . . . been sorry." Mr. Wilder took a few more shallow breaths. "You are glad . . . for my death."

"Sir, I don't mean to contradict you, but I'm sorry for everything." Charlotte let go of the piece of dress she twisted in her fingers. "If I did anything to offend you, I'm truly sorry. Please forgive me." She wasn't sure why she needed to apologize, but maybe it would ease the way for Mr. Wilder to say whatever he'd hoped to say.

"I did not bring you here . . . for apologies." The man gasped for breath, and appeared even paler if that were possible.

"I didn't mean to upset you." The grandfather clock chimed the hour, making her startle. How could Mr. Wilder stand so many noisy clocks? It only served as a reminder that the march of time reigned over each of them as an enemy, relentless and unmerciful. "Sir, do you need your oxygen?"

"No," he growled.

If Charlotte had hoped the man had softened over the years, she had been mistaken. His voice could still grip like the jaws of a crocodile, and his eyes were just as fearsome. The resemblance between Mr. Wilder and his son in appearance had always been uncanny, but they were so far removed in spirit, it was as if they had never been related.

"You have met Miss Anderson. She is a good match for my son." Mr. Wilder's eyes brightened, and he seemed to rally a bit as he talked about Sam's fiancée.

What could she say? "I hope they will be happy." Why had Mr. Wilder brought her to his home? Was it for one final round of torment? Charlotte desperately wanted to ask him why he'd so vehemently opposed Sam's proposal to her those many years ago, but she was determined not to harass a dying man.

"I brought you here because I owe you . . . an explanation." Mr. Wilder closed his eyes for a moment and then opened them again. "Now that my son is marrying a woman who is worthy of our family's heritage, I feel I can be generous and tell you why you were not acceptable. Why you could never marry my son."

At last. The truth. "Sir?" If he was willing to tell her some truth with the last of his energy then she was more than willing to listen.

"I will . . . tell you a story." Mr. Wilder took in several more wheezing breaths. "I love birds, but I have a phobia of them too. Got the fear put in me as a child and have never been able to shake it off. I would go to the cemetery to watch them. Study them. Enjoy their beauty, but because of fear, I could never go near them. Do you understand?"

"Maybe a little." But what did his love and fear of birds have to do with Sam's proposal?

"I threatened you with the scandal about the affair between your father and my wife to make you leave my son, but what

I never told you was why I did it." Mr. Wilder's fingers, which rested on the bed, crawled toward Charlotte's hand like a pale spider. She resisted the urge to recoil. "I knew of your inferior bloodline. Your dark secret," he hissed. "I knew the defective relative that you harbored in your past."

"What could you mean?"

"Your grandmother, on your father's side, was a half-breed . . . born in America, but she was only half white. Her other half was of the Negro race." He spat out the words as if they were a curse.

"Yes, that's true. I never had the opportunity to meet her before she passed away, but I've never kept it a secret. Why should I? I'm proud of all of my roots, including my grand-parents." Was the man serious? Had her grandmother's background really been the only thing that had kept Mr. Wilder from approving of their marriage?

In seconds Mr. Wilder's face flushed with color, and his eyes glinted with anger.

Charlotte leaned over him. "Sir, do you want me to call Lucy in?"

"Call no one." Without warning, Mr. Wilder snatched Charlotte's hand in his. He clamped down on her fingers like a trap snapping shut on the paw of some poor animal.

"Mr. Wilder, you're hurting me." She rose, trying to struggle free, but the man had a sudden, almost supernatural burst of strength. His muscles quickly gave out, though, until she could slip her hand from his damp fingers. "If you do that again I'll need to call for Sam." Charlotte rubbed her hand, trying to calm the pain. How could she discuss anything with such a man? He was heartless. But surely he had loved once. "Mr. Wilder, I know you must have cared for your wife. Doesn't it help you to see my predicament? What if someone had told you all those decades ago that you wouldn't be allowed to marry the woman you loved?"

"I would have been wounded, but then later I would have thanked the person who had done such a deed on my behalf."

What a strange and fruitless reply, unless he had grown to dislike his wife in some way. But there was no reasoning with the man. She sat back down. "I no longer know what to say."

"I'm dying, but I'm not blind. I know why my son wanted to marry you. You're beautiful. Still are after all these years."

Charlotte wasn't in the mood to be grateful for his compliment, since he was bound to use it against her before the conversation ended.

"And I realize . . . there was only a chance you might produce black offspring . . . but I could not allow you to foul our heritage. Legacy, you see, is all I have left. My own father had a saying, 'Negroes are the help we hire, never the children we sire.' " A sneer consumed Mr. Wilder's face, and then he covered his mouth with the oxygen mask.

"Excuse me for saying this, Mr. Wilder, but your words are offensive and unfair."

With quivering hands he yanked off the mask and glared at her. "Doesn't your Christ preach that the truth will set you free?"

"The truth I can handle, but I will not tolerate bigotry. Nor would Christ. And to use the Lord's words for your sinister purposes only fouls *his* good name." Charlotte rose from her chair again. So, that really was it. All the pain and the mystery and the good-byes were about a grandmother she had never even had the privilege of meeting. Talking about bloodlines the way he did made Charlotte feel like an animal with a blemish on her pedigree. Certainly not a respectable woman who was well-liked in her community. "I forgive you, Mr. Wilder."

They were difficult words to say, but she knew they had to be spoken.

His eyelids drifted shut. For a moment Charlotte thought he'd stopped breathing. Just as she was about to call out for Lucy's help, his chest rose, and with a stark movement, he opened his lids and gasped for air. Then he whispered, "I don't *want* your forgiveness."

"I offer it to you anyway." Charlotte backed away a step, but her gaze could not fully sever from Mr. Wilder's stare. His lids were almost closed, and yet she knew he was watching her, assessing her, just like he did with the birds at the cemetery. "I wish things could have been different. That you could have gotten to know me. Over time, you might have grown to like me, and you could have set these other feelings aside."

"Never."

"Life is short, Mr. Wilder, and eternity is forever. You will face God soon. I beg you to talk things over with the Lord. Ask for his forgiveness . . . as I have had to do."

"The only people who need mercy are those who live a life of regret. I do not need a Savior," he said, "but I'm sure you do."

His face ignited with such fury, it seemed the entire inferno of hatred Mr. Wilder had fueled through his lifetime blazed in his eyes all at once, making them appear otherworldly and frightening, as if Charlotte were staring into the mouth of hell.

"The only thing I require now," he hissed, "is your absence."

5

$\mathcal{M}$r. Wilder's words wrung at Charlotte's heart like an icy hand crushing her spirit, but the greater unhappiness was knowing that she'd used up some of Sam's time—time when he should have been saying good-bye to his father. She walked out into the hallway. For one dreadful moment, Charlotte wondered if Sam or Audrey or Lucy could have overheard the conversation, but surely they'd been too far away for them to decipher it.

They all three stared at her when she approached. It was obvious they wondered about the purpose behind Mr. Wilder's summons, but the matter was too private to share. And it would have been too upsetting for Audrey and Sam to know, considering their impending marriage. When she remained silent, Sam and Audrey went inside the room, leaving Charlotte to stand alone in the hallway with Lucy.

"I think I won't go in for a bit," Lucy said. "I'm sure Sam would like to talk to his father without me always being in the room."

"That's very thoughtful."

"I don't think he has long to live. Perhaps just a day or two at the most, so I don't want to interfere." Lucy pulled a rosebud from the pocket of her nurse's outfit and skimmed it against her cheek. "Did you notice there are no cards or flowers in Mr. Wilder's room?"

"Not really, but now that you mention it . . ."

Lucy gestured toward the other end of the hallway. "It's all been put in the kitchen. Apparently, Mr. Wilder doesn't like flowers. I've never heard of anyone in my life who didn't like flowers." Lucy fidgeted with her collar and then scratched the skin on her inner arm.

"You okay?"

"Yeah, but I think the land around my little cabin is infested with chiggers."

"That's not good."

"Or it could be something else. I don't really want to be here . . . in this house." Lucy looked up at the stuffed moose head just above her. "It's so oppressive. Like being in an ancient crypt or something with the walls closing in on you."

"I know what you mean."

"I never would have agreed to come, but lately I've been taking on some in-home nursing jobs for the extra money." Lucy picked at the tassel on the bookmark, letting the bits of fluff drift to the floor. "But actually, I'm thinking of quitting nursing altogether."

Charlotte had wandered off in her thoughts for a second, but she snapped back when she heard the word *quitting*. "But why? You're good at it."

"For the most part, people think I'm a good nurse. That I've found my mission in life, but it's a lie. I never found my calling, Charlotte. Not like you did. You knew exactly what you wanted, and you went after it."

Well, she hadn't gotten all she'd wanted out of life, but it wasn't the time nor the place to speak of her disappointments. "You've helped and comforted lots of people in this town."

"Not really." Lucy smoothed some of her wild curls back into her hairclip, but they came right back to frame her face. "I had such romantic notions about the medical profession when I went to nursing school. I was going to be this great healer like Florence Nightingale. But after all these years I've rarely known that feeling. Too many times patients don't get well, no matter how much medicine they take. Mostly we just manage their pain and symptoms. We give them drugs, but with all the side effects, we're forced to give them more pills. You can only take so much failure before it gets to you. At least I can't. I get weepy all the time." Lucy dropped the rose in her pocket and pulled out a tissue.

"I've never heard anyone talk like that in your line of work. It probably means you have a lot of empathy. Maybe your industry needs fewer pills and more compassion."

"Yes, that's true, but it's slowly killing me. And no guy wants to date me while I'm like this. Guys like Miss Congeniality type girls, and I can't even remember the last time I really smiled or laughed." Lucy fastened her fingers together and then wrenched them back and forth as if they couldn't be undone. "I've never told another living soul about any of this, especially not my parents, but I felt I could tell you."

Charlotte drew Lucy into a hug. "I'm so sorry."

When she released her, Lucy said, "My dad sacrificed a lot for me to go to nursing school. I didn't feel right telling him I was thinking about walking away from it all. He'd be devastated." Lucy chewed on her fingernails.

"Perhaps that's true, but the reason your father sacrificed for you was because he loves you. I'm certain your career doesn't mean as much to your father as your happiness. You should talk to him."

"I suppose I should. But it'll be the hardest thing I've ever done."

"Is there anything I can do?"

"You already have . . . just by listening." Lucy rested against the wall with her palms tucked in behind her. "People aren't good at that anymore. Too many texts and not enough listening."

"You're always welcome to stop by the tearoom. I'll fix you your favorite . . . raspberry sage. And the next pot will be on the house."

"Thanks. I'll take you up on that."

"If you don't love nursing after all, what do you think you'd like to do?"

"Well, remember all those pies we baked in home economics class?"

"Unfortunately, I do. For some reason my crusts came out as tender and flaky as beef jerky."

"Maybe at the beginning of class, but toward the end, we were watching you like you were some kind of cooking show celebrity. All you lacked were the chef's apron and the attitude."

Charlotte chuckled.

"It's true. Anyway, I loved that class. So much so, I'd always wished I'd opened a café in Middlebury. But honesty, you're so good at it, I would be afraid to compete with you."

"But we wouldn't be in competition. Middlebury has been going through a growth spurt lately, with all those people wanting to retire out here. There's plenty of need for another café or two."

"Well, I'll think about it." Lucy looked up and down the hallway and lowered her voice. "You know, there's something about taking care of Mr. Wilder. Well, he's made me want to tell somebody about how I really feel about my career before I'm too old to change. Mr. Wilder has lived such a sad, pathetic life. I don't want to end up like him."

"You're nothing like Mr. Wilder, I assure you."

"Thanks." Lucy bounced against the wall on her hands. "But I'd kill for a smoke about now. If I can make it just five more minutes. That's sixty seconds times five . . . only three hundred seconds. I play these silly games to encourage myself to quit." Lucy looked toward the bedroom door. "Say, tell me if I'm out of line for asking this, but doesn't being here make you uncomfortable? You know, seeing Sam with someone else? I know a long time ago you two were sweethearts."

"I don't mind you asking." Charlotte leaned against the wall next to Lucy and kept an eye on the bedroom doorway in case Sam or Audrey should appear. "I was surprised when Sam came home with a fiancée, but the more I think about it, why wouldn't he? What we had was a long time ago. It's good that he should marry and start a family. I know he loves children. We used to talk about it all the time." She glanced up at the moose head, feeling some peculiar camaraderie with the stuffed beast. She dodged any more of the queries by saying, "I was wondering. Does Doctor Terrell have the results yet on my blood tests?"

Lucy rolled her eyes. "Now, Charlotte. I had this sneaky feeling you were going to ask me that, but you know it's unprofessional of me to give you the results early."

"But you'll probably just call me later today when I get home. What's the difference?" Charlotte raised her hand. "Sorry. I know you're just trying to do your job."

"It's all right. I would do the same thing if I were you. I would want to know as soon as possible." Lucy flicked at the nurse's pin on her lapel as if it were a pesky gnat. "But what if you have questions only the doctor can answer?"

"Why would I have questions? Is there something wrong with my blood work?" Charlotte nearly laughed at herself at the paranoid sound of her words.

Lucy let out a moan. "Look, I guess it doesn't really matter if I tell you now. And at this point if I get fired I'll count it a blessing. Your blood work looks good, except . . . "

"Except what?"

"Your hormone levels. The doctor said the reason you're having hot flashes is because you're going through what's called primary ovarian insufficiency."

"*That* doesn't sound reassuring." Charlotte tried not to over-react, but her mouth went as dry as dust. Maybe paranoia was appropriate.

Lucy licked her lips, and Charlotte knew she was debating whether to say any more. But now without more information she felt like a fish dangling on the end of a pole, waiting for the fisherman to decide if she were a throwback or lunch.

"Well, I've also heard doctors call it premature menopause."

"But that's impossible. I'm only thirty-seven." Charlotte lowered her voice.

"It can happen. I've seen it a couple of other times over the years. That's why I hate nursing. It's almost always bad news."

"You're right. It is bad news. But how did this happen?" Charlotte clasped her arms around her waist, wishing it were a real hug.

"I knew you'd have questions that only the doctor could answer." Lucy pulled a packet of gum from her pocket and offered Charlotte a piece.

"No thanks. Look, I'm sorry to pressure you, but what do the books say about it? Surely you can talk to me as a friend. Otherwise, I'll just scrounge around online when I get home and get such a hodgepodge of information that it'll keep me awake every night until my appointment." Charlotte gave Lucy her most convincing smile.

"Doctors might give you a list of reasons, but they just don't know why." Lucy unwrapped a piece of gum and slid it in her mouth.

Charlotte thought back on previous months concerning her periods. They had been erratic, which was why she'd gone to the doctor, but she'd no idea the diagnosis would be so bleak. She grabbed Lucy's arm and then loosened her grip. "But that means I won't be able to have children . . . ever. I'd always wanted at least one or two. I mean what about medicines for it? Or herbs or exercise or something?"

"I've never heard of anything for it." Lucy covered her hand over Charlotte's. "I'm really sorry."

"I'm not sure what to say. It's quite a blow. I feel run over, Lucy. Like I've been the front pin at Ramer's Bowling Alley, and one of those balls has made a perfect strike, right here, against my heart."

Lucy wrapped her arms around Charlotte. "I wish I could do something. I wish I could fix it."

"Thanks, Lucy."

"Now I guess it's my turn to listen." Lucy gave her back a few reassuring pats and released her.

Charlotte pondered what Lucy had told her.

In the meantime Lucy pulled a cigarette out of her pocket and rolled it around in her fingers. She looked as though she wanted to say something more but didn't.

Charlotte appreciated the fact that Lucy gave her some space. She certainly wouldn't cry now, but later when she was alone, in her special place—her broom closet—there, she planned to cry her eyes out. Seemed so strange to think of life when the man in the next room was dying, and yet it was the absence of life that ripped at her spirit. No children of her own. How could she process such horrible news? Oddly, Mr. Wilder assumed she was fertile, and yet now the opposite appeared to be true. The tragedy, of course, was that she would have had children by now if Mr. Wilder had not stopped her from marrying Sam at eighteen. Now, no matter whom she married, there could be no children of her own. "I guess I do have one more question. What if—"

They were interrupted by Audrey's laughter as she and Sam came out of Mr. Wilder's bedroom.

Why would Audrey be laughing?

When Sam and Audrey joined them, Sam said to Lucy, "He's asking for you. I think it's time for his morphine."

"Absolutely." Lucy gave Charlotte a quick, worried glance and then headed into Mr. Wilder's bedroom.

Audrey circled Charlotte's arm. "As gravely ill as Mr. Wilder is, he still remembered my favorite candy. He had a box of it hidden in the nightstand . . . divinity. Can you imagine?"

No, she really couldn't. "That was thoughtful."

"Indeed. But what made me giggle was his idea of a family. I was thinking maybe one child, you know. But Mr. Wilder said he hoped we'd have at least four or five. Can you imagine?"

Charlotte doubted that a dull knife to the heart could have pained her more. "It would be quite a happy brood, I'm sure. I would love to have had several children."

"Well, I hope you get your dream someday," Audrey said to her.

Lord, help me to get through this day.

Sam looked over at Charlotte. She did not turn away. A world of words passed between them then, but every sentence ended with a question mark.

"It's just that I don't know a lot about the care and feeding of children," Audrey chattered on, "and it's such a huge responsibility. An impossible task when you really think about it. What if something goes wrong? It's like those pet owners you see on the evening news who have way too many dogs or cats, and they can't take care of them all. Of course, in that case they are given over to someone else or to the pound."

Sam ran his finger along a tear in the wallpaper. "Why don't we talk about babies later."

"All right." Audrey stared at him for a moment, then she ran her finger along the same rip in the wallpaper. "Would you like some coffee from the kitchen . . . either one of you?"

"Maybe later." Sam gave Audrey's hand a pat.

"No, thank you," Charlotte said.

Sam glanced over at Charlotte again. "I think my father has worn Charlotte out. Are you okay?"

"I'll be fine." Eventually. Charlotte grasped her fingers around her neck and collarbone. "Seeing your father was a shock, though. I'm so sorry, Sam, that he's so ill. This can't be easy to watch."

"It isn't easy. I just wish my father and I could have been close. I wish for a lot of things now," Sam said in a murmur as if he were speaking to the air.

Was there meaning in Sam's words beyond the regrets he had with his father? Even if Sam had meant something more in his words to her—something revealing about his feelings— why would it matter now? As sure as the sun rising in the east, Sam was going to marry Audrey Anderson, and with the full approval of his father. Charlotte shook off the desperate desire to read more into his words. It would do no good, except to prolong the pain.

Audrey rested her head against Sam's shoulder. "This has been a very hard day on all of us. I wish—"

"Sam," Lucy hollered down the hallway at them. "Your father. I'm so sorry." Her chin quivered, and then she broke out into sobs.

6

"Father?" Sam hurried to Lucy's side and looked through the open door into Mr. Wilder's bedroom.

Lucy touched Sam's arm. "He was gone before I could get to you. I knew you'd want to be with him in his last moments. I'm so sorry you missed saying good-bye."

"It's all right. I'd said my good-byes earlier." Sam placed his arm around Lucy, and her weeping eased. "You've been very good to my father, very attentive. Thank you for that."

"You're welcome," Lucy said. "I wish I could have done more."

Audrey wrapped her arms around both Sam and Lucy.

Charlotte moved back into the shadows of the hallway, wishing she was anywhere on earth but in that one spot. She hadn't helped Mr. Wilder make his peace with the Lord, nor had she done anything to lighten Sam's burden. In the end, Mr. Wilder's news helped no one. It would do nothing but fester in her mind, like a wound that could never heal. If only Mr. Wilder had not asked her to come. If only. Once again, she would be living a life of "if onlys."

Charlotte knew she shouldn't feel sorry for herself. A man had just lost his battle with his own heart and had come to a tragic end.

In spite of her warning to keep her emotions under control, a renegade tear fell down her cheek and dripped onto her palm. She closed her hand on the tear. No more, Charlotte.

As the little huddle among Sam and Audrey and Lucy came to an end, Sam said, "Lucy, would you mind calling the Middlebury Funeral Home? I would really appreciate it."

"Yes, of course."

Sam handed Lucy his handkerchief.

"I'll do it right now." Lucy cleaned up her face and pulled a cell phone from her pocket.

Sam turned to Charlotte. "Do you mind if Audrey drives you back to the tearoom? I'm going to stay in my father's room until they come."

"That would be fine. Thank you. I'm so sorry about your father, Sam." Charlotte wanted to say more, but the words would not come.

Sam gave her a weary but warm smile. "Thank you." He disappeared into Mr. Wilder's bedroom, and Audrey gestured to Charlotte that they could go.

Just as they'd made it to the end of the hallway, Lucy caught up with them. She pulled Charlotte to the side. "I want you to have this." She placed her gold nursing pin into Charlotte's palm. "No more. It ends today."

"Are you sure?" Charlotte placed her hand over Lucy's.

"I am."

"Okay, but I'll keep it safe just in case you ever have a change of heart."

Lucy grinned, and it lit up her eyes through the tears. "You're welcome to keep it in a safe place, but I feel lighter already. My smile feels so good . . . fits on me better than I remembered. See you later."

"Bye."

After Lucy had gone back toward Mr. Wilder's room, and she was out of earshot, Audrey asked Charlotte, "What was that all about, between you and the nurse? If you don't mind me asking."

"I don't think Lucy would want me to mention it, otherwise I'd—"

"No problem. I get it." Audrey continued to walk toward the main living area with Charlotte close behind her. "I'm used to living around secrets."

What could she mean?

Audrey skimmed her fingers along some of the artifacts as they made their way toward the front door. "We'll have an estate sale soon."

Charlotte didn't add anything to Audrey's declaration. Mr. Wilder's body had not even been taken to the funeral home, so maybe it seemed a little premature to chat about estate sales.

Audrey swung open both double doors, closed her eyes against the dazzling sunlight, and breathed deeply. They were greeted not only by bright light but the doleful sound of mourning doves. "It's like their funeral song for us." She looked back at Charlotte as if to scrutinize her frame of mind, her level of grief. "You know, the more I got to know Mr. Wilder, the more I realized how dissimilar he was from Sam. Never could a parent and child be more different.

"That couldn't be truer."

Audrey made no more comment on the subject, but instead led Charlotte out of the house and locked the doors of the Wilder mansion behind them. The clunking of the internal parts and the deep rumble of the door going shut suggested closure and finality of every kind. There would be no more going back. No more woolgathering about Sam as her grandmother might have called it. What was in the past would remain there. But, Audrey was right. The doleful sound of mourning doves felt like a funeral song.

7

With some hesitancy Sam approached his father's body. He stood over him, feeling all the usual mysteries of life and death, but he experienced none of the sentiments that came from deep down when someone says good-bye to a person who was beloved. But out of respect for his father, Sam went around the room and one by one he stopped all the clocks. When he approached the grandfather clock, he paused and stared at the inner parts, remembering it was his father's favorite. He opened the glass door, reached inside the cabinet, and brought the swinging pendulum to a halt. It was a simple act, but strangely painful, as if he'd stopped his own heart.

"I wish we could have talked more," Sam said, releasing the thought into the air. Why couldn't they have made a meaningful connection? It seemed the older his father got, the more broken and impossible their relationship became. For the life of him, he couldn't figure out why, except that his father had held to some pretty strange notions. But more than anything, he wished his father had come to know the Lord. Mr. Wilder's choice had always been to embrace any religious idea that suited his needs rather than following the one true God. That was the biggest tragedy in the moment now. Not just for his lifetime but for all eternity.

Sam stared at his father's ashen face. His eyes were closed and his breath was gone, but even in death, lines of worry creased his forehead. Or perhaps he'd spent so much of his life grimacing that his flesh refused to slacken its hold on anger.

He reached out and wrapped his hand over his father's. He'd forgotten what it was like to touch him, even in the smallest way. His father never approved of hugs—too frivolous he'd always said.

"Mr. Wilder?" a voice came from the hallway, startling him.

"I'm sorry, sir. I didn't mean to scare you." Nelly Washington, his father's cook, stood in the doorway looking at him, her eyes wide. "I'll come back later."

"No, that's all right. Come in. And Nelly, when are you going to start calling me Sam? "

Nelly let a tremulous grin cross her face.

"I know my father insisted on these formalities, but as you can see, he's no longer with us. You're welcome to call me Sam."

"All right. I wanted to tell you that the housekeeper went on home earlier today, but I'll be here if you need me."

"I'm glad. Please come in."

"I'm sorry about your daddy."

"Thanks."

Nelly took a few steps inside the room as if she were walking on shards of glass.

"Are you afraid?"

"No, sir ... . Sam. I just know Mr. Wilder wouldn't want me in here. This was the housekeeper's domain. Not the cook's."

"That no longer matters. Will you wait with me until Edward and Jerald come from the funeral home?"

"Okay. I'll stay." Nelly walked toward him and then went to stand on the other side of the bed. She crossed her arms over her ample middle as if it were armor for protection. After a few moments her dark skin glistened with perspiration. They stood in silence for a moment, and then Sam said, "My father didn't treat you well, did he?"

Nelly pursed her lips and said, "My momma always told me it wasn't right to talk ill of the dead, and I happen to agree with her."

"I understand." Sam looked at his father one more time, memorized the moment, even though it wasn't something he wished to remember, and picked up the corner of the bed sheet. "Do you mind lifting the other side?"

"Of course."

Together they raised the sheet and covered the body of his father, the man known to everyone as Mr. Percy Robert Wilder, and a man he'd never really known.

Nelly took a tissue from the belt of her uniform and daubed at her face. "Kind of warm in here."

"Yes." Sam stepped toward the foot of the bed and Nelly followed. "I hope you'll consider staying on here as our cook. I'd give you a very generous raise. I'm sure whatever my father was paying you wasn't nearly enough. I intend to make amends for him."

Nelly worked her finger back and forth on her lips. "Well, are you and Miss Audrey going to live here in this house?"

"You don't like this place either, do you?"

"Not since the day I first set foot in it."

"And that was a long time ago. I know Mary, the housekeeper, is new, but you've been here since . . . "

"Ever since y'all moved to the Middlebury area. Can't recall what made y'all move out here."

"My father said he wanted to get away from the city. Too many people and too much noise. I didn't like the idea at first, but then later I found plenty of reasons to love the area and the town." Sam tightened his grip on the bedpost. "There are a lot of memories."

"I got one for you," Nelly said. "Maybe you don't remember, but one time you saved my life. I'd taken a spill in the old root cellar out back and busted myself up pretty badly. If you hadn't come looking for me, I mighta died down there in that awful place. I'm sure you nearly broke your back trying to haul me up them steps." She chortled. "And you stayed with me in the hospital. Wouldn't leave my side. Not even when your daddy called you and told you to come on back home. Do you remember?"

"I do."

"You were a little bit of a hero to me that day, and I knew then you'd grow up to be a fine man."

"Not like my father, I guess you mean," Sam said.

"Now I didn't say that."

"You didn't have to say it, Nelly."

"I will add this . . . you was always respectful to your father like it commands in the Good Book, but you weren't afraid to stand up to him when it really counted. When it meant watching out for somebody else."

"I'm afraid these years have put too much of a glow on your memory of me," Sam said. "I'm no saint."

"You're right about that. Nobody is . . . 'cept for maybe my momma." Nelly grinned.

"Do you mind if I ask why you stayed so long when I know it must have been very difficult working for my father?"

"Well, it was good honest work, and sometimes in bad times that's hard to come by. I put it in my mind to stay."

"That shows a sign of good character."

"Or a lack of good sense." Nelly raised an eyebrow.

"You won't convince me of it."

She daubed at her forehead again. "I had some friends over the years who kept quitting their jobs over problems with their employers or coworkers and such, and then they'd get into a new job and it'd happen all over again. Lots of reasons to leave. Never enough reasons to stay. My momma always said you could come and go your life away, so I decided that wasn't how I wanted to live. I thought I'd stay with Mr. Wilder even if it meant I could only find one good reason to be here."

Sam grinned. "And do you mind if I ask what that reason was?"

"God hasn't revealed it to me yet, but as soon as he does you'll be the first to know."

"I'd be honored." Sam motioned to the couch against the wall. "Shall we?"

Once they'd settled on the couch, Sam said, "I don't think I'd want to live here. Too much history in this house . . . too many secrets. Not enough attention to faith or family. Audrey and I haven't talked about it yet, but I'd like to buy a different house out here in the country. Maybe a little closer to Middlebury than this one. And I doubt I'll take any of my father's furnishings or artifacts with me."

Sam surveyed the room. Even though his father hadn't cluttered the bedroom with furniture, he did have one of his treasures displayed on the wall. But it certainly wasn't *his* treasure. An idea solidified in Sam's mind. He rose from the couch and lifted an elegantly framed Confederate flag off the wall. He would put the emblem in Nelly's charge now, since for years, she'd had to deal with the not-so-hidden implications of it. Sam offered it to her. "Please take this and do whatever you want with it. I've always loathed the sight of it, since I know the hateful reason my father displayed it."

Her dark eyes assessed him. "Mr . . . I mean, Sam . . . this is just grief talking. You'll regret giving this away someday. It's an expensive heirloom. It's a piece of your daddy."

"Yeah, but it's not a piece I ever want to remember."

Nelly stayed quiet for a while as if working out a debate in her head. Then she smoothed the folds in her black dress. All right." She reached out and accepted the glassed-in flag. "I think I'll hang it over my bed."

Sam grinned. "That's not what I expected you to say. Why would you want it over your bed?"

"As long as this flag was flying in the South, we had little control over our lives. What one man thinks is freedom can be another's man prison. But now, to have this over my bed, well, it'll be a fitting reminder that my new boss stands for a true spirit of liberty. I'd be most pleased to come work for you . . . Sam. No matter where you choose to live."

"That's good news, Nelly, on such a terrible day. And by the way, I wanted to tell you that you'll be receiving a piece of my father's inheritance. I'll make sure of it. As a thank-you. You see, the fact that you stayed all these years, taking care of him the way you did, well, you're a bit of a hero to me too."

Mist swam in Nelly's eyes. "Thanks, Sam. Those words mean more to me than the money." She tipped her head. "But the money is mighty nice too." She chuckled. "Well, I think I hear the doorbell. I best get it and not make the funeral parlor folks wait." Nelly rose from the couch. "I'll have some coffee ready in the kitchen in case they'd like some before they go."

"Thanks."

Nelly scurried toward the bedroom door as if grateful to be leaving the room, but under her arm, she still clutched the framed Confederate flag. Once in the doorway she turned back to face him. "I'm glad you came home to stay, Sam."

"I really appreciate that, Nelly."

On that note, she vanished around the corner.

Nelly had made him feel welcome. The locals who remembered him seemed pleased to see him too, and he was glad to be away from the city, back in Middlebury. But he'd never imagined how hard it would be to watch his father die and how difficult it would be to see his first love again—Charlotte Rose Hill.

God help me. Was he having second thoughts about marrying Audrey? He still cared for Charlotte. There could be no denying it, and yet he cared for Audrey too. He didn't think it sounded right or biblical or fair to anyone. Life, though, had never been just. Sometimes it felt like a jailhouse with only one key—death.

On the other hand, all those many years ago, Charlotte had refused him, plain and simple. She had let him go with no explanation or turning back. But that look in Charlotte's eyes when he saw her in the tearoom just before he announced his engagement—that was not the look of mere friendship.

He rested his head in his hands. His father had died, and the men were coming to take his body away. Even with that disheartening thought he knew the real reason for his grief. "Charlotte."

8

Charlotte plodded down the outside staircase from her apartment above the tearoom and then sat down on the bottom step. After days of little sleep, Mr. Wilder's funeral, the news from her doctor confirming early menopause, and the strain of helping Audrey plan the reception for Sam's wedding, life did not feel as though it was coming softly in the night. It felt more like it was tramping squarely on her face! It felt as though God had erased her from his memory and his promise to watch over her comings and goings.

She placed her head in her hands and even though she wanted to weep, she didn't. There had been enough tears and wrestling with God in her broom closet. She felt exhausted, and her eyes were puffy to prove it. She'd had to apply two slatherings of concealer to cover her swollen eyes and dark circles. Funny, she'd always thought tea could lighten the foulest mood, the bluest heart, but not today. Not this day.

Charlotte glanced around the gardens and the pathways to the other shops and homes. The area was shrouded in patches of heavy mist, which usually gave the cypress trees a fairy-tale look, but today it just seemed dreary. She was in need of a sunbeam—one of those great shafts of light that would unexpectedly burst through the clouds. It was a glimpse of heaven her grandmother had said, letting us, if only for a moment, imagine life beyond our world, believe in grander schemes and not just the piddling struggles of flesh and bone.

Guess she'd have to make do with the fog. She grabbed the railing, heaved herself up off the stairs, and tapped her cheeks. As sure as church bells on Sunday, her customers would be pouring in soon.

Charlotte opened the back door to The Rose Hill Cottage Tearoom and reminded herself why she was here on this earth—to serve. And on most days to serve the little town of Middlebury was more than enough bliss for one day. For one life. She smiled and walked through the door.

Lil greeted her first, "You look ghastly. Like one of those pale vampires all the girls are reading about these days. I think you should go right back to bed."

Thanks, Lil. "I'll be fine." Charlotte peeked around the corner. "Anybody out there yet?"

"We have a sprinkling. Got that new pastor in from Middlebury Chapel sitting up in front. What's his name?"

"Pastor Wally."

"Unfortunate man." Lil stopped her work at the counter. "What was his mother thinking with that name of his?"

"Now, now. His birth name was Wallace, but it sort of digressed into Wally. But I think it has a nice sociable ring to it."

"Are you kidding me?" Lil shook her spoon in the air. "To be trawled through life as a pastor with a name that either sounds like a fish or a child's imaginary friend can't be easy on the ego. I can tell you that."

Charlotte chuckled. "I suppose it does lack a certain authority, but everyone already likes him."

Lil went back to finishing two orders of chicken salad on greens. "Did a woman show up at the pastor's table yet? You know, another blind date? I wonder if it'll be that new librarian, that Boudreaux woman. Bless her heart. She's a nice lady, but she's got enough hair on her upper lip to compete with the pastor's whiskers, and she's tall enough to polish every man's bald spot from here to Magnolia. I hear she sells lawn ornaments on the side. You know, those little rainbow pinwheels. I applaud the entrepreneurial spirit, but that profession is short-lived, since once everybody in town's got a pinwheel, your career goes kaflewy."

Charlotte chuckled to herself and cut through to the original question. "It doesn't look like there are any blind dates for the pastor today." She loved Lil, but sometimes she served up one too many helpings of narrative. "I have to say, Pastor Wally's been a good sport about it."

"Yeah, but I'm telling you, when you coerce a minister into too many blind dates it's like putting sardines in a scone. It might look okay on the outside, but it isn't going to smell right."

Charlotte grinned. "What do you mean?"

"Pastor Wally is a grown man. He can surely choose a woman for himself!" Lil's silvery waves bounced around outside her hairnet as she waved her spoon.

"Maybe you're right."

"Course I'm right." Lil set the heaping plates up on the top counter. She lifted her hand to the bell as if it were a race to get there, and then with one finger, gave it a timorous little ping.

Eliza appeared and snatched up the plates. "I haven't served the pastor his tea yet. It's Earl Grey."

"I'll take care of it," Charlotte said.

"Thanks." Eliza whisked the mounded plates out of the kitchen.

Charlotte stepped into the blending room, dropped a couple of bags of her finest Earl Grey into a small pot of hot water, and settled the lid back on top of the pot. While she slid the cozy over the container to keep it hot as it brewed, she glanced up at the rows and rows of glass canisters full of tea bases as well as flowers and herbs and fruits—ingredients she used to further tweak and tailor teas to fit the various personalities of her long-time customers. Blending teas was one of the most pleasant pieces of her life, but she didn't know Pastor Wally well enough to make him his signature tea. Not yet anyway. Perhaps someday. There was still much more to be discovered about the man.

Charlotte picked up the teapot and headed to the front of the tearoom where the pastor was seated.

Wally smiled. "Hello." He stood to greet her.

How polite. "Hi there." Charlotte set the pot of tea on the table and shook his hand. She was a little taller, but whatever the pastor lacked in height he made up for in friendly animation. She pointed to the pot. "Let that tea steep for a bit."

"Will do. I hear you blend teas to match your customer's personalities. When will I get to taste your 'Wally' creation?"

Charlotte held up her finger. "Ahh, but I haven't known you long enough to figure out what combination of flavors might be right for you."

Wally pulled out the chair next to him. "Well, if you have a moment you're welcome to sit with me and we can do that very thing," he said in his Georgia drawl.

Charlotte smiled. Hmm. Well, she'd walked right into that one. She liked the new pastor but not in the marrying way. Besides, she was seven years older. According to the local talebearers, Pastor Wally was a mere babe of thirty. But since Sam was getting married, moving beyond the Wilder dream would need to happen soon.

"All right. Thanks." Charlotte sat down across from the pastor, thinking of all the times she'd told her customers to keep an open mind about falling in love. Perhaps she should take her own counsel. She was like the hairdresser who never ran a comb through her own hair. "Tell me, what are some of your favorite things?"

Wally perked up at the question. "Well, I like mornings just like this one. Not quite cold with the mist rising on Middlebury Creek. I like reading for pleasure, which I never have enough time for. My favorite novel being, *To Kill a Mockingbird*."

"Mine too." Charlotte surprised herself with her sudden excitement.

"Is it? You have good taste."

"Thanks." It did help that Wally wasn't wearing his clerical collar. That formality might have been a real hindrance if there ever were any amorous inclinations.

"Let's see," he went on to say, "I also like not having so many blind dates."

Charlotte laughed. Maybe Lil was right.

"The people in my congregation mean well. They really do," Wally said, "but I think I can ask a woman out on my own."

"I'm sure you can." Charlotte poured Wally a cup of steeped Earl Grey. Well, so far so good if this had been a real date. She had given dating a try over the years, but she always ended up feeling like Goldilocks—either finding the porridge too hot or too cold. Never just right.

He leaned over the cup and waved the aroma toward his face. "Irresistible."

"It's the bergamot oil in the tea that you're loving," she said quickly. Maybe a little too quickly.

"From Italy?"

"You knew."

Wally grinned. "Speaking of fragrant. I like the whole smell of this town. What is that?"

"It's the eucalyptus trees. We're close enough to the Texas coast that they do fairly well here. The garden club planted some around town, and they suddenly took off."

Pastor Wally blew on his tea and took a sip. "What's something I can know about you? How did you come to own a tearoom like this?"

Charlotte picked up the tiny vase of rosebuds and smelled them. "When I was a kid I played tea party with my mother, well, like thousands of other little girls. But I loved it enough to see it as a profession. And now I'm living the dream." She tore off several wilted rose petals and stuck them in her pocket.

Wally pointed to her pocket. "Zuzu's petals."

Charlotte laughed. "Yes, I guess so."

"But what made you different from the other girls?" Wally asked. "What made you see it as more than just playtime?"

Charlotte cupped her chin in her palm. "No one has ever asked me that. Let's see . . . " She had to admit their chat was going better than expected. Maybe she would give the pastor a chance. Perhaps she'd been like a little boat that was aimlessly at sea. She was moving, but if she didn't put in a little effort rowing, she'd end up forever adrift. "Well . . . during teatime the girls acted differently. You know, pretending to be all grown up, and everything, but there was a light in their eyes too. Like what we were doing brought them joy. Anyway, I came to see it as a happy profession. And I still do."

"Nicely said."

"Thank you, Pastor—"

"Please call me Wally."

"All right . . . Wally." Things were going well enough that she tried to take her mind off the pastor's mustache, which was a new addition to his face. The wooly thing wriggled so much when he talked it was as if a hamster had taken up lodgings on his upper lip. *Charlotte Rose Hill, you'll never get married if you don't try harder!*

The door to the tearoom opened, and Charlotte glanced toward the newcomer. In spite of all the kind and inquisitive and furry distractions at her table, she was thrilled to see the very person who'd been dancing through her thoughts. Sam Wilder.

When Sam linked gazes with Charlotte, his smile flew around the tearoom like a golden finch and fluttered circles around Pastor Wally's head.

Charlotte rose so swiftly she knocked over her chair. "Pastor, have you met Sam Wilder yet?"

9

*T*rying to regain some composure, Charlotte righted her chair and made the introductions.

Pastor Wally said to Sam, "I heard about your father. I'm very sorry."

"Thank you. Appreciate it." Sam smoothed the lapel on his jacket and then said, "Actually, I'm glad to meet up with you for another reason. I'm getting . . . married. And we decided to have the ceremony at Middlebury Chapel."

"Now, wait a minute." Pastor Wally pointed his finger back and forth at both of them. "Who are we talking about? Do you mean you and Charlotte here?"

"No, no," Charlotte blurted out, feeling breathless.

Sam chuckled. "Sorry, Pastor. I should have been clearer. I'm marrying a woman named Audrey Anderson. Would it be all right for us to visit with you sometime today and discuss the ceremony?"

"Let's see. Sometime later today should be all right. Call my secretary at the church, and she'll get you all set up. And sorry if I embarrassed you both just now. Lately, I've become quite good at it. Too bad that's not what I'm trying to get my doctorate in. It'd be a piece of cake."

"Speaking of cake," Charlotte said, her voice still too high-pitched. "Pastor, how about a slice of my homemade strawberry cake . . . on the house."

"That'll require another thirty minutes on the treadmill." Wally rubbed his middle as if it were a pet. "But it's hard to refuse something that would go so well with the Earl Grey. Thank you."

"Let me get it for you." Charlotte turned to Sam. "Would you like me to seat you? Will Audrey be joining you for lunch? I still owe you both a free welcome-home meal."

Sam took her by the elbow and led her to the other side of the tearoom. "Audrey's not here. I'm afraid I'm in some trouble. I forgot her birthday."

"You forgot your fiancée's birthday?" Edith said loudly from behind a decorative screen.

"Yes, Mrs. Mosley," Sam said to Edith through the screen. "I'm sorry to say I did." He grinned and then turned back to Charlotte. "I know the one thing that would win Audrey over is a box of your cinnamon buns. But I'm paying for them."

"No," Charlotte said, "you're not."

"Yes, I am paying for them."

"No, you're not." Charlotte raised her chin. "And the reason you're not paying for them is because I'm not giving them to you."

Sam looked incredulous. "And why not?"

"Because the last thing a bride-to-be wants to eat before her wedding is a box of my cinnamon buns. They're full of sugar and butter. She'll never fit into her gown."

"That's right," Edith chirped through the screen.

"Hmm. That didn't even cross my mind, and I think she already has her dress."

"You mean you don't know?" Charlotte asked.

Panic consumed Sam's expression. "Should I know something like that?"

"Yes." How could Sam not know that? "It's the most important part of a bride-to-be's journey. It's huge. In hiking terms it's like planting the flag on the summit. She'll go with her mother to a zillion bridal shops, and they'll do this—"

"Audrey doesn't have a mom." Sam shuffled his foot against the floor. "Well, not one who's a part of her life."

"Oh? I'm so sorry to hear it."

"Yeah, it's been hard on her . . . to do all this with no mother to help her. I think that was the reason she sort of latched onto you for assistance."

"I see." Guilt took Charlotte by the throat and squeezed.

"Thank you, Charlotte." Sam tugged on her sleeve. "You've saved me. I would have blown it twice with Audrey. But what do you think I should buy her to make up for it?"

"Go two doors down to the flower shop," Edith hollered through the screen.

"Thanks, Mrs. Mosley," Sam said back to her.

"Listen, Charlotte. I know Audrey wanted to get with you concerning the wedding reception. She wanted to know if she could drop by and work out some more of the details—"

Edith Mosley lumbered around the screen and appeared in front of them. Her big-boned frame loomed over them like an angry Shrek just as it did when they sat in her history class. "Sam Wilder, did it ever occur to you, that considering you were both in love at one time, that Charlotte might feel uncomfortable helping you plan your wedding? *And* it might feel awkward for Charlotte to give you advice on how to win your fiancée over after you forgot her birthday?"

Sam flushed red—actually, the color of burgundy rosebuds. He looked at Charlotte while he said to Edith Mosley, "It was

Audrey's idea to have Charlotte help with the wedding, but I shouldn't have agreed to it. I shouldn't even have come today."

"You got that right," Edith said. "What happened to all that sensitivity? You used to be one of the most thoughtful young men I knew. In fact, weren't you the one who freed all the frogs in science class before they could be dissected?"

"Yeah, that was me," Sam said. "But I was also the one who set off a stink bomb in your history class."

"That was you?" Edith's eyebrows shot up.

"Thanks, Edith," Charlotte said. "I can take it from here."

Edith shook her head and then smiled at Sam. "Glad to have you back in Middlebury." Then she moseyed on back to her seat, mumbling to herself.

Charlotte placed her hand on Sam's arm, and then thinking it might be misconstrued as too affectionate, she pulled away. "I admit when Audrey asked me to help with the wedding I was surprised. But I really don't want her left alone to do this wedding. I feel very blessed to have had a mother who loved me, and it sounds like Audrey has never known that joy. I will help her. I will. It'll be okay, Sam." And it would indeed be okay. Charlotte would make sure of it.

10

Sam sat on the steps of Middlebury Chapel and groaned. He couldn't forget Edith's comment. He had to be more swine than man for allowing Audrey to ask Charlotte to do the reception. When he told Audrey that he'd dated Charlotte in high school, he hadn't mentioned the rest—the fact that he'd proposed to her as well. Since Audrey could be a rather skittish person at times, it didn't feel right to cause her any undue stress. On the other hand, he doubted Audrey would have asked Charlotte to participate in the wedding had she known the whole story.

Stopping by the tearoom had been a disaster all the way around, but it had also been an experiment gone bad. Before he walked down the aisle with Audrey he'd wanted to make certain he could put his feelings for Charlotte safely back in the box where he'd kept them for years. But his little test had only made him more confused, and he'd hurt Charlotte in the process.

Sam lowered his head in his hands and didn't move for what seemed like an hour. When he raised his head it felt as heavy as a brick. He looked at his watch. Audrey was late for their meeting with the pastor. Wasn't it always the groom-to-be who was supposed to be late for everything wedding related?

A man in tattered clothes and a scruffy beard came over and without ceremony sat down next to him on the steps. "Hi."

"Greetings." The man took a sip from a bottle wrapped in a brown paper sack. He offered Sam a swig.

"No, thanks."

"Sure."

They both sat there and stared at a cat lumbering by. Finally, Sam asked the man, "Are you here for the pastor?"

"No, but he's a friend of mine. He lets me sit on the steps."

"It's a good view."

"I can see the town's rose garden from here. I can hear Middlebury Creek flowing and the church bells ringing, of course." The man grinned. "The pastor keeps a cot in the back-room of the chapel when I need it, but as often as I can I like to be outdoors. What do you do?"

"I'm a geologist. Well, I used to be. I'm taking some time off right now."

The stranger brightened. "Me too."

"You're a former geologist?"

"No, the other part. I'm nothing right now." The man tried to piece together his torn trousers, but they just fell apart again.

The homeless guy seemed to have all his faculties. Sound mind and body. How had he ended up on the street? "The good reverend doesn't mind you swigging that beverage on the church steps?"

"Wouldn't matter. It's not liquor." He held up his bottle. "It's a special drink from the tea shop over there." The man pointed across the square to The Rose Hill Cottage Tearoom.

Sam was having trouble believing the man. He must have looked pretty skeptical, since he held the bottle under Sam's nose for a whiff.

After Sam inhaled from the bottle, he said, "I don't really know. Maybe lavender?"

"That had to be a lucky guess. But it's lavender mixed with Earl Grey. Charlotte says it's the tea that defines me." He chuckled.

Who was this guy? Semi-homeless and yet he appeared to be well-educated. He didn't seem to be young, and yet he wasn't old. He was covered with so much beard and long hair it was hard to even get a good look at him. "You know, if you're only drinking tea, why do you hide it in a brown paper bag?"

"I've got to keep up appearances, don't I?"

Sam laughed. "That's funny, but maybe a little foolish too."

The man looked him over. "You've never done anything foolish in your life?"

"Yeah." Sam rested his arms around his knees. "Plenty of times."

"When was the last time you did something foolish?"

"This morning." Sam nodded slowly as he remembered Edith's words.

The man took another sip of his tea. "So what did you do . . . if you don't me asking?"

"Well, first, I allowed my fiancée to hire an old sweetheart of mine, Charlotte, to do our wedding reception without really thinking how it might hurt Charlotte's feelings."

"*Do* you still have feelings for her . . . this old flame of yours?"

"I thought I had things under control, but I didn't."

"Can't put controls on love. All those old feelings came back to you like an old song you can't get out of your head?"

"Yeah. The kind of song you don't want to forget." Sam listened to his own words. "I'm in some trouble here." But the worst part was that someone could get hurt. If his own heart got bruised and broken, he could stand it, since he was no stranger to those feelings. But the idea of hurting either Audrey or Charlotte was unthinkable. He clawed his fingers through his hair.

"You know in a novel when the hero is flawed and he keeps ruining everything," the man went on to say, "but somehow you still want to root for him because there's this one thing about him you like? This one redeeming part of him that makes you cheer for him no matter what? Well, do you have that one thing?"

Sam racked his brain, searching for qualities in his character that would give anyone a reason to cheer him on. All his life he'd sought to be a good and honorable man, and yet he didn't feel it. Not now. "No, I guess not."

The man picked up a fallen leaf that had blown in from a nearby rose bush. "Only men of great character can admit failure."

The man stroked the leaf against his palm. "In the tiniest way, leaves are the hero part of the plant. They take in carbon dioxide and light, and they create sugars, which allow the bush or whatever to grow. The whole process is pretty complex. Seems impossible, and yet . . . "

"Well, I have more going for me than a leaf." Sam chuckled. "I hope so anyway."

The man gestured to the chapel behind them. "Well, you've come to the right place for hope."

"But I didn't come for counseling. I'm here because my fiancée wants to talk to the pastor about our upcoming wedding."

The man seemed to study him. "And she's not the woman you love?"

"Of course I love my fiancée." Sam frowned. "But, I mean, do you think a man can love two women at the same time? I'm not sure I've heard of it. Maybe in the movies, but in real life . . ." He wished his father had been the kind of man he could have gone to for guidance. His father had not only been a man of few words, but the few he had never seemed to be all that wise. Or kind.

"I knew a man once who loved two women at the same time."

"Who did you marry?"

The man grinned. "The *friend* ended up marrying the woman he loved the most."

"Maybe my situation is more complicated."

The man released the leaf in the breeze. "It isn't complicated unless you and your fiancée have love confused with something else."

Confused with something else? What could he mean? Maybe it was time to change the subject. "Seems to me, you'd get more handouts without that paper bag."

The man pulled himself up off the steps. "I'm not a panhandler. I do little jobs for everything I eat . . . even for the cot the pastor gives me. He finds all kinds of janitorial and gardening work for me around the chapel."

"I've offended you. I'm sorry."

"No problem." The man gave Sam a friendly smile and sat back down. "When you said your old sweetheart was Charlotte. Did you mean 'the' Charlotte at the tearoom?"

Back to that topic again. "Yes."

The man held out his hands as if he were holding some invisible object. "It's none of my business, but why did you let her go?"

"She let *me* go. And she would never tell me why. But something made her say no."

"Hmm." The man tugged on his long bushy beard. "That's a curious thing for Charlotte to do if she loved you."

"It was strange, since I think Charlotte *did* love me." *And still does.* Sam reproached himself for saying some of his musings out loud.

"You both loved each other, and you didn't fight for her?"

"I let her go." He had thought of it so many times, countless times, wondering what he could have done differently. What he could have said to make her change her mind. But at eighteen, he had felt helpless, fighting an enemy he couldn't see. Charlotte had been so adamant, so final in her answer, that any more verbal battles would have been cruel and selfish on his part. He looked at the man. He wasn't going to ask for any more advice, but he knew his eyes told a different story.

The man stretched his legs out on the steps. "You'll have to decide like my friend did. You'll either have to put the puzzle away for good, or take it down from the shelf, and you and Charlotte can put it together. See what you have."

Sam stiffened, but he wasn't sure if it came from the ever increasing intrusiveness of the man's comments, or that the concrete steps had given him a backache. Of course, there was a third option—that what the man said held too much truth for comfort.

"Yeah, I can see why any number of men in Middlebury would be enamored with Charlotte Rose Hill," the man continued. "With that sweet personality and those enchanting hazel eyes."

Sam bristled at the man's remark. Seemed awfully intimate talk for someone who just loved her tea.

The man seemed to watch him as if gauging his reaction. "Charlotte also gives me little jobs so I don't hungry," he said. "And she brings me up to one of her front tables and sits me there like I'm somebody. Charlotte is a great heroine . . . in this little Middlebury hamlet."

Yes, she is. A great heroine who once shattered his heart like his rock hammer on glass. "By the way, I forgot to introduce myself."

"I'm used to it. Some people don't think I have a name." The man rose. "These steps will kill your back if you sit too long."

"So, I noticed. I'm Sam Wilder."

"Justin Yule."

Sam got up from the steps, reached out to Justin, and gave his hand a healthy shake. "Good to meet you, Justin."

The chapel door burst open and Pastor Wally strode out. "Good afternoon, gentlemen. Are you busy counseling my next client, Mr. Yule? If you keep doing this I'll be out of a job."

Justin grinned. "Just making the road smoother for you."

Pastor Wally chuckled as he shook their hands. "Is your fiancée still coming, Sam?" He glanced at his watch.

"I think so." Sam looked at his phone. "She hasn't texted me saying otherwise. Maybe she's been held up at the spa."

Pastor Wally and Justin looked at Sam but didn't say anything.

A new silver BMW pulled up in the chapel's circle drive—Audrey's car. "That's my fiancée."

"Nice car," Wally said.

Sam stuffed his hands in his pockets. "Early wedding present."

"Nice wedding present," Justin said.

Audrey got out of the car and clippity-clopped toward them in her spiky shoes. She stood in front of the three of them, out of breath said, "Sorry I'm late. The girl at the salon put on too many coats." She blew on her fingernails.

"No problem. I want you to meet my new friends, Pastor Wally Barns and Mr. Justin Yule."

"I think they're dry now." Audrey shook hands with the pastor. "So, you'll be the man marrying us. Important job."

"Indeed." The pastor smiled.

Then Audrey looked at Justin. She seemed surprised at his furry and threadbare appearance, but with little hesitation, she shook his hand.

When Audrey released Justin he backed away and for a moment he stared at his palm.

Sam said to Audrey, "Since Mr. Yule could use a job, and we need some help, I'm going to hire him to take charge of the greenhouse. It's going to need a lot of work."

Something unreadable lit Audrey's face. "That sounds wonderful." She turned her attention to Justin. "That is, if you would like to work on our estate."

"I would enjoy working in a greenhouse." Justin smiled at her.

"Great." Sam was surprised to hear Audrey already including herself as co-owner of the Wilder estate, but he let it go. "Well, since everyone is in agreement, Justin, you may start tomorrow morning if you'd like. The pay will be generous, and there's a comfortable apartment above the garage. All lodging and meals will be included."

"I appreciate the work." Justin's behavior drifted even further into meekness. Or was it just a more quiet confidence? Sam couldn't account for the sudden change in his temperament.

"Well, that worked out well," the pastor said to Justin. "I'm glad you'll have some work that'll be steadier than mine." He gestured toward the chapel door. "Now, if the happy couple is ready, we can go to my study."

Sam opened the door for Audrey. He said good-bye to Justin, but as he turned to go, he noticed tears glistening in the man's eyes. Perhaps all the talk of a wedding made Justin miss his wife—the woman he had loved the most.

11

Sam followed the pastor into the chapel. Audrey was already busy whirling around, waving her scarf, admiring the beauty of the place. "Oh, Sam, it's so quaint and lovely. Stained glass, wooden floors, and such an ornate altar. I would have been so inspired to have worshiped here. You were so fortunate."

Sam had always thought so, but he'd never known the joy of a family united in faith, since it was his mother who'd brought him to this chapel. His father had always stayed home to read science journals. He'd said that science was the true salvation of the masses, since it gave the people hope through understanding.

Audrey stood at the front of the chapel, pretending to hold a bouquet. Her cheeks were dimpled and her eyes were filled with mirth, all veiled in pomp as she marched down the aisle. Halfway, she stopped at Sam's pew, leaned down to him, and tenderly kissed him on the cheek.

Sam returned her affections by brushing a kiss across her forehead.

Pastor Wally walked up to the front of the chapel. "Since I've been here we've had three weddings. They've all been beautiful. Yours will be too, I'm sure." The pastor motioned for them to follow. "Shall we? My study is at the back."

When they all three had gotten situated in Pastor's Wally tiny study, he flipped through a weekly planner on his desk. "Now, when did you want to do your marriage counseling?"

Audrey looked back and forth at them. "But doesn't that come after marriage? You know, don't couples get counseling when they can't get along?"

"It used to be that way, but since the divorce rate is so high, more and more pastors are requiring counseling ahead of time. I'm only asking for one session, but we discuss things like compatibility and—"

"Well, of course, we're compatible, Pastor Wally. Otherwise we wouldn't be here." Audrey's voice dug a little deeper on that last part.

Pastor Wally folded his hands on the desk. "Please don't misunderstand me, Miss Anderson. I'm not setting out to put you and Sam asunder here. It's just that sometimes an outsider can see things, bring things to your attention that might be a help to you both. And marriages usually need all the help and support they can get."

"Okay. I think I understand now." Audrey looked at her iPhone. "Well, can we do it today? You know, to get it over with? How long does it take?"

"It's just a one, two-hour session. I have time right now if you both are able to." Pastor Wally held his pen in midair, waiting to make a mark on his planner.

"Sure." Sam ran his fingers along the arm of the chair. "That would be fine."

"Okay." Audrey looked at her nails again. "But do you mind if I go to the ladies room first? I've got to take off this nail polish. It got all mushed. I just can't stand . . . well . . . mess."

The pastor replied, "Last door to the right."

Audrey scurried out and left the two men alone in the study.

The pastor bounced a Noah's ark paperweight in his palm as if he were weighing his next words. Sam felt certain Pastor Wally would comment on what Audrey said about not being able to handle mess. It wasn't what she'd meant about life, of course, but he was sure it could have been misunderstood.

Pastor Wally cleared his throat and said, "I wondered if you knew very much about Charlotte."

"You mean Charlotte at the tearoom, Charlotte?"

"Yes. I thought I might take her to a movie sometime."

"You mean like on a date?" That had to be the absolute last thing Sam had expected the pastor to say.

"Well, yes, a date." Pastor Wally squirmed in his chair. "I'm not married, but I would like to be someday. And it's easier to fall in love if you're able to ask a woman out on a—"

"Yes, of course. You don't have to explain." And what more could he say? He had no hold on Charlotte. And he did know the answer to the pastor's question. He'd heard Audrey weasel the information out of her in the car. Charlotte wasn't dating anyone, not seriously anyway

The pastor swiveled around and set the paperweight on a shelf with a stack of books. "I just thought since you know her that you might be aware if she was seeing anyone or not. I don't want to get in the way if she's already in a relationship."

"I'd say you're safe to ask." Sam took off his jacket, since the study had gotten stuffy.

"Thanks." The pastor let out a blustering mouthful of air. "I'll take that as good news."

Audrey popped back into the room, waving her unpolished fingernails. "That does feel better." She sat down in her chair next to Sam. "I'm all ready now."

"Good." Pastor Wally rested back in his chair with an old-fashioned clipboard in his lap. "One of the many questions I ask couples is . . . how to you both feel about having children?"

"I love kids," Sam said, "but if for some reason it didn't work out, I would be open to adoption. If a man and woman are committed to each other, I can't see that there is anything they can't work through."

"Well said. I agree." Audrey looked at the pastor and pointed to Sam. "Just what he said."

"Okay, we'll come back to that question at the end. Let's see." The pastor glanced at his clipboard. "How easy or hard is it for you to say, 'I'm sorry'? Most marriages will need those words often."

Audrey spoke up, "Sam is the best at it. He forgot my birthday, and he's begged for my forgiveness."

"And it is genuine." Sam touched her hand. "By the way, there'll be a nice surprise delivered to the guesthouse today."

"That's sweet." Audrey turned to the pastor. "I do admit at first I didn't handle the whole forgetting my birthday thing very well."

"What did you do?" The pastor seemed to be taking notes.

"I cried." Audrey ran her finger in little circles on her dress. "A lot."

The pastor leaned forward. "But don't you think Sam might have gotten distracted since he was dealing with his father's death?"

"Yes, I'm sure that's true." Audrey's chin quivered. "Look, I know what's happening here. I'm having some kind of off day, and I'm going to make a muddle of these questions. Even when I was in school I didn't do well at tests, and so I—"

"Audrey . . . dear." Sam gave her hand a squeeze. "Whatever you say will be fine. It won't be held against you. I promise. This isn't a courtroom." Although, he was troubled to see his fiancée so distraught. It seemed the longer they'd been in Middlebury the more she wasn't herself and the less often he saw her lighter, happier side. Perhaps she didn't like small town life or living outside of town in the country. She'd always been a city girl, so the change must be wearing on her.

"All right." Audrey chewed on her bottom lip. "I'm all right now."

Sam took her hand, brought it to his lips, and gave it a kiss.

"If I've made this seem too much like a test and not enough like you're getting to know each other better, I'm sorry," Pastor Wally said. "These are just things to think about . . . talk about. Why don't we start fresh with a new question? You're doing just fine."

"I know you're just trying to do your job, and I respect that. I'm sure somewhere on your list of questions is something about our backgrounds . . . our history." She took some tissues from her purse and held them to her nose. "I know you'll find out eventually, so maybe this is the best time to tell you something I've been holding back."

"Oh?" Sam leaned forward.

"I told you I grew up in foster care and that the people who adopted me as a teenager no longer stay in touch with me. This you know. But there's another part I never told you about . . . how I came to be in foster care." Audrey picked at the Kleenexes until they were just a mound of pieces.

"You don't have to talk about this now if you don't want to," Sam said. "It's okay."

"That's right," the pastor said. "If this is a private matter you two need to talk about alone I want to honor that."

Audrey uncrossed her legs and latched onto the arms of the chair. "I've neglected to discuss something that's paramount in my life . . . what will become paramount in both our lives. It's time. I should have talked about this before you proposed."

"Okay." Sam gave Audrey his full attention. "I'm ready, whatever it is."

"Well, sometimes you hear about a child who is abandoned. And on rarer occasions, you hear on the evening news about a baby who is thrown into a garbage dumpster, left to die." Audrey looked at Pastor Wally and then at Sam. Her eyelids fluttered against the tears that flowed down her face. "Well, one of those babies was . . . me."

12

The room fell still. Sam could barely take it in. What kind of a monster could do such a thing to a baby? Sam searched for the right words. "How horrible. I had no idea. But what happened? How were you saved?"

"The place . . . the garbage bin, where I'd been thrown," Audrey continued, "sat behind a popular restaurant in Houston. That was in my favor. People came out back to discard things pretty often, or so they told me. It was a cold night, and the doctors say I wouldn't have lasted until the morning, exposed like that. But a young man came out to dump some boxes, and when he threw them in on top of me I let out a piercing cry. He quickly retrieved me from the bin. The restaurant owners called 911, and I was taken to a local hospital. The incident was reported on the news. At the time, I was six months old."

"Six months old? Oh my. So, you weren't a newborn. Do you have any memory of it?" Sam still tried to take it in, the horror of such an incident.

"Sometimes I think I have memories of my mother and of that night, but it's just bits and pieces. I've had nightmares on and off my whole life, though, about being trapped in a dark hole. I always wake up the same way, screaming." Audrey wiped the damp hair from her face. "But lately I've had another kind of dream. There's a haze all around me, so I can't see very well, but I can tell that one by one, everyone who I've ever known or loved is walking away from me. I try to chase after them, but my feet are caught, and I can't move. I cry out to them, but no one cares. They just leave me there to die."

"Audrey, why didn't you tell me any of this?" Sam asked. "You know you can always talk to me about anything."

"Isn't it obvious?" Audrey pinched at the little hearts on her dress. "I'm afraid."

Every protective instinct in Sam awakened. Seeing Audrey so helpless was more than he could bear. Sam slid off his chair, knelt before her, and took her hands into his. "I am so sorry this terrible thing happened to you as a baby. I can't imagine what it must have felt like, knowing that horror about your parents. But please know, this news doesn't make me see you in a negative light at all. It only endears you to me even more. You turned out so well through such impossible circumstances. It makes me so proud of you."

Audrey burst out crying. "Really?"

"Yes, of course."

Audrey wrapped her arms around Sam's neck and held him to her as she wept. Sam didn't let go, but held her tightly until she had cried out the agony of her memory. When she moved him away, Sam handed her his handkerchief and waited for her to continue.

Audrey cleaned her face and blew her nose through quiet sobs.

"That was quite a miracle," the pastor said, "that young man finding you."

"Yes, I'm very grateful to God. But I do admit, to some residual emotions. It's hard not to have some issues when you've been discarded twice. First by my biological parents and then later by my adoptive parents. I have mostly good days now when everything feels normal, but there are other days when my past forces its way into my present, and then life becomes a struggle. On those days, it's like there's this great weight on my spirit, and I can't get out from under it. I've tried to find my place in the world. React the right way, what people expect. But on those bad days I'm trying to understand how to just 'be.' On those days I get fearful that I won't be what people need, and they might want to throw me away all over again." Audrey's breathing quickened. "I'm feeling kind of dizzy."

"You're breathing too fast." Sam took her by the shoulders. "No one can hurt you now. I'm here. All is well. Can you slow your breaths for me? Audrey?"

"Yes?"

"Look at me, dearest." Sam caught her gaze. "I'm not going anywhere. I won't ever leave you."

"You promise?"

"I promise you."

Audrey nodded and then a smile played at the corners of her lips. "Okay."

Sam knew he would do the right thing—the honorable thing. He'd keep his word till his last breath. He would not desert Audrey Anderson. He could never forsake a woman who'd suffered so greatly and one he cared for so dearly.

Outside the study, the sound of footsteps was faint at first, but then it came more urgently. The door burst open, and Justin Yule rushed inside, looking full of words, but none wanting to come out.

"Justin?" Pastor Wally stood. "What is it?"

"The antique shop. There's a fire truck out front, and I saw smoke."

"Which antique shop?"

"Somewhere in Time," Justin said, "the shop next to the tearoom."

"Oh, Sam," Audrey said, "It's right next to Charlotte's place."

"Maybe we can help." Sam rose from the floor and slipped on his jacket.

"Our volunteer fire department is a good one, but it wouldn't hurt to see if they could use some assistance."

"We should reschedule this and go," Audrey said. "Right now."

13

Charlotte stood amidst the crowd that had gathered in front of the antique shop, straining to see over some heads and a cowboy hat. The smell of smoke was unmistakable, and it appeared to drift from the back of the shop.

Pastor Wally, Justin, Sam, and Audrey all rushed up to her. "What's happening?" the pastor asked.

"A fire, but I don't think it's serious," Charlotte said. "I'm worried about Meredith, though. I know she was working today."

"Who's Meredith?" the pastor asked.

"She's the new owner of Somewhere in Time. Just moved from Houston and bought the place. Why don't we stand over there, and we can get a better view." Charlotte led her little assembly to the side of the crowd. At least now she could see the little painted sign that read, Somewhere in Time. "Wait, wait. I see Meredith now. There she is."

A young fireman plodded out of the antique shop with Meredith bobbing along with him. He'd thrown her over his shoulder, and Meredith was struggling against him, trying to get down.

"I love you guys forever because you put out my fire," Meredith said. "But right now I need you to put me down!"

The fireman stopped not far from them, and said, "I'm not going to set you down this time, Ms. Steinberg, until you promise me you're not going back inside."

"But Rapunzel is still in there." Meredith's face glowed a laborious pink as she reached around to the fireman's other shoulder and gave him what looked like a good pinch.

"Oww." The fireman glanced up at Meredith. "What are you doing?"

"It's the Vulcan grip," Meredith replied. "Set me down."

Several people laughed.

The fireman chuckled, leaned forward, and eased Meredith down to the ground until she got firmly planted back on the earth. "There you go. Now stay put."

"Who's Rapunzel," the pastor asked.

"It's her pet cat," Charlotte whispered back.

The fireman said to Meredith, "We're looking for your pet. Okay?" Then he trotted back into the antique shop.

Charlotte stepped over to Meredith, "How d'd the fire start?"

"A taper candle toppled over." Meredith slipped off her smock, revealing a pantsuit that looked like it had gotten caught inside a paint factory explosion. "Yes, now I'll have to use those chubby candles that are all about safety without the panache."

Meredith turned to the pastor. "Well, clear the decks." She pushed on the center of her red-rimmed glasses and gave him a good look.

The pastor twiddled with his mustache as he fixed his eyes on Meredith.

Charlotte hated to gawk at the two of them, but the sheer intensity of their stare could have reignited the fire!

Then with only a breath of a pause, Pastor Wally took several steps toward Meredith and said, "I don't believe we've formally met. I'm Pastor Wallace Barns . . . at your service."

With debutante flare, Meredith reached out her hand to him. "I'm Meredith Alexandria Steinberg. But my friends call me Cricket."

The pastor did not let go of her hand, and Meredith made no attempt to untangle the union.

Maybe they were checking each other for wedding rings. Charlotte wasn't sure. But Edith, who was a part of the crowd of onlookers, must have thought the elongated connection appeared scandalous, since she stepped forward to ogle their joined hands.

"Well then, Cricket it is," Wally said as he lifted her hand to his lips and brushed it with a kiss before he let her go.

Edith inhaled sharply at the sight. Soon the firemen would have to assist Edith with oxygen. Maybe Meredith as well.

Both Pastor Wally and Meredith's faces grew as red as steamed beets when they looked around and saw the whole crowd was staring at them.

Charlotte squelched a grin. Goodness. There was another fire here, and this one looked serious. She glanced at Audrey and Sam. They too were having trouble holding onto their chuckles. But she glanced around to find Justin; unfortunately, he'd already moved on.

"By the way," Pastor Wally went on to say to Meredith, "I just wanted to mention that if the firemen don't find Rapunzel, might I be of assistance?"

"How gallant of you. Yes, you may." Meredith curtseyed.

Charlotte closed her gaping mouth. Guess she'd just discovered one of the pastor's favorite things. Between the curtsies and their medieval-speak, it was easy to see that Meredith and Pastor Wally had been dipped in the hot tar of attraction and their brains had been feathered beyond recognition. But Charlotte also thought the whole scene appeared touching, and maybe she felt just a wee bit envious too. Not because Wally's flicker of interest in her had now been doused, but because she'd only known that kind of attraction once, and nothing even close had ever come again.

Charlotte backed away a few steps to give the couple some breathing room, but continued to watch them, especially Meredith. She was such an exotic for Middlebury—a dark-haired beauty with her olive skin and big onyx eyes. And if that wasn't enough, Meredith had an energy about her that was like a power line eruption, sparks spraying everywhere she went. Pastor Wally seemed enraptured by it all.

"I would love to visit your church on Sunday. Which one is it?" Meredith said to Pastor Wally as she linked arms with Charlotte and pulled her back into the little circle.

He pointed across the street. "Middlebury Chapel."

"Oh, that one by the town square. It's like something from a postcard. So pretty with its white steeple and arched windows. I listen to the bells every day. You bring heaven down to earth when you play them. It must be perfection for weddings . . . the chapel."

"It is. Actually, I was just discussing that with my new friends. Let me introduce you." Wally looked around. "Oh, well, they seem to be busy talking to someone in front of the tearoom. Maybe another time."

"Of course." Meredith touched Wally's sleeve. "I would enjoy meeting any of your friends."

"Cricket." Wally smiled at Meredith. "While we're waiting to go inside to search for your Rapunzel, I'd love for you to tell me a little bit about yourself."

Charlotte grinned for so many reasons she couldn't count them all, but just hearing the pastor call Meredith by such a snuggly name right off was enough to make her smile.

"Well, let's see." Meredith said. "I'll make it easy on you and give you the short version. I'm a widow with no children. I'm a Messianic Jew. My family is as close as too many matzo balls in a teacup. I like Mozart, superheroes, storms with lots of thunder, and Earl Grey . . . extra hot."

Pastor Wally chuckled then—and his laughter rose as merrily as the bells that rang at Middlebury Chapel.

14

*P*erhaps it was the peal of laughter that did the trick, but Rapunzel ran out the front door of the antique shop and up to Meredith's feet. "Ohh, sweetie." She scooped up the cat and held the fluffy white kitty to her heart. "My darling, baby. Mommy's here. Were you frightened in there? I know you were."

Pastor Wally gently ran his hand along the cat's fur. "I don't think I've ever seen a cat like this before, except maybe on *American Pet Lovers.* What breed is she?"

"You watch that show too? How wonderful. Rapunzel is a domestic long-haired cat." Meredith pretended to cover the cat's ears. "But she's a mixed breed. Doesn't matter in the least to me. I love her so." She showered the animal with affection, making little kissy noises along with the cat's purr.

Since the fire was behind them, Charlotte suddenly remembered all the things she had to do, including preparing the new spring menus. Time to go. She excused herself and then glanced over at Audrey and Sam, to say good-bye. But they were both locked, head to head, in a tight discussion. No problem. Charlotte swung open the door to the tearoom and strode inside. She pulled out a tissue from her pocket and daubed at her face. Hmm. Another hot flash to remind her of the doctor's not-so-good news, but there was plenty of work to do besides stewing over what couldn't be changed.

Customers had filtered back into the tearoom from all the excitement and had resumed their eating. Fortunately, her staff was busy taking care of them. She stepped into her office to work on the new menus when the phone rang. She picked up. "Rose Hill Cottage Tearoom. May I help you?"

"Yes, you may," the female caller said. "I'm Dee Hollingsworth, and I'm with Morland Publishing in Austin. Are you Charlotte Hill?"

"Yes, I am." She sat down.

"I'm senior editor here, and we've heard really good things about you and your tearoom."

"I'm always happy to hear that kind of news."

"Actually, one of our editors was there a few weeks ago, and she hasn't stopped talking about it since. The food, the décor, the hand-blended teas. We were wondering if you might be interested in writing a cookbook for us."

Charlotte smiled as she curled the phone cord around her finger. "Yes, it has crossed my mind, but I've never really known where to start."

"Would you be interested if we helped you?"

How would she squeeze the cookbook in around all her other work? But it would be good for business, and it might even bring some publicity to Middlebury, which the local chamber would appreciate. As a side benefit, it would mean a potential distraction from all her recent cares. "Yes, I can do it. I would love to."

"Good deal. Well, it might be helpful to meet you in person. My secretary will call you and set up a time for me to drive down from Austin, and we can discuss the details then. Does this sound agreeable?"

"Sounds great." She and the staff might have to schedule some spring cleaning before Ms. Hollingsworth arrives, but other than that. . . .

"In the meantime you can be thinking about your very best recipes as well as your most popular ones. The ones customers love so much that they'd be angry at you if you took them off the menu. We'll want to use those for our project."

"All right. I can do it." They made a bit more pleasant chatter, and then Dee Hollingsworth from Morland Publishing hung up. Charlotte set the phone down. My, my, my. Life really was a daily surprise. It could be a boulder falling on one's head, or it could be reaching down and finding the perfect polished gem among ten thousand rocks. At first glance this one looked like a gem. She fingered the stone in her pocket. Hopefully this would turn out to be one of the smooth things in life that would bring her delight.

Eliza popped her head around the corner and said, "Obadiah is out here by the backdoor, and he's whimpering, asking for you."

"Obie's whimpering? Why didn't you send him on back?"

"Well, I heard you on the phone, and I know everything has been keeping you from the new menus, so I thought—"

"That's sweet, Eliza, but Obie is like family . . . top priority."

Eliza made a waving gesture outside the room, and the sound of Obie's cowboy boots clomped on the wooden floors until she saw his sad puckery little face. He'd just turned nine years old, but sometimes he seemed thirty-nine when he had the weight of the world on his shoulders—or at least the weight of his home life.

"Hi there. Come on in, Obie." Charlotte closed her laptop and ruffled his sandy-colored hair. His Wild Bill cowlick became even more pronounced, but it was kind of adorable.

"Eliza, why don't you bring us a couple of chicken salad sandwiches."

"You got it." Eliza disappeared around the corner.

Charlotte tugged on Obie's sleeve. "Well, now, what's got you so upset?"

Obie didn't answer but instead crawled under her desk and curled up with his arms folded around his knees. "It's not so dangerous under here. The space trolls can't find me, since their radar can't go through metal." He looked up at her, his big brown calf eyes glistening. "Can I stay down here under this desk forever?"

"Well, for now you can stay down there, but you wouldn't want to be there forever. I'm sure the space trolls will tire of looking for you anyway. They have other more important things to do."

"Like what?"

Oh, dear, now she was in for it. "Uhh, well, they get hungry just like you do. They're probably off ordering chicken salad sandwiches just like us."

Obie laughed. "Space trolls don't eat sandwiches."

Charlotte looked down at him and grinned. "What do they eat?"

"They eat humans!"

"Oh, dear." Charlotte got down on the floor near him and leaned against the desk. "Obie, I love your imagination. It's one of the many things I like about you, but for now we need to talk about something serious. Your momma told me things weren't going well at home. I'm worried about you both. Is everything okay?"

"Yeah . . . maybe . . . not sure."

The question Charlotte knew she needed to ask Obie caught in her throat. The words never seemed right coming out of any person's mouth. "Has your papa been hitting you or your momma again?"

Obie lifted his shirt up over most of his face, but left his eyes peeking out at her. "Uhh . . . no."

"Is that the truth?"

"They yelled a lot. All the time." Obie scrubbed one of the heels of his boot against the floor until it made several angry looking black marks across the floor. " 'Cept now he's gone."

"Your papa left?"

"Yeah. For good. He won't ever be back. And I'm glad. I'm glad he's gone."

Charlotte wasn't sure how far she should go with the questioning. If it would somehow prove helpful for Obie to talk about it, or if it was just invading his home life. "Where did your papa go?"

Obie shrugged. "Don't know. I'm not going to call him Papa anymore. He made me call him that. But my real papa's in heaven."

"Yes, that's true." And it was so unfortunate, since his real father had been a fine Christian man, he'd loved Obie, and he'd given stability to their home. "Does your mother know you're here?"

"Yeah, she said I could come over." He uncovered his face. "She's so busy crying all the time I don't think she has much time left for me."

"I know your momma loves you."

"Yeah, I know." He pounded his little fists together softly. "Then why do I feel so bad?"

"Good question." Charlotte ran her fingers through her hair, pushing it away from her face. "Well, Obie, I've wondered the same thing lately. But people, adults in particular, make a lot of mess, and the bigger the mess the longer it takes to clean it up."

"Mess. That's what my momma calls my room."

Charlotte grinned.

Obie tightened and loosened the Western bolo tie around his neck, the one she'd given him for Christmas. "So, when that papa man left us . . . it was his mess. His bad."

"Yes. Families are supposed to watch out for each other. They're supposed to . . . " Charlotte felt close to tears, but the little guy had already had to deal with so many female emotions, she wasn't going to make him suffer through any more.

"They're supposed to what?"

"Families are supposed to love each other."

"Oh . . . that." He picked at the patch on his jeans.

"Yeah, but love isn't always easy." Charlotte realized she was ruminating on her own life and moved on. "Just remember, Obie . . . you are very lovable. Promise me you'll always remember that about yourself. Okay?" *Oh, Lord, how this little guy has suffered.* He's endured the loss of his real father, and now a makeshift father—his mother's latest boyfriend—and now he has to deal with a mother who doesn't act like she even cares about him. And here *she* sat, hoping to have a family someday, while so many other people tossed their children away as if they were old clothes to be dropped off at the thrift store. There was a lot more unfairness in this life than there was justice.

"Okay. I promise to think I am lovable." Obie looked up at Charlotte and almost smiled.

Eliza came around the corner with two sodas and a couple of sandwiches wrapped in wax paper. "Here you go."

Obie reached out for one of the sandwiches. "May I have some barbeque chips too . . . since I'm so lovable? Please, please, please?"

Charlotte grinned. "Yes, you may."

"And may I have some of Miss Charlotte's tea instead of the soda?" Obie asked Eliza.

Charlotte gave Obie's boot a wiggle. "A boy after my own heart."

Eliza winked at Charlotte. "What kind of tea would you like, Obadiah?"

He pressed his finger hard against his chin as if in deep thought and then said, "I'll have English breakfast tea with milk and honey . . . please."

"I'll have the same," Charlotte said. Okay, that was impressive for a kid who loved barbeque chips.

Eliza grinned. "You got it."

As Charlotte reached up for her sandwich she studied Eliza's latest hairdo—which was more about chaos than style. Charlotte usually tried to compliment the waitresses on their hair and makeup, but Eliza's mini pink Mohawk didn't tempt her toward that end. In fact, Eliza's hair had already frightened a couple of the older patrons. She'd have to find a way to tell her without hurting her feelings.

"Cool hair," Obie said to Eliza.

Charlotte dropped her chin to her chest. *Well, my job just got harder.*

"Thanks, Obadiah," Eliza said.

"Is everything going all right in the tearoom?" Charlotte asked, hoping to move the conversation away from the topic of hair.

Eliza patted the doorframe. "Going as smoothly as warm lard on ice."

"Great image, Eliza. Working on your metaphors and similes for English Lit?"

"Yep," she said and then disappeared.

"She's funny." Obie made a snuffling sound.

They munched in silence for a while, and then Obie looked up at Charlotte and asked, "What if Momma leaves too? Leaves without me and doesn't ever come back?"

"She won't do that. Your momma loves you." Charlotte looked at her sandwich and lost her appetite.

Obie took another big bite and said through chews, "Why can't you be my momma?"

Oh, no. Charlotte had feared those words ever since she first took Obie under her wing a year earlier. She set her sandwich down and got his full attention. "I was never meant to replace your momma. I'm just a good friend. Okay?"

"Yeah. Okay." Charlotte would love being Obie's mom, but their discussion wasn't helping him bond with his mother. And now that the man in his house had left for good, Obie would need that special bonding with his mother more than ever. "I have an idea. Lil gives classes on cooking. Maybe for your birthday present this year, you and your mom could come for free. You both might think it's fun to cook together. Would you like that?"

"Yeah."

"Well, then tell your mom when you get home. Okay?"

"Okay." Obie took several bites and then with his mouth crammed full he said, "Can I play in that little house you got in your garden?"

Charlotte wasn't sure which to correct first—Obie's manners or his grammar. She let it go for now. "Why do you want to play in an old outhouse?" She'd had everything boarded over inside the outhouse, and yet a precocious child could find trouble in a room full of pillows. "I don't think it's a good idea for you to play in that outhouse by yourself, but sometime I'll go back there with you and we'll explore it together. Honestly, though, there's not much to see. It's just a tiny empty room now. Why are you so curious about it?"

"My mom says your outhouse is just for purdy in your garden."

"It is. That's why I left it there and painted some flowers on it like it was part of the garden. But I'd still like to know why you're so interested in it."

"I can see it from my bedroom window, and I saw lightning strike it."

"Really?" Charlotte was never sure when Obie told the truth or a big fish story.

"And so now I think it must be a time-travel outhouse. You know, maybe there are dials in there and you can go anywhere you want . . . even far, far away. And we could go together."

Ohh, so that's where the conversation was going. Charlotte sighed. She wasn't making any headway after all.

Obie rolled the last bite of his sandwich into a ball, leaned his head back, and dropped the wad into his mouth. Then he gazed at what was left of her sandwich.

"Want my half? I'm not that hungry after all."

"Thanks." Obie accepted the sandwich and dug into it with gusto.

Eliza appeared at the door again. "Sorry I don't have the tea ready for you. But I think you'd better get out here."

Thank goodness. Now she wouldn't have to answer any more questions about the outhouse. "What is it?"

"Ida and Beatrice are here at the same time. And on my watch. I mean what are the chances of that?" She stuck her tongue out and snorted. Not Eliza's most feminine gesture. "Anyway, a customer told them off. She said they were silly for not speaking to each other for years. Now they're speaking all right, but it's not 'G' rated."

Hmm. Maybe staying under the desk forever really was a good idea. Charlotte rose off the floor. "We're in a pickle, Obie."

He chuckled. "Is it one of those big green rubbery ones like you buy at the movies?"

"It is indeed."

"And," Eliza went on to say, "Deloris Cobb wants to know if it's okay to pay her bill in fresh eggs and homegrown tomatoes."

"Is that all?"

"No. Some mother's little dumpling is dismantling the shelves of stuff animals. He's performing surgery on one of the bears, and stuffing is going everywhere."

"So, things are running as smooth as lard on ice, huh?" Charlotte gave Eliza a good-natured grin.

Obie crawled out from under the desk. "This is too cool."

15

Audrey found herself working alongside Sam in an effort to prepare the house for sale. There was so much to organize, so much to sell, so much to clean, she felt overcome by it all. There was little time left for wedding planning with all the extra work. They needed more workers than Justin and the housekeeper; they needed a whole team of folks working around the clock.

Audrey tossed several old kitchen strainers into the give-away bin. It hadn't been her wish to put the house on the market. She'd hoped to convince Sam that they could refurbish it and make it a showplace. But during their rescheduled counseling session with Pastor Wally, she discovered that Sam was more interested in a home than a palace, so Audrey relented. Then she remembered that Sam's unpretentious ways and his love for home and family were the finest things about him. She wouldn't stifle his best qualities. The very qualities that would guarantee her emotional safety, that would help her recover from her past.

She picked up a tarnished compass and stared at it. Which box should she put it in? The one for valuables, the thrift store, or the trash bin? Since so much of what Mr. Wilder had owned seemed valuable, she hated to be foolish and give away a fortune unknowingly. But there was so much of everything. And yet too much of nothing. Perhaps that was the way Sam's father had lived his life.

"Sam," Audrey hollered across the living room. Her voice echoed around the big room. "What about this old compass on your father's entry table? Is that an antique or should I toss it in the thrift store heap?"

He looked at her over a stack of boxes "Put the compass in with the valuables. You know, I should probably have a professional do this sorting, but I keep thinking we'll find something extraordinary. You know, something that'll explain why my father became the way he was. Why he lived his life like all those NO TRESSPASSING signs he posted everywhere on the property."

"It'd be like finding the sled, Rosebud, in the movie *Citizen Kane*?"

"Yeah." Sam nodded. "Maybe a little like that."

Audrey came up behind Sam and slipped her arms around his neck. "I've gone through everything in the entry and the closet. What do you want me to do next?"

Sam folded the lids down on a box, rose from the stool he'd been sitting on, and took her into his arms. "Tell me something."

"Anything."

"Have I made you happy?"

"Happy?" Audrey pulled back to study him better. "Why would you ask such a question?"

"When I think of all you've suffered in your life, you surely need more than I've given you."

"You're my rock, steady and safe. That's what I need." Audrey gave his chest a tender poke with her finger. "Half the women in the world are looking for that quality."

"Half the women, huh?" Sam grinned. "What are the other half looking for?"

Audrey chuckled. "A wild ride I guess, but I'm not interested in the carnival. It's too garish to me . . . and frightening."

"You sure it isn't just another way to say that I'm boring?"

"No. Not at all." She latched onto the loops of his jeans and gave him an affectionate tug. "It's just that some people are on a Ferris wheel, and some aren't. I prefer to have my feet on the ground where they belong. I had enough treacherous rides when I was a child, enough to last a lifetime."

"Yes, I'm sure you did."

Audrey stroked her finger along his chin. "Sam Wilder is all he should to be. You're humble and honest and . . . loyal. Things I admire." Things she couldn't live without. "So, do you feel better?"

Sam kissed her hand and then her mouth. "Well, *now* I feel better."

Audrey laughed. But somewhere deep down, her laughter got smothered in fear. What was troubling her? Because of her past, could she have confused love with a voracious need for stability and financial security? Maybe she didn't know her own heart.

"By the way," Sam said, breaking into her thoughts, "I just heard back from two of the antique dealers. They're coming in a few minutes to look at several of Father's collections. Look, I know you like plants better than antiques, so maybe you'd rather work in the greenhouse for a while. You could see how Justin is getting along."

"Good idea. I will." Audrey hurried toward the main hallway and then turned around. "Sam?"

"Hmm?"

"I just wondered about something. When you sent Justin out there to put the greenhouse in order, did you know he had a degree in botany?"

"Not at all. How impressive. We should feel fortunate to have him working for us."

Audrey toyed with the lace collar at her neck. "But for all his knowledge, he's hard to read. Sometimes he's talkative, and other times it's like he's disappeared in his head. And I have no idea where he went off to."

Sam looked up from his work. "Well, the pastor told me he thinks Justin has some sort of tragic past he can't talk about."

"I certainly understand that part."

Sam stared at her and then smiled.

Audrey couldn't make out Sam's expression. "Why are you gaping at me?"

Sam chuckled. "I just thought how providential it seems, that Justin's come to work for us. Maybe you can help him, be an encouragement to him."

"Maybe I can, and maybe he'll come to trust us enough to open up and tell us what went wrong in his life."

"I can tell you're taking a real interest in him. I'm glad."

Audrey wanted to hug his neck again, but she stayed put and let him work. "I wonder how Justin ended up on the streets."

Sam held up a snowshoe and then dropped it in the trash pile. "Well, Justin wasn't really on the streets. There was a cot available when he needed it, and he did odd jobs for a few of the people around town . . . like the pastor . . . and Charlotte."

There was that name again—Charlotte. She seemed to be everywhere, doing everything. She was no doubt a good woman, a new friend, and with her generous help the wedding would be wonderful, but Charlotte was also everything Audrey knew she could never be. Jealousy, an emotion that chased Audrey, and one she usually ran from, caught up with her.

Audrey walked back into the room with Sam. "Everyone's help is generous, of course, but it's so temporary . . . not enough to move him forward in a career or fulfill his destiny."

"Well, that's a tall order. I'm not sure if we can help him with his destiny, but for now he's got a full-time job fixing up our greenhouse, and he's sleeping in the apartment above the garage. I'd say we're giving him a good start." Sam lifted a baseball glove out of a box, held it up, and then placed it in the valuables pile.

Audrey smiled. Sam really was a sentimentalist. Such a nice quality. She could never marry a man who didn't want to make the world a more beautiful place. Sam was bound to love her idea then—a plan that had just hatched in her mind. "But I mean maybe we could do something more for Justin. He's covered with so much hair and beard he's like this burly beast of a man who's been living by himself in the mountains, and he's finally come down into town to see what he's been missing."

Sam chuckled. "Well, that's funny."

"When I first met him I thought he was much older."

"I think the pastor said he is in his mid-thirties."

"Just like us. Amazing." Audrey wandered around the open boxes, peeking in each. "It wouldn't be appropriate for me to do it, but maybe later today, you could drive Justin into town and get him a haircut and shave. Maybe even a good set of clothes."

"Maybe . . . although a subject like that would need some diplomacy."

"Hmm. Something I don't have."

Sam looked at her. "What do you mean?"

"Well, war broke out in Charlotte's tearoom because of me." She gestured with her hands as if she were playing charades.

"After Meredith's fire, while you went off to the hardware store, I did some shopping and then went into the tearoom to talk to Charlotte about the reception. I couldn't get with Charlotte right away, because one of the waitresses said she was busy taking care of some child in the backroom."

"I can see her doing that."

"Doing what?"

"Taking care of the neighborhood kids who need some looking after . . . when no one else is paying attention."

Audrey kept the groan to herself. "Yes, it's very kind of Charlotte."

"But continue your story . . . about the war you started at the tearoom."

"Well, while I was sitting there waiting on Charlotte, I noticed these two older women who were sitting across from each other, giving each other the evil eye. I asked the waitress about it, and she told me the two women, Ida and Beatrice, hadn't talked to each other in years. Something about one of the ladies owning a peach tree that stretched over onto the other lady's property and she'd been picking all the peaches on her side. But it made the owner so mad, she cut down the tree so nobody could have *any* peaches. And then the two women refused to talk to each other. For years. Over that. How stupid. Imagine!"

Audrey blew at her bangs. "Honestly, small town people have way too much time on their hands. They're constantly poking around in other's business like a pack of bloodhounds sniffing for a foxhole. And they get petty and peevish over a basketful of peaches. Living here isn't going to be easy I can tell you that."

"But I hope you'll be able to settle into life here eventually. There's a lot to love about this countryside as well as the townspeople."

"Oh, I will." *For your sake. Eventually.*

"Good."

Audrey studied him as he went back to work. Had she ever really noticed how ocean blue his eyes were? Of course she had. But they looked unfamiliar suddenly and so deep they seemed unreachable.

The story about the two older women being trapped in their pride left her thinking about her childhood again. Thinking about dark confining spaces and voices. Were they real glimpses from her youth, or were they merely images that her mind had manufactured in an effort to cope with the past? It was another facet of her life that she didn't know how to share. Sam would simply never understand that part of her. How could he? She barely understood any of it herself. "Well, I'm off to the greenhouse." Audrey let go of her troubling thoughts, fluffed the ruffles on her blouse, and pulled her iPhone out of her pocket.

Once in the kitchen, Audrey had Nelly brew a cup of hot tea for Justin, and then she headed out one of the backdoors. When she'd made it to the courtyard, she took the bridge over the koi pond and then the winding cobblestone path to the greenhouse.

Audrey opened the door and peered inside. She loved the building with its copper and glass roofing, cathedral ceiling, and cedar beams. And the floor-to-ceiling glass windows made it look as though it was still part of the outdoors. To her, the greenhouse was a work of art all by itself, like an exquisite vase holding a bouquet of flowers.

She heard the sound of sweeping and whistling. She stepped inside, but stayed still. Justin had such a pretty warbling sound, so musical, she longed to listen.

But then the melody came to a close, and her hand faltered, making the teacup rattle in its saucer.

"Is someone there?" Justin asked.

"Just me. Audrey."

"Oh? I'm right back here sweeping behind the clay pots." He showed himself, and came to meet her.

"I made you some tea." Audrey offered him her gift. "Well, I had *Nelly* make you some tea."

"Still, I appreciate the thought." He took hold of the saucer, but before Audrey could let go of it, the cup made a nervous rattle.

Justin didn't seem to miss the tiny noise, since he looked up at her with keen interest and said, "I'm sorry if I make you uneasy."

"No, not at all. I just, well . . ." Audrey laughed. "Maybe you do make me a little nervous."

"I like your honesty."

"Really?"

Justin took a sip of his tea, but without taking his gaze from her, which made her even more nervous.

Time to browse. Ahh. The smell of earth and growing things. Better than Paris perfume. Audrey glanced around the greenhouse, at the rows of tables, now cleared off and the tangled plants cleaned up and pruned back. "You've done a great job with this place. It was a disaster just a few days ago."

"It's a real joy working here. Some of the best things in life are in this place. I can't thank you both enough."

"We should be thanking you." Audrey gazed at one of the orchid plants and then touched one of the translucent petals, always amazed that they felt sturdier than they looked. With humans it was usually the other way around. She noticed a sketchbook on the worktable. Does he draw as well? Just before she opened it, Justin placed his hand over the book, barring her from seeing inside.

"I'm sorry." She looked up at him. "I'm just being nosy." His sudden nearness, the intimacy of being inside his personal space, made her step away from the table. "So you sketch?"

"A little."

"May I see?" she asked. "Please?"

Justin paused for a moment and then slowly opened the sketchbook.

Audrey turned the pages and studied the absolute perfection of his pencil drawings. "How wonderful. You draw with such precision." She inspected the sketches more closely. "I mean, they look just like the flowers. How do you do it?"

"I am determined to make it right. To *get* it right. That's all I can attribute it to." His expression seemed riddled with a dozen nuances, but she felt uneasy about digging too deeply with her questions.

Audrey ran her finger along the flawless lines of a rosebud, which had just begun to open. Since many of the drawings were of roses, it was obvious he had a great love for that particular flower. "But you *do* get it right."

"My sketches lack vision . . . passion. They're just a reflection. I think they should be more, much more to be good."

Audrey examined him while he wasn't looking at her. It seemed to take him a moment to unwind from the intensity of his words. Yet another layer of Justin Yule. "In Houston I used to work as a secretary to the owner of a nursery. But when we were short of help, sometimes I had to run the front counter. That's when I met Sam. He was buying a basket of flowers to hang on the balcony of his apartment."

Justin took a long swig of his tea. His strong hands handled the tiny cup as nimbly as if it were a gardening tool. "Are you a great lover of plants too, or was your work at the nursery just a job?" He set the cup and saucer down on the table.

"I am a lover of plants. Maybe because plants can't talk back. They can't hurt you, at least not emotionally." Before Justin could question her, she said, "Nelly told me you come into the kitchen for lavender tea. What's so special about lavender?"

"The flower has a lot of stage presence on the garden scene. And it's a good stress reliever."

"Do you feel stressed?"

"Being alive is stressful." Justin gestured toward the sketchbook, which she now held tightly in her arms.

Embarrassed, she handed him the book. But he hadn't really answered her question.

"Did you know Texas grows lavender commercially?" he said. "They discovered that our hill country is similar to Provence."

"No, I hadn't heard that."

"Charlotte Rose Hill makes her lavender tea with a touch of—"

"You love her, don't you?" Audrey clasped her hand over her mouth.

"Who?" Justin frowned. "You mean Charlotte?"

Audrey stepped back a little, her face flushed. "I don't know why I would say that. Lately, it's like I've been injected with some kind of weird blunt serum. But that's no excuse."

"I'm curious. Why did you say I loved Charlotte?"

"I don't know. Maybe the way you said her whole name. It's very lyrical, isn't it? Very floral. But then everyone seems to love Charlotte—" Audrey didn't mean to have an edge to her voice, but it was there just the same.

"You sound jealous." Justin looked at her. "But why should you be?"

Audrey took the broom and began to sweep at nothing. She didn't like the way Justin gazed at her sometimes. It was as if he saw things she wanted to hide. Sam never looked at her that way.

"Of course I love Charlotte," Justin said, "but I don't love her in a romantic way."

Audrey gave the broom a pugnacious swoop against the concrete floor. "Maybe I *am* jealous . . . of how treasured she is by everyone who meets her. I don't get it. How does one person become so beloved by so many people? A champion to widows and orphans. I'll bet she even befriends every stray animal in town."

"I think she has from time to time." Justin looked away, pained.

"Please don't think I meant you. I wasn't implying anything. I would never—"

"Slip of the tongue perhaps?"

"No, I promise you . . . " No use in going on. He wouldn't believe her. Her spirit stung with what she'd always called invisible tears. She didn't mean to hurt Justin, but words had never come easily. Nothing had. Even the way she saw herself. When she looked in the mirror she couldn't see the pretty young woman people claimed she was. She could only see something discarded, like an unwanted plant—a weed to be tossed in the fire. "It's just, well, you were going to tell me that Charlotte is like this rare flower, and—"

"No," Justin said. "I might have said the opposite. Charlotte wouldn't want to be anything pampered or put in a special vase on a pedestal. I'm sure she'd rather be a big bouquet of carnations. Something common but generous that could be enjoyed by everyone."

"Of course!" *Oh dear.* She took a deep breath and sighed. Her temper had gotten the better of her. Again. It was becoming obvious that the goodness of Charlotte and Sam was eating away at her like ants in a sugar bowl. The two of them were so similar, so wonderful, she couldn't fathom their qualities. Couldn't emulate them or even touch them. Once again, as she had felt her whole life, she was on the outside of a warm and cozy circle, merely looking in.

Justin seemed to examine her. "You know, photographers say that people always have a better side."

Audrey shrugged. "What do you mean?"

"This isn't your best side," he said softly.

Audrey got Justin's second meaning, which made her skin sear hot again. Not from anger but from disappointment—in herself. "I understand. You're right." She tried to hide her feelings, but it was no use. She had come undone. Tears, no longer the invisible kind, dribbled down her cheeks. "I don't know what's wrong." Her voice became a squeak. "One minute I'm blissful and the next I'm a basket case or I'm insulting someone." Audrey let the broom fall. The handle knocked over the potted orchid, which then rolled to the floor and smashed into pieces. She felt a fresh batch of tears coming as she looked down at the perfect orchid with its petals now dirtied and crushed. Her fault. Always her fault. Feeling like a willful and unlovable child, she collapsed on the floor in a heap next to the wounded orchid.

Justin sat down next to her. He lifted his arm and then hesitantly placed it around her shoulder as if she might break as well. "This is my fault. What I said was too forward, and it was unkind. Sometimes I'm too outspoken. Please forgive me."

"Nothing to forgive. Apparently, my personality needs something. I'm sure God is working on me, but if I were him I'd squash up the clay, toss it back onto the wheel, and start all over again. Recently I've been avoiding mirrors. I don't like looking at myself." Audrey hiccupped and rubbed her eyes.

"No one is perfect, Audrey . . . including Charlotte."

"Yes, I know that has to be true."

"One of the waitresses told me that sometimes she sits in a closet to pray . . . and cry."

Hmm, that's kind of sad. "I wonder why Charlotte's crying." Audrey sniffled. "I don't have a tissue. Do you have a handkerchief?"

"Sorry, I never carry one." Justin reached into his back pocket and pulled out a rag, which looked tattered and covered in axle grease. "I don't think this will work."

"No, thank you." She sniffled again. "Sam always carries a handkerchief."

"Well, I'm not Sam."

No, you're not. "I don't know what's come over me. I shouldn't even be here with you. I barely know you, and here you've seen me like this." Audrey wiped her nose on her blouse—an act she hadn't succumbed to since age five. "A meltdown is a very private thing. I should be having my meltdown in front of Sam." She pulled out from under his arm.

"I'm not an expert, but I think this sometimes happens before a wedding. I think it's common . . . unless." Justin got up off the floor, took her hands, and gently lifted her to her feet.

"Unless what?"

He backed away. "Nothing."

Maybe he thought she was going to clobber him with a pot. Audrey's arms thrashed around until they landed tight against her ribcage. "Your face doesn't say it was nothing." She picked up the broom.

Justin gestured toward the broom. "I'll clean up the mess."

"No, I'll clean it up. It was *my* fault," Audrey said, "because I'm being a silly child."

Justin took hold of the broom and tugged, but Audrey didn't feel like letting go.

They stared at each other and then stumbled backward, letting go of the handle as if it had burned their hands.

Audrey stared at the broom on the floor. "What was that all about?"

"I don't know." Justin picked up the broom and backed away. "But I think you being here in the greenhouse with me . . . is no longer appropriate."

"You're right. I'd better go." Compared to Justin, perhaps Sam was a simpler man. Justin had stage presence like his beloved lavender plants, but he was also complicated and a little bit like standing too close to the edge of something. "Before I go, I have a message from Sam. Easter is coming, and he wants to have a holiday dinner. Along with a few other Middlebury people, he wanted you to be there."

"Maybe I shouldn't."

"No, I want you to come too. Please. Nelly will have dinner at six."

Justin frowned and then slowly nodded. "All right. If you're sure."

Audrey wasn't sure about anything, but her mouth went so dry it was hard to say much more. When she made it to the door, she turned around.

Justin gave her a forlorn smile, and a two-finger salute.

Without thinking she gave him a two-finger salute right back. Where had that come from? There was something about the gesture that jogged her memory. In spite of his mane and beard, there was something about him that she recognized— something from the past. "You know what? You look familiar to me. I thought the day I met you that I'd known you from somewhere, but now I'm sure of it. Perhaps it—"

"I need to go." Justin set the broom against the table.

"Why do you need to go?"

"I'm sorry, Audrey. I need to leave now." And then Justin picked up his sketchbook, turned around, and walked away from her.

"What do you mean? Are you leaving for good? But why?"

"Please tell Sam I'm sorry," Justin said over his shoulder as he walked out of the backdoor of the greenhouse. He didn't say good-bye, and he didn't say where he was going or if he was ever coming back.

Audrey stood there, gaping after him, feeling lost and dejected. Somewhere in her mind, a drop of pure panic seeped through her, and the fear made her feel like a child again, lost and forsaken.

16

Charlotte could hardly believe it was a mere two days later when she sat across from Austin editor, Dee Hollingsworth, at one of the corner tables in the tearoom. The plan to do a cookbook was moving beyond just an idea. Charlotte watched in amazement at the woman's intensity. Dee breathed so deeply of her tea it seemed she was trying to sip it through her nose. She also did more sampling than real eating, but Dee assured Charlotte that she was impressed with everything.

When Dee rested back in her chair from her study of Charlotte's cooking, the woman tugged on the lapels of her suit like Abraham Lincoln and stared at the table of food like it was the Emancipation Proclamation. "My editor was right. You have a gift for tearoom cuisine. It's not the usual fare, and even when you offer chicken salad it's not predictable. You've got an ingenious combination of ingredients in there." She shook her finger at her. "A concoction of spices that I can't quite make out."

"Some of the local women have been trying to ferret those ingredients out of me for years."

Dee eyeballed her. "Well, I'm sure you know they won't be a secret for long." She took another nibble of the lobster quiche.

As she chewed, her eyelids drifted shut. "Oh, this is inspiring enough to make me want to quote Keats."

Grinning, Charlotte took a sip of her favorite tea—jasmine green—while Dee went off into a place of savoring Shangri-La. On first impression, Dee was a rather stark woman with her short, black cropped hair, piercing glances, and surefire answers; but there were plenty of things to like about the woman too, especially the fact that she loved her recipes so much.

Dee daubed the napkin on her lips. "Back to business. We were thinking of a cookbook with a small-town theme. We could entitle it, *The Rose Hill Cottage Tearoom Cookbook*. We'll do a photo shoot here, of course. Not just the food, but some interior and exterior shots too. Also we'll start a blog. This will get everyone ready for their visit to the country to meet Charlotte Rose Hill and her irresistible fare. Well, that is, after you approve the advance, which you'll find more than generous, and after you sign the contract, which I brought with me." Dee opened her leather briefcase, pulled out a wad of papers, and set them in front of Charlotte. "You might want to have an attorney look this over before you sign it, but it's a standard boilerplate contract. I can e-mail you a copy as well."

Charlotte had no idea what a boilerplate contract was, but she doubted she needed an attorney. "I'll read it thoroughly before I sign it."

"Good deal. Assuming the recipes have already been tried several times, there shouldn't be any reason you can't turn in the manuscript within say, five or six months. I hope that's agreeable to you. The book will come out next spring. We're a regional publisher, but because all things Texas are so popular, we'll do a national campaign, especially online. But marketing can go over those details with you later." Dee gave her fingers an impatient looking flutter. "So, what do you think?"

Well, except for her head spinning from all the new information, Charlotte couldn't think of one good reason to say no. She had created enough recipes over the years to fill several cookbooks, and since it had been a hidden dream of hers, she took in a deep breath, gripped the edges of the table, and said, "Okay, where do I sign?"

Dee narrowed her eyelids to slivers and grinned. "That a girl." She woodpecker-tapped her pen on a saucer, which sat at the edge of the table. "I'm curious about something. While you were in the little girl's room, some older gentleman who looked a little like Santa Claus left this saucer for you with these little carnation petals in it. He claimed it was tradition. What's up with that?"

"Oh, you're talking about Mr. LaGrange. Every morning he comes in here for tea and to read his paper. But first he stops by the flower shop and buys a red carnation to put in the lapel of his jacket. Just before he leaves the tearoom, he puts several of the petals on his saucer for me."

Dee leaned closer to her. "You sure he isn't a little bit in love with you?"

Charlotte chuckled. "No, no. He's old enough to be my father. It's just his way of thanking me for my hospitality."

"So, what do you do with those petals later when he's not looking?" Dee asked. "Toss them?"

"No, I'm saving them." Charlotte slipped the petals into the pocket of her apron. "When I have enough I'll make some potpourri and give it to him."

Dee shook her head and made a funny squeaky laugh. "Oh, now that story is pure small town." She pointed the pen at her in excitement. "I have a terrific idea. Maybe we could add some of those charming stories about your patrons to the cookbook. People will eat it up, no pun intended. The whole gingham, wholesome town square thing is so hot right now. What do you think?"

Charlotte opened her mouth to reply, when Dee said, "By the way, I was hoping you had enough time today to give me a little tour of this shopping complex. I love the way it's set up. You know, a cluster of old houses made into shops with cobblestone walkways connecting them all in the back. It's so clever. So Southern . . . just like your tearoom."

Charlotte looked at her watch. "I don't think it would a problem. Sure. I'd love to show you around."

"Good deal."

Eliza strode over to their table and tapped her knuckles together. "Charlotte. It's Wednesday."

"Yes, Eliza, you're right. It is." Charlotte gave her an overly bright smile.

Eliza gave her a funny look back. "Yeah, but isn't this the day when Obie's mom lets him come over here after school. You know, so she can work a little later?"

Charlotte gasped. "It is. You're right. I forgot. Where is Obie?"

"I don't know." Eliza put her hands on her hips. "I don't see him out back playing in the garden or anything."

"The outhouse." Charlotte rose out of her chair. "He might be in there."

"You have an outhouse?" Dee asked.

"Not really. The seat inside has been boarded up. It's just a decorative garden ornament now. But Obie has been curious about it lately. Why don't we check there first, and then I'll call over to his house." Charlotte said to Dee, "I'm really sorry. Do you mind waiting a bit for our tour?"

"I understand. I have two kids at home, and they get into every kind of mischief. I'll go with you." Dee got up from the table.

"All right."

The three of them headed through the kitchen and then out the backdoor. Charlotte broke out into a run, thinking Obie might have gotten himself trapped inside. That was it. She was going to have the door of that outhouse nailed shut.

Dee followed close behind her. When Charlotte reached the tiny building she flipped up the wooden latch and peered inside. "No. He's not here."

"Where else do you think he might go?" Dee asked.

"Well, his house is nearby, but he doesn't stay there when his mom's not home."

Someone hollered across the street, seizing Charlotte's attention. A car horn blared as tires screeched. Suddenly, a man shoved a boy out of the way of an oncoming car. "Obie!" Charlotte ran toward the boy, her heart hammering

The man toppled onto the pavement while Obie ran toward the sidewalk.

When Charlotte reached Obie, she threw her arms around him. "Are you all right?"

"Yeah."

"Good. I want you to stay with Eliza, so I can check on the man who's injured."

Charlotte glanced toward the street. The man lifted his head. Obie's rescuer could be seen clearly now—it was Justin Yule! She ran into the street, and knelt down next to him. She looked back at the man who'd been driving the car and hollered, "Call 911!"

"Got it." The man pulled out his phone.

Justin reached out his hand to Charlotte, and she clasped it in hers.

"The ambulance is coming. It'll be all right." She brushed his bushy hair away from his face, looking for blood. She didn't see any. *Thank God.*

Justin lowered his head and clutched his arm. "Would you help me up?"

"Help you up? No, I most certainly will not. You're not going anywhere without an ambulance," Charlotte said. "You were hit by that car."

"Just knocked down. I've got my bearings now."

Charlotte gave him her nastiest scowl. "But they always say—"

"I want to get up. I just need a little help." Justin attempted a smile.

"The medics will be here soon."

When Justin tried getting up on his own, Charlotte rolled her eyes. "Justin Yule, you are such a mule."

Justin chuckled and then winced. "You're a wise woman, Charlotte, but this time I'm going to need to challenge your good sense. Now, please, will you help me up?"

Charlotte got up off the pavement, and with her hand under Justin's arm, she helped him to his feet.

Justin wobbled a little, but then let her go. "I'm fine. But how's the boy?" He looked toward Obie, who stood on the sidewalk with Eliza. "You okay, little man?"

Obie gave Justin a vigorous nod. "Yes, sir."

Charlotte gave his arm a pat. "You saved his life."

Justin didn't reply but hobbled off toward the other side of the street.

Charlotte shook her head at him. What a unique man.

The driver, who still stood outside his car, hollered to Justin, "Hey, buddy. Don't you want to wait for the paramedics to check you out first? You look injured."

Justin said, "If they want to talk to me, just tell them they'll have to hunt me down."

"Hey, sorry I ran you and the kid down like that," he yelled to Justin. "It all happened so fast."

"It wasn't your fault," Justin shouted back as he continued to limp down the other side of the street toward the chapel.

Justin, you poor, dear man. Charlotte then gazed back at Obie and hurried over to him.

"He's shivering," Eliza said.

Dee took off her suit jacket and wrapped it around the boy's shoulders.

Charlotte knelt down in front of him. "Obie, are you okay? Did the car hurt you?"

"I'm okay. That man pushed me out of the way of the car."

"Yes. I think Justin Yule may have saved your life. But what in the world were you doing out in the street?" Charlotte asked. "You know, that's off limits without an adult."

"I know," Obie said.

"The reason I'm upset with you is because you could have been hurt or killed just now. People love you, Obie. I love you. Okay? I know you're used to walking around behind these houses and shops on your own, but promise me right now that you won't go out into the street without an adult."

"Okay." He sniffled. "I promise."

Dee pulled some tissues out of her purse and handed them to Obie.

"I saw you in the tearoom, but you looked real busy," Obie said to Charlotte. "I thought I could tell Mr. Wally about Momma." He blew his nose.

"Your momma? Is she okay?"

"I don't know." Obie covered his face with his hands. "She can't get up."

Did Obie know what he was saying? "What do you mean she can't get up?"

"Momma won't wake up," Obie whimpered. "She was on the couch. I shook her and shook her, but she wouldn't wake up. She fell over on the floor. Did I hurt her?"

Oh, dear Lord, help us. Was it a drug overdose? Charlotte stroked Obie's hair back from his face. "No, I'm sure you didn't hurt your momma, but we'll need to go to your house right now to see about her. Okay?"

"Okay."

Charlotte rose and looked toward the street. The driver had parked alongside the curb and strode toward them.

"Hey, how is the little guy?" he asked.

"I think he's fine, but something's wrong with his mom. Can you please wait for the ambulance and send them over to the house with the green shutters, the one just behind my garden over there." Charlotte pointed to Obie's house.

"Absolutely," the man said. "Will do."

"You're welcome to go back if you need to, Dee. I'm so sorry." With Obie alongside her, Charlotte started walking swiftly toward Obie's house.

"I'll come along," Dee said, "Maybe I can help."

"I will too," Eliza said.

"Okay. Let's take a shortcut." Charlotte broke out into a run through her garden. "We'd better hurry!"

17

Charlotte sat in her broom closet on a little round stool in the midst of the dust and the quiet and the warm light of the bulb. It was her usual spot to talk to God when life got demanding, but today was different. Life felt more than challenging—it was overwhelming. It reminded her of an ice storm, the way it weighed down the branches to their absolute breaking point. She fingered the river stone in her pocket, noting its unusual heaviness.

"If it's all right to say this, Lord, please give us a breather down here. We've had two funerals recently. We've had more than our share of grief and trouble."

The face of Obie's mother flashed into Charlotte's mind again, making her shudder. It would be a long time before that image faded. Obie's mother had passed away a couple of hours before the paramedics had arrived, so there was nothing they could do. The cause had been an overdose of sleeping pills. The suicide note on the coffee table had simply read:

Can't live without your papa.

Always know your mother loves you, Obie.

Humph. Not much love for a child to live on for the rest of his life. What was the woman thinking? She may not have had her boyfriend, but she still had a child to raise, to love.

Charlotte willed her hands to stop writhing in her lap as she raised her gaze to the endearments sitting in her closet—the oval-framed photo of her parents when they were first married, a rubber mouse squeeze toy, and the quirky little sign Eliza had embroidered that read, "God must love dust. He created us."

She reached up for the mouse and let it dangle by its tail between her thumb and forefinger. Then she gave it a squeeze, making it squeak. The goofy thing made her grin as it always did. It had been Obie's way of breaking into the tearoom family. After school, on a busy afternoon, he'd put the rubber mouse on the kitchen floor. Then he waited for the female staff to go ballistic. They did not disappoint him. It was one of the highlights of his school year to watch those women scatter and yelp. But in the end, the incident endeared him to the whole staff at Rose Hill Cottage.

Charlotte set the rubber mouse in her lap as the first of the tears fell. Obie had wanted her to be his mother, and yet now that the opportunity had presented itself, he made no mention of it. Perhaps Obie thought she was too busy to care for him— too unworthy. She was furious with herself for not being there when Obie needed her the most. She would have stopped her meeting with Dee in a heartbeat to help the boy, but apparently he did not know that. Not well enough anyway.

Or perhaps the reason for Obie's sudden silence on the subject was that he now enjoyed the safe and joyous confines of foster care in Roberta's house. Charlotte knew Roberta well, a stout middle-aged woman full of warm hugs and quiet wisdom, and she knew for a fact that Obie would receive the best care and love any woman could give a child. Perhaps God sent her a message—that it didn't matter about early menopause or that she had never married. And maybe Obie was in the right place. The tearoom was her spouse and offspring after all. The town needed her, and that would be enough. It had to be.

"Well, God, I felt very content with my life before Sam came home. The past has been stirred up, and I am—" Charlotte stopped her petition to the Almighty, thinking she'd heard the scratching of a real mouse. She listened. There it was again.

"Charlotte?" a tiny voice came from the other side of the closet door.

"Eliza, is that you?"

"I know you said people shouldn't bother you while you're in the broom closet, but I think this is important."

"It's okay." Charlotte rolled her eyes. Couldn't she ever have a moment to herself? The tearoom was closed. "What is it?"

"It's Audrey and Sam," Eliza said.

Great day in the morning. Can't I be tortured in peace? Oh my. Fear gulped her up. Were Sam and Eliza on the other side of the closet door? Had they heard her prayer? "Tell them I'll be out in a minute. I'm sure it's about the wedding."

"No. It's not about the wedding," Eliza said. "It's about Justin Yule. I know you like to watch out for him, so I thought you'd want to know."

"Now what?"

"Justin has disappeared."

18

Charlotte's shoulders sagged. *God, is this what you call a reprieve?* "Okay, back away from the door," she said. "I'm coming out." She pulled the chain on the light, paused in the darkness for another blissful second or two, and then gave the door a kick.

Sam stood just outside the door, but Eliza and Audrey were nowhere in sight.

Charlotte groaned to herself. *So much for keeping the broom closet a secret, Eliza.* "I guess you're wondering why I was in the broom closet with the door shut," was all Charlotte could manage.

"I had a place like this when I was growing up. The attic."

"Well, you had youth for your excuse, but I'm all grown up now." Charlotte slipped her hands into her pockets to keep from giving away any emotions.

"I know you weren't in there reading comic books, although that might be fun. You were talking to God." Sam closed the closet door. "What's he saying?"

"Well, lately he hasn't been saying anything I want to hear."

Sam stared down at his hands. "I know exactly what you mean."

Really? You do? "How much did you hear in there?"

"Not much. Mostly muffled words." He smiled.

Charlotte studied him, but she didn't want to look too deeply into those blue eyes—it was perilous—like getting caught in an electrical storm holding an umbrella. And it did funny, abnormal things to her heartbeat. Yes, she had a heart condition. It was called Sam Wilder! *I thought this letting go would get easier, Lord, not harder.* "Where is Audrey?"

"She's out in the car. She's pretty upset. Audrey is still obsessing about Justin. She blames herself that he left, but I don't believe it. It wasn't her fault."

"We shouldn't leave Audrey out there if she's upset. Why don't you have her come inside, and we'll go to my apartment upstairs. I'll make a cup of tea for you both. I'll have some things to tell her about Justin. It might make her feel better."

"Thank you," Sam said.

"It's no problem."

He touched her arm. "Thank you for everything. Well, for being a friend to her."

"Of course." Charlotte tried to funnel her thoughts into a safe mode, but in spite of her determination, the spot on her arm warmed and prickled where Sam touched her.

Ten minutes later Audrey and Sam were sitting in her small apartment above the tearoom. She offered them homemade butter cookies, and she poured them some tea at the kitchen table, using her very best tea set and her finest blends. Sam had always been used to space and luxury, and Audrey had been introduced to his world of plenty, so she wondered what they thought of her modest abode. But to be fair, though, Sam had never been one to flaunt his family's wealth. In fact, in high school he seemed embarrassed about his family's money.

"Your home is comfortable and welcoming," Sam said. "I like it."

"Thank you."

"And this is the prettiest tea set I've ever seen." Audrey dropped a few sugar cubes in her beverage. "Where did you get it?"

Charlotte sat down between them. "It comes from Provence."

Audrey touched the pot's fat belly and its delicate handle, which was gilded in gold. "You've been to France?"

"No, never been out of Texas, but I hope to fix that one day. It's just hard to get away from the tearoom. Sort of married to it." Charlotte may have seen something flash through Sam's expression, but she ignored it.

Sam poured a generous amount of cream in his brew and stirred, clinking his cup with the dainty spoon. "As you may already know, Audrey and I hired Justin to help us get my father's house and property ready for sale. He's been working on the greenhouse."

"How was it going, before he left?" Charlotte lowered a thin slice of lemon into her tea with the silver tongs.

"It was going well," Sam said. "Justin was doing a great job, and he enjoyed the work." He fidgeted with his teacup, nearly spilling it. "Audrey managed to find out that he has a degree in botany."

"That's impressive." Charlotte blew on her tea. "I could tell Justin was an educated man, but I had no idea he'd graduated from college."

"How long have you known him," Audrey asked.

"A year or so," Charlotte said. "Justin can be talkative at times, but if you ask too many questions about his past he gets uncomfortable."

"Audrey mentioned that." Sam picked up the teacup by the outer rim and drank his beverage down in gulps. "Great tea."

"Thanks." Charlotte grinned. A man handling a teacup and saucer was always as entertaining and unpredictable as watching a water buffalo trying to do a pirouette. "I do know

Justin well enough to know he has some quirks. But he's also a hero. Did you hear what happened in town with Obie?"

"We heard some of it, "Audrey said. "That Justin ran out into the street to save the boy's life. It sounds so miraculous. Is it true?"

"It's true," Charlotte said. "Justin got hit by the car, but the boy is fine."

"Nelly didn't mention that part to us. How badly was Justin injured?" Sam asked.

"After a moment or two, Justin got up and walked away. But he was limping." Charlotte refilled Sam's teacup. "I insisted Justin wait for the ambulance, but he didn't want any medical attention. He just hobbled away."

"That was so gallant of him. It should have been on the evening news," Audrey said. "And it was a good thing Justin left our employment when he did, since it made him walk into town to be there when that boy's life needed saving." She took a nibble of her cookie. "But I wish he would have come back. I will always blame myself. That I said something to make him run away. He didn't come back to pick up his check. I'm sure he could use the money. And he didn't take any of his belongings. We'd been letting him live in the apartment above the garage."

Charlotte wasn't sure how much to say. "If you don't mind me asking, what did you say to him? Was it something connected to his past?"

Audrey's eyes held a look of despair. "I told Justin he looked familiar to me. And he did. I thought the same thing on the day I met him too, but I didn't say anything then. Anyway, that's when he walked out. He apologized for leaving, but he said he had to go."

"I can't imagine why that would matter, except it might be connected to some of the past that he doesn't like to talk about." Charlotte gave Audrey's hand a pat. "But how could you have known? You're not to blame."

Sam absently toyed with the cookie on his plate but made no comment.

What was Sam thinking? To what faraway place had he gone?

"Justin still hasn't come back to the house, and it's been days." Audrey's fingers laced in knots. "What if his wound got worse, and he can't get to a hospital? He might be lying in a ditch somewhere."

Audrey's expression seemed so distraught it made Charlotte steal a glance at Sam. "I think he'll be okay. I saw Justin briefly yesterday at the graveside service. The one for Obie's mother. Justin still limped but not as badly as before." Charlotte wrapped her fingers around the cup to warm them. "He didn't visit with anyone, but he stayed back and watched."

Sam grimaced. "We heard about Obie's mom. I hope the boy will be okay."

"It'll be a hard adjustment, but he's in good hands with a woman named Roberta. I know her. She's a fine woman. She'll be watching out for him until something more permanent can be found."

"Justin was there at the gravesite?" Audrey asked.

"Yes." Charlotte fingered the lace on her linen tablecloth. "I only saw him at a distance. He may have wanted to make sure Obie would be all right."

"How sweet of him." Audrey stared into her empty teacup as if searching for something. "You know, we did invite him to join us for Easter dinner tomorrow, and he did promise to come."

Charlotte poured Audrey another cup of tea. "Then you'll see Justin tomorrow."

"How do you know?"

"Because that is something I do know about Justin. It's hard for him to break a promise. It must have been difficult for him to leave the greenhouse that day. To walk out on his job and your generosity. And so I doubt he'll want to disappoint you both again. Hopefully, on Easter you'll get a chance to talk to him."

"Thank you for making me feel better." Audrey reached out to Charlotte's hand. "We would like you to join us for Easter dinner too. Wouldn't we, Sam?"

"Yes, of course," Sam said.

If Sam had some uncomfortable twinges about her being at the dinner, he hid them well. She grinned back at him, but she really felt like cringing all the way to her toes.

"Sam lost track of his old friends from high school," Audrey said, "and I don't have any friends except for you and Nelly, so I've invited some of the people we're getting to know from the tearoom. And we'll be inviting Obie and Roberta too. So, what do you think? Will you come?"

Charlotte still felt a "no" on the tip of her tongue, but if Sam and Audrey were going to make their home in Middlebury, she would have to learn to cope with seeing them together. No better time than the present to start dealing with what was obviously meant to be. "Yes, of course. Would you like me to bring something?"

"No, not at all," Audrey said. "I'm sure you'd appreciate a rest from cooking for the day. Nelly will have it all under control."

"Nelly is a terrific cook," Charlotte said. "You're lucky to have her."

Audrey scooted her chair out and started collecting the tea dishes.

"Thank you for inviting me." Charlotte hoped her smile came off as sincere. Then she remembered the promise she'd made to herself to work a little harder at dating and thought of a really nice guy she knew in Houston—one she'd dated on and off again through the years. "I have one question about the dinner. Would you mind if I brought a date?"

The grasp that Sam had on his teacup must have loosened, because the fine porcelain cup fell from his fingers to the floor and smashed into a hundred heartbreaking pieces.

19

Tomorrow arrived and Sam felt it might be safer to steer clear of the galley. It appeared that two women in the kitchen could turn hazardous. And laboring over an Easter turkey was like delivering a baby—lots of attention on the oven with a thousand and one things that could go wrong.

Nelly had made turkey dinners before, but never for such a big crowd. The whole turkey episode had turned two affable female temperaments into something entirely new. Except for the heavenly aroma wafting out of the kitchen, it was a scene he wanted to flee from.

"Sam!" Audrey cried from the kitchen. "Where are you?"

He knew better than to stay within earshot, but now it was too late. He'd have to go back in now. Sam stepped into the kitchen. "Yes?"

"I can't believe it. The turkey I bought for Nelly is no good. She says she can spot a tough old bird baking even before anybody cuts into it. I mean, it was the cheaper store brand, but that's all they had. I ruined our meal." Audrey stamped her foot, which was adorable, but also slightly troubling since he didn't know what to do about it.

"Gravy is always the answer, right?" Sam asked. "Just make extra giblet gravy and have everyone smother their pieces with it. No one will know."

That suggestion, as fine as it was, sent Audrey into tears. "Guests will be arriving any second."

Nelly slapped the turkey with her basting brush as if she were giving it a spanking. "Now, looky here. I'm tougher than you, you old geezer. You just need somebody to show you who's boss." She looked up from the oven, her face covered with a sheen of perspiration and perseverance. "Now, you go on Audrey, and make sure the table is ready. I'll do the rest in here. Don't you give it another worry."

"Okay, thanks, Nelly. You're a peach," Audrey said.

"I'm feeling like one of those sour green apples right now, but come feasting time it'll all come together. And if the turkey is too much of a workout for their jaws, they can eat ham." Nelly bent over the beast and slathered a whole stick of butter over the golden-tinged bird.

Audrey scurried into the dining room, and Sam reluctantly followed.

She flitted around, putting the finishing touches on her Easter decorations. Bouquets of colorful flowers and glittery eggs littered the long mahogany table. Audrey straightened things that looked straight and fluffed things that already looked fluffy. Once again Sam wasn't sure how to help with the details. He felt more comfortable moving furniture and cleaning out closets than ruffling pastel bows on the napkin rings, but he gave it a try anyway. He picked at a bow, hoping it would look like Audrey's, but the stupid thing deflated defiantly.

Then the doorbell rang. No sweeter sound had ever been heard.

"I'll get it!" Sam said. Maybe he'd said it a little too gleefully.

"I'll go with you." Audrey took off her apron, paused briefly in front of the dining room mirror, shook her head and then walked on. "We should welcome our guests together, even if the meal is a disaster."

"You heard Nelly. It'll all be fine."

"It's a good thing we got the living room cleared out from all those boxes. Of course now the den and library are a mess." She looked him over and whisked something off his lapel. "And I'm glad I talked you out of wearing those jalopy jeans you always put on. You look so much better in khakis and a sports jacket."

Sam grinned at her. "And I feel so much better too . . . like a real man." He opened the door before Audrey could give him a playful punch or reply with something snarky.

Pastor Wally and Meredith Steinberg stood before them holding a box, looking giddier than anyone had a right to be. Sam broke out into smiles. He couldn't even account for such joy in seeing them together, unless it was because the pastor now had someone else to pursue besides Charlotte. He dismissed his train of thought as inappropriate. "Welcome."

"Happy Easter. So glad you could come." Audrey leaned toward the box. "Is that mewing I hear?"

Wally sat the box down. Three kittens of various colors looked up at them.

"Ohh," Audrey said. "Kitty-cats."

The animals were cute, but Sam hoped they weren't supposed to be an Easter present. He'd always been more of a dog lover.

Just behind them, coming up the walk, were Obie and Roberta.

After some hearty greetings, Meredith said, "Mr. Obie, you're just the person I need. I have something I think you might want to see."

Obie stopped in front of the box and brightened a little. "Baby cats."

The mewing pleas of the kittens were enough to melt the coldest heart. "Actually," Meredith said, "these three kittens don't have a mother."

Obie's face crinkled. "Like me?"

"Yes, and it would be a great help to me if you could find a home for two of the kittens." Meredith moved the box a little closer to him.

"But what would happen to the last one?" Obie reached down, and with timid strokes, petted the calico kitten.

"Well, I was hoping you might keep one of them and raise it yourself." Meredith picked up the calico kitten that Obie was petting and placed it in his arms. "I called Roberta ahead of time, and she gave it the thumbs-up."

"Really?" Obie looked up at Roberta. "For real?"

"Yes. For real." Roberta gave him a shoulder hug. "Meredith called me today, and I said yes. But can you take the responsibility of finding homes for the other two kittens? Do you think some of your friends at school might be interested?"

"I can find homes for them." Obie nodded. "I can do this."

Meredith smiled. "I knew you were the man for the job."

Obie gently lifted the kitten to his cheek.

"Which one do you think you'll keep?" Wally asked.

"I think this calico one. It's the skinniest, and it licked my finger. Maybe this one needs me the most."

"Good thinking." Wally stroked his finger under the kitten's chin.

Obie's face reflected such hope compared to when he'd first arrived that it warmed Sam's heart to see it. What a resilient kid. He'd been through some terrible circumstances. The situation reminded him of Audrey's youth, and yet at least Obie had plenty of people around him who cared for him.

Obie set the kitten back down inside the box. "Can I take them inside by the table as long as I leave them in the box? Please, please, please?"

"Well, it's up to Audrey and Sam," Roberta said.

Audrey opened the door wider. "Why don't we put them in the kitchen where it's extra warm, and you can give them some milk."

Obie picked up the box and hugged it to him. "Okay."

"Let's take our party inside," Audrey said. "The food's almost ready."

Everyone resettled in the entry, and after they were all enveloped in chatter, the doorbell rang again.

Edith and Mr. LaGrange were at the door, all dressed up in Easter finery, looking prickly and awkward.

"Thank you for the invite." Mr. LaGrange tipped his hat and looked around. "Sure glad we beat those storm clouds."

Edith raised her chin at Mr. LaGrange and then said to Sam, "We didn't come in the same car. It was just a coincidence we arrived at the same time. And the weatherman said there was no chance of rain."

"No one is going to accuse us of a tryst, Edith." Mr. LaGrange sniffed the air. "Something smells good."

"Well, it certainly isn't that stogie of yours. You'll have to put out that nasty thing at once." Edith twisted her purse strap like she was trying to wring its neck.

"Anything for you, my lady." Mr. LaGrange gave his hand a flurry and bowed. Then he flicked his cigar in the flowerbed and ground out the glowing butt with his shoe.

Edith huffed.

"Glad you both could come." Sam couldn't tell if Edith loathed the man, or if she was giving him a hard time for fun. But since Edith hadn't shown a sense of merriment in her history class, or maybe in her whole life, he guessed the former option.

Sam opened the door for them, and after some encouragement, they joined the others who'd now gathered in the living room.

Before Sam shut the door another vehicle pulled up—one he didn't recognize. Must be Charlotte and her date. Hmm. He yanked on his necktie, since it suddenly felt like a noose. Whoever invented neckties should be hung with one of them. Perhaps Edith's foul mood had doused his fine spirits, but he wasn't so naive as to swallow all of that as truth. Bottom line— he was getting married, and he should rally behind Charlotte to do the same. And as Charlotte's self-appointed big brother, he would have to monitor the situation. Heavily.

The stranger's vehicle, a small pickup, wasn't expensive, but it wasn't a beater either. Charlotte's date opened her door and helped her out. He seemed like a gentleman, but the man was dressed a little too cowboy-ish in his Western shirt, frayed leather vest, and boots. Guess he was a real *Dukes of Hazzard* kind of guy. But what did he think the dinner was—an Easter roundup? He must be a redneck. There were plenty of them around, and one could spot a redneck instantly—since they were more bow-leg than brain. Sam sighed. He felt ashamed of his thoughts. But not *that* ashamed.

Sam conjured up a smile as the couple came up the walk.

Charlotte carried a white lily in a pot with a blue bow, and she was dressed the same way—a white dress with a wide blue ribbon around her waist. Had she planned it that way? To be so coordinated? To look so charming? "Hi, Charlotte."

"Hi, Sam. I'd like to introduce you to Lou Maverick." She gestured to her date.

Lou Maverick? What was that—the guy's stage name for rodeo days?

"And Lou," Charlotte said, "this is Sam Wilder."

Lou reached out and shook his hand. Sam thought his grip seemed a bit wonky, but he overlooked it. Sam led them all into the entry, so he could quiz Lou a bit further.

Charlotte handed Sam the potted lily. "Happy Easter."

"Thanks." On closer inspection of Charlotte's date, the man had a bald spot, a buffalo frame, and a topsy-turvy face that some women might call handsome. Some, but probably not Charlotte.

"You're welcome," Charlotte said, sounding way too formal. "Lou just came from a performance . . . at a Houston theatre."

"I didn't have time to change." Lou looked at his clothes and smirked. "Sorry. I usually wear a suit. But Charlotte makes up for my shortcomings. I told her she looked so lovely in her dress that she could romance the Easter eggs right out of their hiding places."

No matter how true the statement was, Sam just wasn't up to chuckling.

"Thanks." Charlotte shuffled her purse from one arm to the other. "Actually, the reason Lou is dressed this way is because his family owns the Maverick Theatre."

Maverick Theatre, huh? He'd been there years before. Good shows. But actors were more notorious than rednecks could ever think to be. At least rednecks had a sense of moral decency—on occasion. If Charlotte was going to marry, which he hoped she would, then she deserved someone who'd cherish her. Someone who'd take good care of her. Actors didn't have two nickels of loyalty to rub together. They probably didn't even *have* two nickels, period.

"So, you were playing a cowboy in the production?" Sam asked Lou, trying not to simper too much.

Lou gestured with his hands. "Just for the day."

Did he have a tongue depressor in his pocket—with a happy face sticker on top? Surely not.

"Lou is very modest." Charlotte stepped closer to him. "Today he did a special performance for a group of disadvantaged kids."

"True," Lou said. "But I'm not an actor. I never did follow in my family's profession or go into business with them at the Maverick. But I do support them."

Sam got "curiouser and curiouser." "Well, Lou, what *do* you do for a living?"

"I'm a doctor." Lou smiled. "Pediatrics."

Charlotte smiled.

Sam smiled, but he wanted to ask the man to leave immediately. Preferably sooner.

20

Sam knew he was a grown man, and he had to put childish attitudes away, so instead of saying something that reeked of adolescent gibberish, he said with a butler-like demeanor, "Let's join the others. Dinner is ready."

After everyone had gathered in the dining room for the feast, Nelly continued to hover over the table and fuss over the food.

Audrey must have known what he was thinking since she pulled out a chair and nodded toward Nelly to sit down. Sam went to stand behind the chair with Audrey. "Nelly?"

"What?" Nelly stared at the two of them. "What's that chair for?"

"For you." Sam motioned for her to sit down.

"I don't know," Nelly said. "Mr. Wilder never allowed me—"

"I am not Mr. Wilder. I am Sam. Now please have a seat before your wonderful cooking gets so cold no one will want to eat it."

Nelly's scowl thawed. "Well, if you put it that way." She straightened her shoulders, smoothed her new Easter dress, and allowed Sam to seat her at the table.

"If we need anything else, Nelly, we can take turns going to the kitchen." Sam glanced around the table at the guests and announced, "I'm sorry that Edith's daughter and Lucy Loman couldn't be here today, but we're very happy all of the rest of you could come." When they were all seated, Sam offered a hand to Meredith and to Mr. LaGrange who sat on either side of him. They clasped hands with him.

Edith elbowed Mr. LaGrange, who then pulled off his hat, leaving behind some serious hat hair.

Sam grinned to himself. Everyone followed his lead and held hands, even Obie joined in, making an unbroken circle around the table.

Sam looked at Mr. LaGrange. "Sir, would you like to say grace?"

Mr. LaGrange cleared his throat. "Well, that would be kind of hard since I'm an atheist."

"You are?" Sam asked. "I guess you're right. It would make prayer seem pretty pointless to you." He turned to Wally. "Pastor, do you mind?"

"Of course." Wally bowed his head.

After a stirring but short prayer, Audrey and Nelly started passing heaping bowls of food around the table.

Sam took a big helping of dressing, his favorite part. So, one of Charlotte's friends was an atheist. Yeah, that was so like Charlotte—there was no one she wouldn't befriend.

Nelly loaded her plate as she eyeballed Mr. LaGrange. "I've never known an atheist before. So, how is it that you can sleep at night?"

Mr. LaGrange chuckled. "Pretty well, with some melatonin from the health food store."

"Well, how do you explain miracles and such?" Nelly asked, taking a big bite of her sweet potatoes.

"It's very simple really." Mr. LaGrange aimed his fork at her and grinned. "When something good happens you call it a miracle. When something bad happens you say it wasn't God's will. Or it was God's will. Whatever fits the moment. I merely call them what they both are . . . pure chance."

Nelly pointed her fork right back at him. "Well, all I know is, when I see what looks like a miracle, my soul cries out to thank somebody. And I can't see how that deep craving in my spirit can be a random thing." She ran her knuckles over her heart. "Even when times are tough, and I've seen some pretty rough times, it sets things right to be thankful to somebody. The reason it feels right is 'cause our souls were designed that way."

"I agree," Lou chimed in. "As a doctor I see cases all the time that have an unpredicted outcome . . . incidents where children are healed . . . events that can't be accounted for any other way than a miracle."

"Humph. Well, I may not believe in miracles," Mr. LaGrange said. "But I know how to be thankful. And today, Nelly, I'm mighty thankful for your sweet tea."

He took another sip. "So, what's the secret to your sweet tea?"

"Well, honey," Nelly said, "I always say that if the spoon can't stand up straight in my pitcher of sweet tea then 'bout another bag of sugar ought to do it."

Chuckles flowed around the table.

Sam grinned at Nelly and raised his glass of sweet tea to her. "I realize this isn't Thanksgiving Day, but I still want to say how thankful I am for Easter and all the love it represents. For dear friends like you. Oh, and of course, for my bride-to-be."

"Aww, that's as sweet as Nelly's tea." Audrey raised her glass to him.

"Oh, and one side note, pastor," Sam said. "Audrey and I greeted everyone as a couple today, but I want to make it clear that I live here, and Audrey lives in the guesthouse. Just thought I'd add that tidbit of information in case anyone wondered."

"I wasn't worried, Sam." Pastor Wally buttered his roll. "You seem like a principled man to me."

"Thank you for your vote of confidence. I hope I can live up to it." Why had he said that? He sunk his fork into a slice of ham. New subject. "By the way everyone, after we get this house cleaned up and cleared out, we're going to put it on the market. If you know of anyone who might be interested, let us know. But Audrey wants to have the wedding reception here, so we have to hold onto the house until then."

Audrey went around the table refilling everyone's glasses with tea. "But, Sam, I hope I'm not the only one who wants our wedding reception here."

"No, of course not. I think it's a great idea." Sam dug into his salad and leisurely glanced at Charlotte. Her head dipped toward her date—Mr. Redneck Actor Turned Doctor Maverick. She clearly took pleasure in his company. Even so far as to cleaving to his every word. But it seemed obvious to Sam now—that no matter how fine or accomplished a man, there was no one he would fully approve of to marry Charlotte.

"I don't know how we'll sell this house, though, since I doubt there's anyone in Middlebury who could afford it." Audrey sat back down, her chair scooting loudly on the wooden floor.

"True, but I'll bet you'll still be able to sell it," Meredith said, as she helped herself to the creamed squash. "A Realtor friend of mine claims more and more Houstonians will want to retire out of the city. She says folks like it out here because it's not too far away from the city, but it's still real country. And the land prices haven't skyrocketed. At least not yet."

Edith grunted. "Well, I for one have lived here my whole life, and I can't say it pleases me to think we might get overrun by a lot of city folks. They bring the city vices with them."

"And they bring in scurvy and warts too," Mr. LaGrange added. "Don't forget that, old woman. Oh, and I forgot, city people bring in restless hair syndrome too."

Edith tapped her foot against the wooden floor—it was her one-of-a-kind tap—a gesture she'd sharpened in history class and used on the unfortunate souls who learned the hard way that Mrs. Mosley had zero tolerance for spontaneous humor. "We already have the hair problem here in Middlebury, thanks to you." Edith gave Mr. LaGrange's arm a slap with her napkin and pointed to his head. "And stop calling me old woman."

Mr. LaGrange made some little mumbly noises and shrugged like he couldn't care less about his hat hair. But the second Edith turned away, he smoothed it down.

"Well, I bet city people don't bring in lice," Obie said. "At school we have lots of those."

Some chuckles rippled around the table as well as a few flickers of concern.

Mr. LaGrange picked up a small wad of pink Easter grass from the table and tossed it on Edith's head when she wasn't looking.

Sam tried not to stare at the tiny comedy/drama next to him. How random was that? Surely Mr. LaGrange wasn't interested in Edith. She was a Baptist for goodness sakes! But he was certainly acting as asinine as a lovesick schoolboy.

In spite of the fact that Edith had nodded and turned a few times, the grass still remained hanging onto the back of her hair. It seemed odd to let it stay there as she chatted—gave him sort of a rebel feeling—but if he mentioned it now, Edith would just get riled up again.

"Edith, I hope you don't hate Houstonians too much," Audrey said. "Since I'm one of them."

"Does it mean you have vices?" Obie asked Audrey. "I don't know what that word is."

"It means bad habits," Roberta said quietly as she offered him the basket of rolls. "And I'm sure Miss Audrey doesn't have any of those."

"We've all got vices," Mr. LaGrange said. "Even Miss Audrey."

"Oh, my stars, what a thing to say to our hostess." Edith looked back and forth, felt around on her hair, and pulled the pink grass from her head. The glare she gave Mr. LaGrange could have melted asphalt.

He ignored her while he chased his peas across his plate. A few of them flipped onto the floor, but he made no attempt to retrieve them.

Audrey daubed at her mouth with a napkin. "No, I'm sure Mr. LaGrange is right. I'm sure I do have vices."

Sam grinned. "We just don't know what they are yet."

Everyone around the table perked up and stared at the foolish person who uttered such an acerbic comment. *Me.* Sam thought maybe he'd died during those moments. He wasn't sure, but he could just imagine the doctor trying to revive him, with Audrey telling him not to work too hard at bringing him back to life. Had he just been thinking out loud? "I was just trying to banter with you, Audrey, but after it came out of my mouth, I realized how it came off. Will you forgive me?" He said the words directly to Audrey, and he said it with every bit of sincerity and humility he could muster.

Everyone waited for her reply.

Audrey smiled. "Of course I'll forgive you. That's what marriages are made of. Forgiveness."

"I thought marriages were made of love," Mr. LaGrange said in a blustery voice.

Nelly leaned forward in her chair and gaped at Mr. LaGrange. "Yes, marriages *are* made of love, LaGrange," she said. "But let's not forget about the merits of forgiveness. 'Cause without it, we would have asked you to leave half an hour ago." She cocked her head at him while she stabbed a cherry tomato with her fork. Then Nelly puckered up her lips to keep from grinning until a laugh finally erupted from her mouth like a bursting dam.

Mr. LaGrange chuckled, and it too escalated into roaring laughter.

Everyone at the table joined in until the whole room was filled with mirth. Sam laughed too. What in the world would his father have thought of the day? Of Audrey serving Nelly on Easter Sunday? Of his unused dining room filled with people and laughter? He would have hated it all.

Without seeking her out, Sam caught Charlotte's laughing gaze. In that one moment, there was such a rush of emotion that it stampeded right over Sam's heart. There was no getting around his feelings. But he also knew that even amidst the turmoil, even amidst his inability to wipe away the past, come June, he would marry Audrey. He would never again allow her to be abandoned. His will would stay as strong as iron on the matter. But he was equally sure of something else—being a spectator at one of Charlotte's date nights was not something he wanted to partake of again. Sam broke their gaze by taking a long swig of tea, but he swallowed funny and came up sputtering.

Meredith patted him on the back. "Are you all right?"

"Well, I'm—" The doorbell rang. Good. Saved by the bell twice in one day.

"It must be Justin," Charlotte said softly. "I knew he would come."

"That's the man who saved my life." Obie reached for the silver tray of deviled eggs, which were just out of reach. "Maybe I could ask Mr. Justin if he wants a kitten."

"That is a very good idea." Roberta scooted the tray closer to him, and they both took several eggs from the tray.

"Charlotte, do you mind getting the door?" Audrey said. "Justin might feel less timid if he sees you first, since you're a friend of his."

Charlotte rose from the table. "I'd be happy to."

Lightning flashed through the drapes, and then a second or two later, a deep grumbling thunder rolled its way through the room.

"Gracious," Nelly said. "My momma used to say that thunder was like a potato wagon rolling over a bridge, but I think that one was rolling right over my bones."

"That's funny," Obie said.

"I think we're in for some rambunctious weather today." Meredith reached for the bowl of olives. "But then I've always loved a good storm."

"I like a good storm too." Nelly's grin held a trace of concern. "As long as nobody gets hurt."

21

As Charlotte walked from Sam's dining room toward the front door, the words, "I shouldn't have come," played over and over in her mind. And it was true. Every time she felt strong enough to withstand the coming marriage between Sam and Audrey, her courage got dashed on the rocks of sentiment. *Oh, Lord, why am I so frail in spirit?*

And Lou, dear Lou was such a good man. He would be the perfect husband for some woman, but Charlotte could already tell she wasn't meant to be that woman. There wasn't anything in particular Lou did or didn't do that settled the matter in her heart. It was just a subtle knowing that they were not meant to spend their lives walking side by side. But in the end, it was less complicated than that—Lou simply wasn't Sam.

Charlotte opened one of the heavy oak front doors, and even though she was fairly certain Justin would keep his promise to attend, the man standing before her was not Justin. "May I help you?"

The man winced and then offered her a half-smile. "I know this will be hard at first, Charlotte. But give it a minute, and you'll know me."

"I'm sorry. You must have me confused with someone else." Then Charlotte got a little worried. "How do you know my name?"

"It's me, Justin Yule," the man said.

"But . . . " Charlotte thought the man was playing some sort of practical joke on her. The man on the porch looked handsome and clean shaven with short groomed hair and expensive clothes. He reminded her of an Eddie Bauer model. He looked nothing at all like Justin Yule.

The stranger limped inside and into the bright entry light. Charlotte took note of his shuffle. That limp was certainly a part of Justin, at least until he healed. She gazed into his eyes and gasped. "Justin. I can't believe it. I see it now. It is you. But I don't understand. Why did you . . . "

Audrey came up from behind them and gasped. "Justin."

Charlotte turned to Audrey. "How did you know it was him right away?"

She smiled warmly. "I just knew." Audrey stepped over to Justin, hugged him, and then suddenly pulled away. "I'm glad you came. I was so afraid I'd frightened you off for good."

"I'm here. I promised I'd come." Justin stroked his chin as if he were still marveling that he had a face under all his bushy hair.

"You shaved off your beard and cut your hair." Audrey wound her arms in front of her and laced her fingers in a demure way. "You look so . . . "

Charlotte knew Audrey wanted to use the word handsome, but perhaps it felt inappropriate considering her fiancé sat in the next room.

"It was time," Justin straightened his shoulders, "to make a few changes."

Audrey said, "If it's okay to mention it now, I do know where I've seen you before. You're from local TV, and you were always just known as the Plant Doctor. That's why no one recognized your name. And that salute of yours, well, that was your signature good-bye to viewers."

"Yes, that used to be me." Justin lowered his gaze and shuffled his feet. "Not anymore."

"What happened?" Charlotte asked.

"I think all of you deserve to know," Justin said. "If I could—"

"Please, we would love for you to eat with us in the dining room. Then you may tell us your story . . . if you choose to." Audrey led Justin into the dining room, and said to everyone, "Let me reintroduce someone to you . . . Justin Yule."

Sounds and murmurings and shouts of surprise trickled around the room.

"Are you the same man who saved my life?" Obie asked. "You sure look different."

"I feel different. I'm glad to see you looking well, Obie." Justin limped over to Charlotte and sat down next to her.

"I used to watch you on TV all the time," Nelly said, pouring Justin a glass of sweet tea. "You're that plant guru guy. When you'd do your shows, people would think you were talking about plants, and you were, but you always tied it into life so snugly it was like wrapping up in one of my momma's quilts." Nelly pressed her hand against her chest. "Got me here, every time, Mr. Yule."

Audrey added, "I never missed a show."

"If you're such a big TV personality why did you come out to Middlebury and pretend to be a homeless guy?" Mr. LaGrange pushed away from the table. "Makes us all feel a little duped."

"I don't feel duped," Wally said. "But I do wonder what happened to you, Justin, to drive you to something so desperate. Are you able to talk about it now?"

"Yes, I think so." Justin fiddled with his napkin but didn't place it on his lap. "It's time."

"Would you like me to get you a plate of hot food before you begin?" Nelly asked. "You look hungry. Of course, I always think everybody looks hungry."

"Thank you. I would love to have some in few minutes." Justin smiled at Nelly. "But right now I have a need to get this out."

Charlotte gave Justin her full attention. For a long time, she'd wondered about his past, his story.

The table went quiet, including Mr. LaGrange.

Justin took a sip of his sweet tea. "I built a good life in my twenties and thirties, doing what I loved . . . teaching people about growing things. I was successful and happily married. I had what some people might call a perfect life. But then my wife, well, she passed away."

Justin moved the sweet tea away from his hand. "We used to ride bikes every weekend, my wife and I. It was one of the many things we loved doing together. But while on the road, she swerved at the wrong time . . . and was hit by a car. She died instantly. Well, she and the baby. My wife was three months pregnant with our first child when it happened. But she wouldn't have lost her balance that day had it not been for me. I had distracted her. I was arguing with her about spending too much money. She got upset with me and swerved in front of that car. It happened so fast. Her life was taken so quickly, it still frightens me."

Justin grasped the edge of the table. "I've played that scene over and over in my head, but the outcome is always the same. I lost the one person I loved most in the world that day as well as our child . . . and it was my fault."

Charlotte closed her hand over Justin's. "I'm so sorry."

"We've all done things we've regretted deeply. All of us," Pastor Wally said. "No one can escape it."

Justin looked up, his face troubled. "Yes, but did the mistake cost someone his or her life?"

"You're right. It isn't all that common, but you're not alone," Wally said. "And you couldn't have known she would swerve. You wouldn't have wished it on your wife or child."

"Never, but the car hit them just the same. And it destroyed me that day too. I quit the show and became sort of a displaced person, trying to find meaning in my life. Trying to forgive myself. I lived off my savings, but then that money dwindled. I lost contact with my family and friends. I think they were glad to be rid of me. By the time I arrived in Middlebury I was lost. I looked like a homeless man. Since that's how people perceived me, I just let them think what they wanted to. And then after a while, it fit. I could no longer identify with my old self or with anyone successful. That man was gone. And somehow it was a relief . . . the way I sort of disappeared from myself."

Everyone around the table seemed mesmerized with Justin's story.

Mr. LaGrange broke the silence by saying, "So, what turned you around? Made you want to get yourself all cleaned up today?"

Thunder interrupted them, but it growled more gently this time.

Justin looked around the table. "It was the town, I suppose. The people. They gave me love when I needed it. Most of them, that is. Sometimes people said some pretty hateful things to me. They didn't understand what happened. But they were very few. Mostly, people offered me work or encouragement. Especially Pastor Wally and Charlotte. They were kind enough to bring me back from the edge. And then there was Obie." Justin looked over at the boy.

"I think I understand what happened." Obie patted his roll against his mouth. "You couldn't save your wife, but you could save me. We sort of rescued each other."

Justin nodded. "You're a smart young man to figure that out. And it helped me to know I still had a reason to be here. I could still make a difference. It was another step back toward living again . . . and in forgiving myself."

"Word about what you did for Obie spread pretty fast around town," Wally said. "Sounds like an ordained moment."

"A miracle," Audrey murmured.

"It was heroic . . . what you did for Obie." Meredith raised her glass to Justin. "And I feel honored that you would trust us enough to share your story after all these years."

A sniffle or two could be heard, and Charlotte noticed one of them was hers. But beyond hearing Justin's amazing story was the pleasure of seeing Meredith and Pastor Wally together. Guess they got over their age differences. *Good for them.*

"Well, thank you all for listening to my story," Justin said. "By the way, Obie, I hadn't gotten a chance to say it before, but I'm sure sorry about your mom."

"Yeah. Me too," Obie said.

Justin smiled. "It's okay to *feel* when somebody dies."

"Okay." Obie took a bite of his roll.

Up until that moment, Roberta had been rather quiet, but she daubed her lips with her napkin and asked, "Justin, what will you do now?"

"Will you go back into TV?" Meredith pulled off her Easter egg earbobs and set them on the table. "I mean people loved it . . . the show."

"Thank you. To be honest, I don't know if I'd ever be able to go back. I'm still a shell of a man, but at least the shell feels alive again. It's more than I've felt in a long time. I'd like to keep working in your greenhouse, Sam. If it'd be okay. I'm sorry I ran off the other day. It wasn't right."

"No problem," Audrey said. "You taking off like that, the way you did . . . well, it saved Obie's life. Such an inspiring moment."

"Yes, it is," Sam said. "But the job is still yours, Justin. Well, that is, as long as we have this house. I don't know if we can afford you now, though. I mean, to have the Plant Doctor all to ourselves is quite—"

"Same pay." Justin held up his hand. "It was more than generous."

"People will see you differently now." Audrey toyed with the charm bracelet on her wrist. "I mean between the new way you look and the buzz that's bound to happen, are you going to be okay with all the attention?"

Justin slipped his napkin onto his lap. "I'll do my best."

The rain came in torrents then, and the sound of it was like an audience of a million clapping all at once. Somehow applause seemed right for the moment.

Mr. LaGrange leaned over to Edith and mumbled, "No chance of rain, huh?"

"We didn't bring an umbrella," Obie said. "Coool."

Charlotte grinned at Obie. Somehow Roberta had managed to tame that cowlick of his. Probably took a whole tube of hair gel. And Roberta had groomed Obie into a handsome young boy. It was obvious he thrived under Roberta's care. It was a bittersweet joy to think of it.

Mr. LaGrange unpinned his carnation from his lapel, gave it a sniff, and set it next to Edith's plate. "Well, I'm afraid I have to go now." He set his napkin on the table with unruffled civility, but his face had gone as red as rhubarb pie. "Thank you . . . for your hospitality."

"Leaving so soon?" Audrey rose. "But you'll miss Nelly's grand finale."

"No, thank you. And please, don't get up. I'll let myself out." Mr. LaGrange scooted his chair back and rose. "I have one thing to say before I go. I can swallow that delicious dinner. It went down just fine, but listening to you people talk incessantly about ordained moments and miracles is something I just can't stomach. Not when everyone here neglects to talk about Justin's wife or Obie's mother, the woman who killed herself. Where was the miracle for them when they needed it?"

Mr. LaGrange pressed the tips of his fingers to his chin. "Your religion has put you inside one of those sculpted Easter eggs made of sugar. It's pretty to look at, but if you really need it, you discover that it has no real purpose. It's just a sweet lump of nothing." He rapped his knuckles on the table. "Please excuse me. I guess I'm having an *un*inspired moment." And then Mr. LaGrange walked out of the dining room, let himself out the front door, and walked into the stormy Easter night.

Aghast seemed too puny a word to describe Edith's expression.

22

Sam drank down the last of his morning coffee and looked over his laptop at Nelly. She was busy in the kitchen as always, scurrying around. He had no idea what she was up to, except that she usually had something going into the oven or coming out of it.

Nelly was singing, "Swing Low, Sweet Chariot," and that meant she was in a good mood.

"Nelly?"

"Hmm?" She looked back at him. "My singing bothering you?"

"No, of course not." He folded up his laptop.

Nelly lifted the coffee pot toward him. "You need some more of my exceptionally good coffee?"

Sam chuckled. "No, thanks. It was good, though." He drummed his fingers on the table. "Uhh, I was just wondering about something."

"Wondering can be dodgy business," she sing-songed. When Sam paused, Nelly glanced up from her work. "What is it?" An anxious look eclipsed her smile.

"The fish you serve us at dinner doesn't taste like store bought."

"Oh." Nelly's smile returned. "That's because they aren't. Those fish are from your daddy's pond out back. I mean *your* pond out back."

"I knew it." Sam slapped the table. "It had to be. And who does all the fishing?"

"I do."

"Yeah, that's what I thought. You are a woman of many talents, Nelly. My father took you for granted in so many ways."

She turned back to her work at the counter and made no reply.

"Audrey texted from the guesthouse last night and said she was going to sleep in today. And I noticed we're having a fine spring day. I haven't been fishing in years. Want to go with me?"

Nelly looked at him as if he'd lost his mind, but then she nodded. "All right. The fish might be biting, and I haven't been out to buy us any meat for tonight's supper. So, your idea might work."

"Great." Sam rinsed his mug out in the sink and patted her on the back. "Let's do it."

"Right now?"

"Yep."

"Okay. I guess I can do that. For once, the oven's off." Nelly removed her apron and followed Sam out the back door.

They gathered up some fishing gear in the toolshed, and headed out on the path to the pond. Once on the bank they both baited their hooks.

Nelly pulled her rod back and gave it a flick, sending the line sailing across the pond with ease. She glanced over at him as he fumbled with the reel. "Need some help with that?"

Sam grinned. "You can just tuck that smirk right back into your pocket."

Nelly chuckled.

"I think I've got it. I haven't done this in a long time." Sam tried hurling the line toward the middle of the pond, but the worm and bobber landed pathetically close to the bank. Annoyed with himself, he let them set there in the mire.

"Fishing for crawdads along the muddy banks, are you?" Nelly squelched a grin as she casually reeled in her line.

"Maybe. Just in case we run out of bait."

Nelly smiled a smile big enough to rival a politician's.

Sam glanced around here and there, searching for any signs of poison ivy. Good grief. He'd gotten to be such a wimp in the city. Being outdoors would be good for him. But before he brought up the real reason for persuading Nelly to go fishing with him, he said, "I'm sorry about Mr. LaGrange at the dinner. Kind of tinged the holiday meal with sadness. He had a valid question about suffering, but he lacked . . . delicacy."

Nelly looked at him with her signature droll expression. "Yeah, that LaGrange is a piece of work. He has as much finesse as a sumo wrestler at a tea party."

Sam chuckled. "True."

"Charlotte says that maybe all LaGrange needs is some extra love."

"Sounds so much like Charlotte. She's something else, isn't she?"

"Uhh-huh. She still is." Nelly cleared her throat.

Sam reeled in his line. "But what do you think about Mr. LaGrange?"

"I think love is always good," Nelly said. "That was my momma's watchword. It's my motto too. But in LaGrange's case, he might benefit from a good beating with this fishing pole."

Sam threw his head back laughing.

His father had clearly missed out by not talking to Nelly, by not getting to know her beyond her cooking. But then before he left for college he couldn't recall spending time chatting with Nelly or any of the other employees. Had he adopted some of the same attitudes as his father without knowing it?

"But wasn't that just like God?" Nelly said. "To send us an atheist for Easter dinner? You know, stir things up a bit."

"I think it is like God."

Sam breathed in the cool air, wishing he could just enjoy the moment and not bother Nelly about secrets.

After a few minutes, Nelly said, "Just so ya know, there are a couple of things I'll miss about this place when you sell it. This pond and that fine stand of pecan trees over there. The meats off those trees were so sweet and thick you could make a meal out of them. And they make the best pecan pie on this side of the Mississippi. Yes, indeed, I'll miss those trees and this here pond. Well, and of course I'll miss the bluebonnets. But that's a given. This year they look like somebody spilled out a knapsack full of jewels, don't they?"

"Yes, they do."

Nelly finished bringing in her line and then recast. The bobber landed on the slivery smooth plane of the pond, only breaking the surface enough to tease some fish into thinking the worm might be an easy meal. "Oh, and one more thing I'm gonna miss. Those black swans over there that glide across this pond. I remember one time your daddy came home from Melbourne, Australia, on business, and I overheard him talking about the botanical gardens there and how they had black swans. Anyway, he had to have some right away, so he hired a man to bring them in."

"I don't remember much of that, but I'm glad for the swans. They're peaceful looking creatures." Sam tried casting again, and this time, it didn't plop, but flew out toward deeper water with at least a measure of dignity.

Nelly took in a deep breath. "Was there something in particular you wanted to talk about?"

"What do you mean?"

"I just get this feeling you brought me out here to do more than fish and chew the fat. Just wondering if you meant to say more."

Sam grinned. "Well, I've heard that wondering can be dodgy business."

"So, I'm right then."

"I just thought if I—"

"You just thought if you brought me out here to my favorite spot you could schmooze your way into asking me some questions."

Sam chuckled. "You're too smart for me, Nelly, and way too intuitive."

"Probably."

A dragonfly whorled by him, skimming the grasses, light as air, and it reminded him of how weighty his spirit felt with what he was about to say. "Okay. I'll give it to you straight. Because of my father, there have been way too many secrets in his house. Let's bring some out into the light. Okay?"

Nelly released a bulky sigh. "The problem with secrets is . . . once they're out, you can't never put them back. But . . . all right. I will tell you this, not because I love gossip, but because I believe the truth sets us free. Trying to figure out whether to tell you or not has been like this hornet's nest of debate going on inside my head. But better now than after you marry."

"I think we need to sit down." Sam pulled up two Adirondack chairs, and after they set their poles aside, they settled in underneath a maple tree.

Nelly sat quietly for a while, and then said, "I wish your father had come out here. He owned it, but he never enjoyed it. Never let this pond work its magic. He was always tied up in that house with his treasures or what he thought were treasures. He loved everything old. I think it was because he felt more comfortable with the ways of the past. I understood it a little myself, but some things have to change, or they can get a stranglehold on you and your family." Nelly looked over at Sam. "I do have a point to all this. Back when you and Charlotte were in high school, you used to bring her home sometimes."

"That's right. The first few times, it went well. My father seemed to be impressed with Charlotte, and she was even invited to dinner. All was going well. I thought I had his approval if we were to marry. He knew I loved her. But something must have gone wrong. When I proposed, Charlotte said no. It was the biggest blow of my life. I don't think I ever truly recovered from it. And I always wondered if my father had somehow influenced Charlotte."

Nelly gripped the arms of the chair. "I believe he did, Sam."

"What happened?"

"I didn't hear the conversation when you two were dating, but I did hear what your father said to Charlotte on his deathbed. As you know, there's a door at the back of his room that leads to the hallway that goes to the kitchen. Well, that backdoor was ajar."

"Really?" Sam raised an eyebrow. "You were eavesdropping?"

"I hadn't intended to, but the sudden harsh sound of your father's voice made me curious, wondering why he would speak to Charlotte that way. I felt sorry for her, but yes, after I heard his furious tone, I leaned closer to hear."

"I'm glad you did." Sam picked up a pinecone and turned it around in his hand. "Charlotte never volunteered to tell me what he said that day, and I couldn't demand that she tell me. It wouldn't have been right. But I could tell from her pale face when she came out of my father's room that it hadn't gone well." Sam ran his hands along the arms of the chair. "So, he didn't offer her the apology I'd hoped for?"

"I'm sorry," Nelly said. "There was no apology. But before he died, your father felt Charlotte had a right to know the reason why she could never marry you."

Sam squeezed the pinecone, which sent stinging pain through his palm. "Nelly, it's impossible for me to guess at my father's reasoning."

"I will tell you. Your daddy said that Charlotte's grand-mother on her father's side was half African American, and he said he wouldn't allow any son of his to marry into a family with such a polluted bloodline. He didn't want to have a black grandchild or even worry that there was the possibility of it."

"Oh, no," Sam groaned. "I knew my father was, well, prejudiced, but I had no idea he'd taken it to such extreme levels." He dug his fingernails into his scalp. "I'm sorry you heard it, Nelly. I apologize for my father's heartlessness and his ignorance."

Nelly laced her fingers together. "It was just fear talking. People do the most outlandish things when they get consumed by it."

"That's being too generous on a man who was cruel." Sam rose out of the chair and threw the pinecone into the pond. Then he picked up his fishing rod, tried to break it over his knee, and when it wouldn't snap in his hands, he threw it into the water. He looked at Nelly.

She drew back." You're not going to throw me in next, are you?"

"No." He grinned.

"I've never seen you with a temper before. It's kind of scary," Nelly said.

"It's scary to me as well. All of it. How could my father do that? It wasn't his decision to make! I didn't know about

Charlotte's grandmother, but that information about her heritage wouldn't have mattered to me in the least. Because of my father's insane bigotry and his need to control everything . . . he ruined our chances for joy. It's as simple and as evil as that. And when I think of what Charlotte might have thought when he said that to her, it grieves me all over again. Surely she didn't think I felt that way too. I hope not."

"I'm sure Charlotte knew that you weren't anything like your father."

Sam stuffed his fists into his pockets. "But my father must have been so angry back then that Charlotte felt she had to say no to the proposal. She felt she had no choice. Nelly, when you were by the door, did you hear any more? Anything at all?"

"No. I'm sorry. I was so surprised at the way he was talking to Charlotte that I accidentally dropped the pen in my hand. It made enough of a clatter I thought they might find me out. I just hurried down the hall then." Nelly took a tissue out of her pocket and daubed at her forehead. "I'm pretty sure there was more to their conversation, but that's all I heard."

"Still, I feel it's only part of the mystery. But to talk to Charlotte about it now . . . to gain more information about our past, it wouldn't help anyone. I could ask her to forgive my father for what he did, but it wouldn't change our history." Sam gazed out over the pond. So serene. A flawless veneer. Is that what his father had wanted to present to the world? What he thought would be an unblemished family? *God, help me not to hate my father.* Sam kicked the tackle box, making it tumble down the bank.

"We're back to that again, huh?" Nelly clasped her hand around her throat.

"I'm sorry. I'll calm down, eventually." He gazed up at the sailing clouds and let his eyes lids drift shut. "I'm sorry about so many things." He opened his eyes again and tore at some of the spring leaves, which hung low on a branch in front of him. New growth. New life. So easy for trees. Infinitely harder for humans. He stepped away from the branch and the reminder.

"Sam?"

"Yes?"

"I'm about to say something, and it might be considered what my momma would call a "come to Jesus" talk. Can you handle it?" Nelly asked.

"Sure." Sam grinned. "I promise I won't throw anything at you."

"Good. That's good." Nelly fanned the tissue in front of her face as she shook her head. "Maybe now that you know the truth, you can let it go just like your fishing pole out in the water. You're engaged to be married to Miss Audrey who's a fine woman. Is there something else you need to talk about?" Nelly rose out of the chair.

"What do you mean?" Sam frowned. Why had he said it? He knew exactly what she meant.

Sam couldn't tell if Nelly's facial contortion—a scowl—was from sympathy or disapproval. Maybe it was a little of both.

"You're a good and admirable man, Sam Wilder. The best. But sometimes even good guys need a little help, so that's what I'm offering. So, here it is. You talk about the past like you want to resurrect it, not look at it and bury it proper." Nelly put her hands on her hips. "Seems like a man who's about to marry the true joy of his life . . . a man who's been given a second chance at love, wouldn't be writhing around, like some dying creature, talking about the past like it's more important than the future."

23

*T*he bell jangled on the front door of Meredith's antique shop, making her look up from her work. *Okay, clear the decks.* It was her favorite customer, her favorite everything. The good reverend had come to pay her a visit. And here she'd been worried he'd forgotten to drop by with it being the afternoon and all. She christened him with her brightest, warmest smile. "Hello, Pastor Wallace."

"Hello, Cricket."

Meredith took a leisurely sip of her cream soda as she watched the pastor. He looked so distinguished in his clerical collar and his mustache that she released a little cherub sigh. And, well, the way he said her name in that deep southern accent made her dissolve into a puddle inside her Crocs. Yes, she was being as syrupy as a paperback romance, but she didn't care one whit. Meredith stuffed the lemon wood polish and the rag under the counter and fingered her cameo brooch.

Instead of walking right up to her to give her a hug, the pastor strolled around the shop, humming something classical and glancing at a row of old books and miscellany. "I noticed something." He gave the keys on an antique typewriter a couple of strokes.

"And what's that?" Meredith wanted to add, "my darling," but she hesitated. In life, timing was everything, and since timing had never been her strongest suit, among other things, she approached gingerly. She truly hoped their bond might bloom into more. But she'd leave the "darling" off for now.

"You used to call me Wally, and now it's Pastor Wallace. Why is that? Most people . . . the more they get to know each other, the more informal their greeting gets toward each other. Not the other way around."

"Well, you see," Meredith tapped her lips with her finger, "I'm not most people."

"Yes, I noticed that the moment I met you," he said. "Do you realize we've seen each other every day since the fire?"

"I do," Meredith replied. "In fact, would you like to come over for my stuffed cabbage this evening?"

"Will it be as incredible as your roasted chicken and challah bread?"

"Even better. And I'll have lox and bagels too. What can I say? I love it . . . to feed you."

"Then we're sailing in the same blissful boat together, because I love being fed by you." The pastor's grin was full of lingering delight as if he were recalling every juicy bite of her roasted chicken. "By the way, I love these antique telephones you have all over the shop. What are they?"

"Well, the one in front of you is a Kellogg wall telephone . . . 1901. It's my favorite."

"Oh?" The pastor picked up the receiver and as if he were calling her, he said into the mouthpiece, "You say it's your favorite? It always feels good to be a favorite."

Meredith reached for the handset on the brass French telephone sitting on the counter and said into the mouthpiece, "My favorite . . . by far. I don't know what I'd do if a customer came in and bought the thing. I'd be devastated and cry like a baby."

"Well now, we can't have that," he said. "Maybe you won't have to give it up."

The pastor's gaze was so happily steeped in double meaning that mist filled her eyes. "But I'm in the antique business, and pieces come in and pieces go. It's the nature of business. And well, life."

"So, what are we to do?" His expression seemed to say that he already held the answer to his question.

Meredith grinned. "Guess we'll have to improvise."

"Well, what if—"

"What if what?" Meredith gripped the phone.

"I know we agreed to go out as friends. To take this slowly. To see if what we have together could mesh with family and friends and the congregation." He fingered the phone's cord. "They are all important people, but in the end, this is about us."

"Yes, I agree. *Us* is good." Her cat, Rapunzel, strolled over and rubbed up against her leg. She wanted to be held. *You're the joy of my life, princess, but not right now.*

"If you are in agreement . . . I think we can officially be more than friends."

It was those very words she'd dreamed about at night. Meredith took in a deep breath. The smell of lemon oil had to be the finest aroma on earth. "Yes, yes, yes." She nearly nodded her silly head right off her neck. "I am so ready not to be friends with you."

Wally laughed, and then she joined in. What a musical sound they made together. Their laughter was like the trill of flutes or a duo of songbirds. If Wally's parishioners knew his thoughts about now, he might shock a few members,

especially if they'd entertained the idea that he was more sermon than sentiment.

"So, what do you think . . . does this mean you'll be my
sweetheart?"

"Sweetheart . . . what a delightful word. So vintage and so
endearing." But even as she'd been swept off to lofty heights
with that one word, more practical words weighted her down.
The brain-chant, which she knew was inevitable, began its
harsh refrain. *You're. Too. Old.* "I guess it's time for the talk."
Meredith hated the way the words scudded out of her mouth
when his had been so lilting.

The pastor put the receiver back into the hook. "Sounds
serious."

"It might be." Meredith set the handset down in the cradle.
"I don't know if you have spent much time thinking about
this, but I have. What do we do about . . . my age? I'm a decade
older than you. Maybe it's not as noticeable right now, but it
will be in a few years. I know what you've asked me today isn't
a proposal, but it is—"

"But it is one step closer," the pastor said.

"And in a small town like this, don't you think people will
talk, you know, about the vast difference in our ages?"

"First of all, it's not that vast an age difference. I'm sure it's
not uncommon."

"You're right." Meredith fingered the cameo on her collar. "But it's usually the man who's ten years older than the
woman, not the other way around."

"True." The pastor took a few steps closer to her. "But if it
doesn't bother me, what does it matter?"

"But—"

The pastor held up his finger. "In answer to your other
question, knowing the nature of people, yes I'm sure they'll
talk about the difference in our ages. That's what folks do in

small towns, they gab like there's a full pitcher of it in the morning that they're expected to empty by the end of the day. In general, I care what they say, but on this particular subject, I'm not asking for their opinion. I'm asking *you* to be my sweetheart, not the whole town of Middlebury."

Meredith grinned. Wally was arguing his points well, and he looked so cute the way his mouth curled when he got revved up. She relaxed a little in her hope, but she had at least one more round. "This is easy for you to joke about now while there's still some blush on the lilacs. But what happens when the perfume and the color fades? And I don't just mean my appearance. When you're fifty, I'll be on my way to being a retired senior citizen. I'll be creaking with arthritis while you'll still hiking up mountains.

"Actually, I don't hike. I swim."

Meredith wagged her finger at him. "You know exactly what I mean, Pastor Barns."

Wally walked up to the counter. "Then I'll refer you to my grandmother's Bible."

"You mean there's scriptural advice on men marrying women old enough to be their aunts?"

He chuckled. "I meant that I'd let you open my grandmother's Bible and you could see the flowers she'd pressed inside. They're the wildflowers I picked for her when I was a little boy, and since she wanted to keep them near her heart, she pressed them into her Bible. She gave it to me right before she passed away, and those flowers are still there. When I look at them, yes, they're faded, but because of all the fond affections attached to them, to me they're still running over with beauty. And that's the way you will always be in my eyes."

"Ohh." Meredith sniffled. "Do you know how exquisite you are?"

The pastor straightened his shoulders. "You mean physically?" He chuckled.

"No, spiritually."

"Hmm. I don't know whether to argue with you or kiss you."

She tiled her head. "When in doubt, always kiss me, Reverend Barns."

Wally reached out for her hand. "Our first kiss needs to be special."

Meredith accepted his hand and came around the counter to meet him. "Something special. Let's see. I have just the thing." She led him to a rack of vintage clothing and dressed him in a black tailcoat and top hat.

Wally looked in the standing mirror. "Not bad. But let me see what might be right on you." He chose a cathedral wedding veil and attached it to her hair. Then he helped her slip on a pair of lace gloves. She giggled. *Imagine, a mature woman of forty giggling.* The thought made her giggle again.

When they were dressed they turned and looked into the mirror together.

"It's a good look on us." Wally's brown eyes twinkled.

"One step at a time, Reverend Barns." But the sight of them looking like a bride and groom on top of a wedding cake made her heart do the most delightful rumba. "I don't think I've told you, but I love the way you have such an affection for your little flock. I'm just glad I came along so some of it could spill on me."

"Well, the way I feel about you isn't exactly the way I feel about my other parishioners."

Meredith knew she was fishing for sweet nothings, but oh how she loved hearing his words. "I think we're ready now. You know, for what you mentioned earlier." She moved closer to him and fingered his clerical collar. "But are you sure it's not sacrilegious or anything for me to kiss you while you're wearing your uniform?"

"No violations or fines I assure you."

Meredith grinned. They'd spent so much time grinning at each other since he'd walked in the door that her face was beginning to ache. But it was a suffering she could cope with.

"And are you sure you won't mind this bristle brush on my upper lip?" He gestured to his mustache.

"Tickly has its benefits."

He chuckled.

Meredith removed her glasses and slipped them into her pocket.

Then Wally brought his lips to meet with hers in what Meredith could only describe as a sublime union. She lifted the veil around them, closing them in a cocoon of Victorian lace. The kiss was so light, so delicately sweet, it reminded Meredith of the meringue on top of one of her mother's pudding tarts.

After Wally pulled back, she longed for the irresistible creamy filling that rests just below the surface, so she took his face in her hands and kissed him back with all the passion she had held back. His top hat tumbled off his head and bounced somewhere beyond their bliss. It was a good kiss. A grand and messy kiss—just like life would be for them. When she released him, she suddenly realized she might have overstepped her bounds with such a gooey kiss.

Meredith panicked. Her lace-covered fingers rose up in horror. "Was it too much? Please tell me it wasn't. I can tell you this, though, it could not have been more genuinely Meredith."

Wally grinned and took her hands into his. "Do I look upset in any way?"

Meredith sighed and shook her head. "If you want us to be more than friends, I guess you'll have to put up with all of me, including my kisses."

"The problem with you, my dear, Meredith, is that your kisses will be just like ice cream . . . one sweet round will never do."

"Mmm." Meredith reached up and smoothed Wally's hair. It wasn't hat hair, but hair that'd been mussed during their moment of abandon. "Are you sure you want me for a sweetheart, though? I'm such a fumbly, bumbly kind of person. Always too early or too late. Always too something. Sometimes I like to wear mannish-looking apparel." She lifted her polka-dot tie for proof. "I like to paint rooms in the middle of the night. And sometimes, I even lick my plate." She expected a raised eyebrow or two.

"And this is supposed to put me off?" Wally took her into his arms, and she snuggled in close.

"Oh, you are so good. And I don't just mean pastor good. I mean *man* good."

Wally laughed. "And you are woman good." He eased her back and kissed the tip of her nose.

"You know who else seems good? Good together, that is?" Meredith said, thinking out loud.

"Who?" Wally leaned down and grazed a soft kiss along her neck.

"Sam and Charlotte."

"Hmm?" Wally seemed to come back to reality. "What did you say? You meant Sam and Audrey."

"No, I meant Sam and Charlotte. Didn't you see the way they were looking at each other at Easter? Enough to catch an igloo on fire."

Wally chuckled. "I did notice it a little, now that you mention it."

"I heard the two fell in love in high school, but for some reason, it didn't work out."

Wally stroked his chin. "I didn't know that."

"And I'm thrilled for Justin's newfound life, but the way he and Audrey were gazing at each other seemed to be beyond friendship." Meredith took the veil off her head and placed it back on the pedestal. "I just hope after the wedding there aren't some serious regrets for everyone. It would be a hard way to live, especially being so close in a small town."

"Yes, it would, but you're making some pretty big assumptions here." Wally picked up the top hat and set it on a display table.

"Charlotte and I are gradually becoming friends. Do you think it would be all right for me to talk to her about it?"

"Maybe." Wally unbuttoned his vintage jacket, and Meredith helped him slip it off.

"I come from a long line of matchmakers, you know, so I'm trained to see things other people miss." She hung the jacket back on the rack. "In fact, my mother says I was born on this earth to be a *yenta*. That's a matchmaker."

"I knew that." He shrugged. "Hey, I saw *Fiddler on the Roof*."
Meredith grinned.

"I don't have a problem with matchmaking. But remember, in order to bring Sam and Charlotte together, that means breaking up an engaged couple. Very delicate stuff . . . very serious consequences," Wally said.

"Yes." Meredith peeled off her lace gloves, fluffed them, and set them back on the display case. "But wouldn't you also agree that painful breakups aren't as serious in the long run as a lifetime of regrets or divorce?"

"Absolutely true. But promise me you'll be careful choosing your words if you do talk to Charlotte. I'm new to this congregation, and for the most part, people are happy to see me succeed. But there are always a handful of folks who seem to enjoy amplifying my blunders. I'd hate for those people to misunderstand and think the pastor and his sweetheart were out there meddling in Middlebury." He paused and then added, "Just something to think about . . . and pray about."

Meredith went over to him and tugged on his sleeve. "Oh, is that what I'm doing? I'd hate for you to think I'm a busybody." She couldn't stand the idea of having their first spat right after their first kiss, yet it would be so much easier to welcome happiness if the people around her were happy too.

Wally pulled her close. "No, Cricket. I think you want to do whatever it takes to ensure the happiness of others. So few people have that quality. I see it in you, and it's one of the many things that make you so enchanting."

"Mmm, nice." Meredith walked her fingers up his arms. "Hard to be upset when you word it so sweetly."

"But being from Houston, I'm sure you know how much big city life is different from small-town living. Houston is like an aquarium, and Middlebury is like a fishbowl. It is cozier here, but just like a real fishbowl, sometimes when you're not paying attention, the water can get dirty really fast."

Meredith chuckled. "I'll be careful. I do know how to watch myself, since my family is a lot like a small town."

Wally's hand drifted outward as if he were addressing a big audience. "When am I going to meet this town of yours?"

"Soon. I've told them all about you. They're dying to meet you." At least Meredith hoped so. She prayed so.

Rapunzel curled up around her leg again, and this time, Meredith picked her up to give her a lovey kiss or two.

Wally stroked Rapunzel under her neck. "I have to go. I've got to finish my sermon. But I'd rather stay. You know, being with you is like somebody giving me a whole strawberry cake from the tearoom and saying I could eat it with no thought about how my suit would fit come Sunday morning."

Meredith laughed and set Rapunzel down. "I love it that you think in food metaphors . . . just like me. Got it from my sisters. If we're not eating we're loving or arguing or eating leftovers. But now you'll have to get back to your sermon. I will not be responsible for the spiritual collapse of Middlebury, so I'll have to insist you leave." She turned him around and pushed him toward the door.

Wally chuckled. "All right. I'm going, but perhaps one more kiss would help sustain me through my work."

"What will we do if your parishioners catch us?" She giggled.

He raised a mischievous brow and replied, "Guess we'll just have to improvise."

So they came together again for some sweet affection, and Meredith thought how charming it was that the word *affection* rhymed with *confection*. Meredith also surmised that Wally wanted to show her how much he too enjoyed the yummy pudding along with the meringue. With those thoughts teasing her mind and his kiss delighting Meredith's whole being, the bell on the front door did its jangling thing again.

Wally didn't rush to disengaged, but when their kiss was complete, Meredith looked toward the door. An older lady stood gaping at them, the purple feather on her red hat twitching to beat the band.

"Good afternoon, Mrs. Langley," Wally said.

"And what is all this, Reverend Wallace?" She gave her fingers little flutters in front of her, trying to motion toward the earlier canoodling offense.

Tufts of Wally's hair stuck up in all sorts of entertaining ways like a cockatoo, but the older woman did not appear to appreciate the amusement. Wally did not seem embarrassed nor did he shy away from her question but replied simply, "That, Mrs. Langley, was your pastor kissing his sweetheart."

24

Charlotte turned the sign on the tearoom door to closed and sat down at the table across from Audrey. "All right. Everyone's gone home. We're ready. Let's talk reception."

Audrey glanced at her iPhone. "I don't know what's keeping Sam. He was helping Justin with something in the greenhouse, and he must have lost track of time."

Charlotte felt revived knowing Sam might not come to the planning meeting for the reception after all. "There's no problem. Most grooms don't want to make these decisions anyway. It's mostly the bride's choice."

"I know, but I just thought it would be fun for us to do this together." Audrey opened and closed the clasp on her dainty handbag.

She was going to wear that thing out. "I understand. Would you like some coffee or tea while you wait?"

"No, thank you." Audrey moved the vase of roses over to the side. "Let's go ahead without Sam."

Charlotte placed a menu in front of Audrey. "These are the various menu options we have for receptions. As you can see, the tearoom's fare is more casual than what you'd find at a hotel or wedding facility. If you were hoping for something more elegant, you won't hurt my feelings if you need to—"

"No, this is perfect." Audrey tapped her fingernails on the menu. "Sam and I talked some more, and we decided on a more casual setting for the reception. I think it's more his style, and I want to honor that. After the ceremony at the Middlebury Chapel, the reception will be in the Wilder backyard. Or I should say, 'their grounds.' We're going to hire a company to put in a large tent with tables and chairs. We'll have it overlooking the pond. I'd like the reception to look like a garden tea party. That should be different and pretty. Don't you think?"

It wasn't quite what Charlotte had expected Audrey to say. She seemed to have changed her opinions over the weeks she'd been in Middlebury. Perhaps she was acclimating to small town life. Or falling more deeply in love. *Lord, let me put my past aside now, and concentrate on Audrey. This is her time for joy.* "Hmm. A garden party look sounds nice."

"And I'll have a harpist playing the whole time. Should add a nice ambiance." Audrey glanced at her iPhone and sighed.

"I'm sure it will. It sounds beautiful."

Audrey smiled. "Really?" She pressed her hands against her cheeks. "Thanks."

Perhaps since the young woman had no mother figure in her life, she craved her approval. "Okay, while you're looking over the menu options let me say a few words about the wedding cake. Honestly, Cheryl at Owen's Bakery is better at it than I am. It's the bulk of her business, and you'll love her prices. If I were you, I'd go to Owen's Bakery just around the corner on Maplewood Drive. She has a huge book of designs you can choose from."

Audrey leaned forward. "That's kind of you, Charlotte, to be more concerned about our wedding than your pocketbook. I can tell you right now, that's not how they operate in the city. Thank you."

"You're welcome." Charlotte was relieved she wouldn't have to bake and decorate their cake. It was just another part of the wedding, but in some ways, it seemed an intimate piece of the celebration. Her hand would probably start shaking on the rosebuds or the trim, and then she'd be forced to redo it. Wasn't a happy prospect. What was that pattering sound? Charlotte looked under the table. "Are those your shoes making that noise?"

Audrey chuckled. "Yes. Sorry."

"No need to apologize. Are you okay? Probably best that you passed on the caffeine, eh?"

"I'm just a little frazzled today. I'm fine." She glanced at the door again and pointed to something on the menu. "I think Sam would like this one right here, and I—" She stopped when the bell jangled over the door. "There he is. There's my Sam."

Charlotte hadn't seen Sam since Easter, but what a difference a few days could make. He had circles under his eyes, and he looked pale. She couldn't believe Audrey hadn't noticed the difference.

"Hi. Sorry I'm late. I hope you started without me." Sam shambled over to them and sat down at the table across from them. "Hi, Charlotte."

"It's no problem. We didn't wait." Audrey gave his arm a squeeze.

"Hi, Sam. You doing all right?" Charlotte asked.

"Me? Yeah, I'm just tired."

Charlotte handed Sam a copy of the menu selections for the reception and then draped the gauzy sweater around her more tightly. Why couldn't she have worn something less casual and less drab? She definitely needed to upgrade her look. She always wore the same boring earth-toned skirts and sweaters.

But then she reminded herself that the way she looked no longer mattered. At least it wouldn't matter to Sam, nor should it.

"He's been overworking himself actually," Audrey chattered on. "Sam's always trying to get the house in order. But the more we dig, the more stuff we find to sell or to give away or to clean."

"True." Sam stared at the sheet Charlotte handed him. "Beyond my father's affinity for antiquities, I think he was a hoarder. I think he was a lot of other things too." He twiddled with the vase of roses, lifted them up to his nose, and gave them a whiff. "In some ways, I'm getting to know my father for the first time. I'm learning all sorts of things about him that I never knew. Discovering some unsavory things . . . from the past."

Sam's expression was like an arrow, shooting straight through her heart. She didn't turn away, but under the table she dug her fingernails into her palm to control her emotions. What had Sam meant, that he'd discovered something unsavory from the past, and why did he look at her in that knowing way? Could he have uncovered something—like the real reason she'd refused his proposal all those years ago?

As if emerging from a daydream, Audrey broke the silence and said, "Well, you sound kind of cryptic." She pointed to something on her sheet. "Why don't we talk about the food for the reception?"

Sam set his copy of the menu aside. "I will be happy with whatever you choose."

"Well, okay," Audrey said. "If you're sure you don't mind my choices."

Some desperate part of Charlotte wanted to brush everything off onto the floor and ask, "Are we certain we're all doing the right thing here?" But knowing cruelty sometimes went hand in hand with recklessness, Charlotte left everything as it was and held steady to the expected course.

She reminded herself once again that Audrey was younger and would never hear the words, "early menopause" from her doctor. She would be able to have children, and those children would bring Sam a great deal of joy. There was some consolation in that knowledge, but with romance popping up everywhere like spring tulips, the comfort from that awareness dwindled by the day.

"Charlotte?" Audrey touched her hand. "You okay?"

"Oh, sorry." Charlotte took in a deep breath. "I got lost in my thoughts for a minute."

"Sam's been doing that a lot lately too. Must be springtime," Audrey said. "It can make people wistful."

The rest of the meeting went well as far as Audrey's menu choices for the reception. She didn't appear to notice Charlotte's occasional lapses in focus but seemed to have enough nervous chatter for all of them. Sam remained quiet most of the time, but chimed in with a smile or a nod when it was required.

When the meeting came to a close, Charlotte said good-night to them both. Audrey thanked her again and again for her help. It was obvious Audrey was trying extra hard to make her life work—the wedding, friendships, everything—she just hoped it didn't send the poor woman to the Middlebury Hospital with a nervous breakdown.

When the door was finally shut, though, Charlotte felt the full force of the evening. The word *weary* came to mind. And she felt lonelier than she could ever remember.

Charlotte closed the front blinds and then groaned as she remembered all the cleaning and sprucing up she had to do before the upcoming photo shoot. The cookbook would indeed become a reality. What a godsend, but she would have traded a thousand blessings to go back in time to relive that one day when she said no to Sam. Her answer would have been different. Their lives would have been joined as one.

She shut off a few of the lights as tears threatened. Charlotte pinched her nose to control her emotions, but it did no good. She ran into her broom closet, pulled the light chain, and shut out the rest of the world. Then she let the tears flow. After all, that's what God had created them to do—to pour out and not stay dammed up inside. She plucked a few tissues out of a box and blew her nose.

Lord, I've been trying to do your will, but to no avail. That's prayer talk for I'm failing. Miserably. Middlebury was just too small a town for all of them to coexist in joy. Maybe she could move to New Zealand. Would that be far enough? She wished fervently that Sam had never come back to Middlebury. It was too awkward and heartrending. There were too many memories. And too many ongoing fantasies of how things could have been. And now it would only get worse, since Sam had uncovered some of the past.

Charlotte took the little rubber mouse from the shelf, gave it a squeeze to make it squeak, but this time it didn't make her smile. Why had she told Sam she would be glad to handle the food for the wedding? Edith had given them a way out. What had she been thinking—that her emotions would settle down like silt at the bottom of a pond? Oh, how she wished she'd taken the escape route when she'd had the chance.

She yanked some more tissues out of the box and covered her face with them. She would have to force her emotions into a distant mode and remind herself daily, hourly if she had to, that Sam would never be "her" Sam again. He was to become "Audrey's" Sam. If she didn't force her feelings somewhere else, eventually she would be longing for another woman's husband, not fiancé. She would be morally adrift. Perhaps she already was.

Lord, let the meditations of my heart come under your control if Sam and Audrey's choice is right and good. But if there's a chance you're trying to show us a better way, a finer plan before it's too late,

*please let us all see it clearly. And so there is no unnecessary heart-
ache, please let that revelation begin with Audrey.*

Charlotte cleaned up her face and opened the closet door.
Seconds later, the bell jangled over the door.

Meredith Steinberg poked her head inside. "Hi. I just closed
up shop. I wondered if I could buy us some tea, and we could
have some girl time. What do you think?"

Charlotte was so glad she'd forgotten to lock the door and
so happy to see Meredith she almost burst out crying again. "I
think it's the best thing I've heard all week."

"Oh, good. What fun." Meredith stepped inside and looked
her over. "Wow, you look like you've had a rough day. You
really *do* need some girl time."

"Truer words have never been spoken." Charlotte gave the
woman a hug.

Meredith hugged her back with the biggest bear hug she'd
ever had. She didn't know her new friend all that well yet,
but she was looking forward to the prospect. When Meredith
released her, she said, "But instead of tea, how about some
French roast coffee and a big decadent dessert? My treat."

"You're on, my friend."

"Good." Charlotte locked up. "My apartment is upstairs. It's
comfier up there."

Meredith patty-caked her hands together. "Oh, this will be
so much fun after a grueling day in the antique business. I
sold several pieces today. Big honking expensive pieces, but
I can't imagine why. I know just enough about antiques to be
dangerous."

Charlotte chuckled. "That still amazes me. Now tell me
again why you bought the store."

"Well, after my husband died, I needed something to do
with my time. You know, stay occupied so I wouldn't lose my
marbles. I was driving my family crazy, so they suggested

I change my life. Maybe move to a small town, away from Houston. Buy a little business and run a shop. It seemed like a good idea. Then when I saw this place next door, I fell in love with it instantly. My husband adored antiques. Maybe that was the real reason I bought it. I could still feel close to him for a little while longer as I said my good-byes. You know, kind of like the way I used to sit in his closet and smell his cologne a few more times before it faded forever. "

Charlotte shut off the rest of the lights in the shop. "I've never been married, but I did lose my parents, so I know about that ache of missing them and the part about hoping to lock those smells and memories away." She pointed toward the kitchen. "I have a set of stairs inside and outside. We'll just use the ones at the back of the kitchen. We can head up now if you'd like."

"Oh, Hon, you left the light on in this closet." Meredith looked inside and then pulled the light chain. "Wow, that's quite a little utility closet you have there." She shut the door. "Very cozy. You've got a place to sit and everything. What do you do in there if you don't mind me asking?"

"Cry, reminisce, talk to God. I've been in there more in the last few weeks than I have over the last year." Charlotte wasn't sure it was wise to reveal too much about her recent troubles, but maybe a good airing of her feelings to a friend would help.

"Do you want to talk about it?" Meredith asked.

"I just might tell you some of it, depending on how intoxi-cated I get on my devil's food cake."

"Oww, my favorite cake. So, you actually make it with booze?"

"No, just lots of dark chocolate and pure butter."

Meredith rocked her head back and forth. "Oh, yeah, baby, bring it on."

Charlotte chuckled. After they'd climbed the stairs, and she'd let Meredith into her little apartment, she asked, "Do you still miss your husband a lot?"

"I miss him all the time, but in the midst of my sorrow, I found Wally. Spending time with him has taken some of the sting and lonesomeness out of losing Joey."

"I'm glad for you. Truly." Charlotte led Meredith from her living area to her kitchen. "You two seem to spend a lot of time together. Is it getting serious? Oh dear, I sound pretty nosy. You don't have to answer that."

Meredith waved her off. "It wasn't any nosier than my questions. We're going to have a girly night, so that means we can talk about anything. In answer to your question, yes, it's getting more serious. There's no marriage proposal or anything. We're taking it slow, but we're calling each other sweethearts."

"Mmm. That's good news," Charlotte said.

"We think so too." Meredith glanced around the kitchen. "Charming apartment. Feels like a hug. I like it."

"Thanks. I call it my cubbyhole, but I love it."

Meredith set the table while Charlotte brewed a pot of her best French roast and put out two bowls of devil's food cake. "You can't have the coffee without real cream. And I know this sounds crazy, but my purple potatoes taste great along with the cake." Charlotte opened the fridge and brought out a few more snacks and goodies and set them on the table.

"I love it that you brought out the mustard, just in case we need it. That's the way it always was at home. We ate mustard like it was another food group. In fact, when I was in school, I never could relate to the other girls who brought their white bread and mayo. It was like these little albino sandwiches with no soul."

Charlotte laughed. "By the way. I like your accent."

"I got it from my family. We call it New York with a Texas twang."

"Well, it's unique to Middlebury. I like it."

Meredith gestured with her hands over the table. "Look at this feast." She took a sip of the coffee, kissed the tips of her fingers, and then let them fly open. "Ohh, this is the best coffee, and that's saying something because my mother makes a wicked brew." She took a bite of the cake. "Oh, and this is heaven, Charlotte . . . the cake."

"Thanks."

"I'm officially swooning here." She gestured as if conducting an orchestra. "You are the maestro of cake bakers, my friend."

Charlotte laughed.

"Listen, darlin', don't let anybody ever tell you that dessert doesn't take the edge off a bad day. It's just the lie those size 4 girls tell themselves to keep from bingeing."

Charlotte chuckled. Oh, it felt so good to laugh again.

"I think I've seen this cake on your menu, but you should offer this coffee in your tearoom too."

"Actually, I do. But most people don't notice it. They come in for my blended teas. They know they can get coffee all over Middlebury, but tea is one of my specialties." Charlotte took a big bite of her cake.

"It is indeed." Meredith licked her fork. "And speaking of special, I can already tell that you and your tearoom are special to a lot of people in this town."

"I always hope so."

"And I've noticed that you're especially special to someone in particular." Meredith adjusted her glasses and looked at her with the intensity of a laser.

"Oh? Who's that?" Charlotte took a big sip of her coffee.

"Sam Wilder," Meredith said.

Charlotte choked on her coffee.

Meredith slapped her on the back. "Oh, honey, are you all right? Now just look what I've done."

25

$\mathcal{M}$eredith felt awful that she'd rushed at Charlotte with her declaration about Sam Wilder. Must have felt like a mountain lion springing on her in the midst of a pleasant stroll. "I'm so sorry."

"It just took me by surprise." Charlotte took a sip of her coffee. "I'm fine now."

"Does this reaction have anything to do with why you've been spending so much time in the utility closet?" Meredith put up her hands. "You know what? I think I'm wiping you out here. You see, I'm used to being this way with my sisters when we get together. We're like this kamikaze sisterhood when it comes to our emotions. We tell each other everything. We hold nothing back. But maybe you're not used to that."

"Well, I am an only child. But I did say that I would talk about this if I got woozy enough on my cake." She took another big sloppy bite. "I might be there." Charlotte got a tiny dollop on her nose and chuckled.

Meredith grinned, glad that her new friend could recover so quickly from the onslaught. She took another bite of the cake and tried not to moan with each mouthful.

"Here, try this along with the cake. These are gourmet purple potatoes with my caramelized pecans." Charlotte reached over and spooned a bite into Meredith's mouth.

She tasted it all together. "Okay, I'm going to moan now. I can't hold it back. I never would have thought to put those flavors together."

"Good, isn't it?"

"You could make a million bucks off this taste."

"Thanks." Charlotte pushed her bowl away, but took a sip of her coffee. "Okay, now I'm going to tell you about Sam."

Meredith sat still, not wanting to break the spell of camaraderie.

"Sam Wilder and his family moved here to Middlebury when he was a junior in high school. We fell in love, and we both knew what we felt for each other was more than a summer fling or a fleeting infatuation. It was something lasting. But as time went on, something changed. Not with Sam, but with his father."

Meredith listened as Charlotte told her about Mr. Wilder's recent deathbed confession and his objection to her grandmother's heritage. Her heart wilted with sadness at the story, the unfairness of a man who could disapprove of a marriage over such narrow-minded reasoning. But Meredith did understand very well how bigotry could become hideous if left unchecked. "Couldn't you have just married Sam anyway? I mean, I know it's always best to have the family's blessing, but sometimes you gotta do what you gotta do for love." Meredith hoped she wouldn't have to eat those words soon, concerning Wally.

"But there's more to the story." Charlotte laced her fingers across her chest and squeezed. "Sam's father knew we'd probably get married without his approval, so he wanted a guarantee that I would walk away."

"Oh. Surely he didn't offer you money. But then I know you wouldn't have taken it."

"I think Mr. Wilder would have offered me money, but you're right, he knew I wouldn't take it. In the end, his guarantee that I would walk away was tied to a scandal."

"Oh, dear." Meredith let her chin drop into her cupped palm.

Charlotte went on to explain that Mr. Wilder claimed there'd been an affair between her own father and his wife, Sam's mother.

"Oh, my." Meredith shook her head.

"Mr. Wilder threatened to tell everyone. He claimed the scandal would tear both families apart and destroy Sam's close relationship with his mother. Mr. Wilder was willing to tell all, risk everything, just to force me to walk away. His motivation and prejudice were intense." Charlotte's shouldered drooped. "And his ploy worked. I admit I was a fool for believing him, but I was so young. Too young to know if he would follow through with his threat or if he was just bullying me. In the end, I did believe him, and I couldn't do that to our families. I couldn't tear them apart for my happiness. I was angry at my father, of course, for what he did . . . for having an affair with Mrs. Wilder and ruining my chances for happiness. And for confusing me. You know, making me wonder at times if marriage was even a good idea at all. I wanted to scream at him for what he did, or flee from home. But in the end, I said nothing to my father or to anyone. I did nothing. Except that when Sam proposed to me, I said no, and we went our own ways after graduation."

"I'm so sorry." Meredith thought it sounded like a terrible dream one couldn't wake up from. "I wish you or Sam could have fought it. Such a shame Mr. Wilder would win a war that he had no right to start." Meredith took another sip of her coffee, but it had gone cold.

"I felt that way too." Charlotte's hands folded together on the table in a limp, little nest. "Mr. Wilder could be a very intimidating and persuasive man. I just didn't know where to turn. Most girls would run to their mothers for advice, but it wasn't something I could talk to her about. It would have killed my mom had she found out that Dad was having an affair with Mrs. Wilder . . . no matter how brief."

"What an impossible situation for you. And all you'd done was to fall in love." Meredith let her fist drop onto the table, and it rattled the spoons. "Sorry."

"That's all right. Sometimes I felt like pounding things too, but I didn't. Maybe I should have. For years I buried it inside, and I started to grow bitter. But fortunately I had the dream of opening up this tearoom. I bought this old house and fixed it up. I poured myself into this place, and it helped me to forget." Charlotte rose and poured them both fresh cups of coffee. "I've been content."

Meredith looked up at her, tears burning her eyes. "Only content?"

"I've had joy too . . . that is, until Sam moved back home."

Meredith blew her nose into her napkin. "So, you never told anyone? And Sam has never known?"

"I never told anyone. I don't think Sam ever knew any of it. He would have been very angry with his father I'm sure. He would have insisted we fight it. But I wasn't ready for him to walk away from his family. And I thought it might break up my family as well. It just seemed like too much trauma for too many people."

"Had you ever thought that maybe Mr. Wilder lied about the affair? Just making it all up to scare you? To get you to leave his son?"

Charlotte twisted the paper napkin in her hands. "It had crossed my mind. My mother and father as well as Sam's parents were older, and so it seemed even harder to believe that something like this would happen. You'd think they would be, you know, more settled in their marriages and hopefully wiser. I didn't want to believe any of it, of course. But Mr. Wilder had me cornered pretty well. He knew I'd have to risk a lot to find out the truth."

Meredith's temper prickled like a mad porcupine the more she thought about the story—a young innocent woman who was forced to walk away from love. "One more thing that I can't wrap my mind around. If Mr. Wilder was so paranoid about having a grandchild of color, it looks like he would be equally fearful about launching a scandal that could destroy his family."

"Or maybe he wasn't as worried about gossip surrounding his wife as much as guarding his own racist views. Or maybe Mr. Wilder felt the affair was all about his wife, and that he could endure the scandal if it reflected poorly on her. Maybe he was angry and jealous enough to ruin her. He knew the news would hurt his wife, or it would be enough to silence me. Maybe he thought he would win either way." Charlotte dropped some sugar into her coffee. "Believe me, I've thought of every angle of this over the years. That's why the tearoom was such a blessing, keeping my mind occupied."

Meredith felt like slamming something again. "It's so awful that a person like Mr. Wilder could have won anything. It's so unfair. But have you ever wondered why Sam didn't badger you with questions? Or maybe why he didn't figure out on his own what made you go away?"

"Actually, Sam did ask a lot of questions back then, and I managed to answer him without lying. He wasn't angry at me, but he was devastated. I guess the town felt too small for us back then, so he moved to Houston, went to college, and made a life for himself there." Charlotte stirred her coffee. "I will say this too . . . as of recently, I think Sam is aware of pieces of the past. I can tell from subtle things he's said. But how much he knows is anyone's guess."

"Now I know I'm getting pushy with this question," Meredith said.

"Well, that didn't stop you before."

Meredith's eyebrows shot up.

Charlotte patted her hand. "I'm teasing. It feels good to talk about this. But I'm glad you were an outside party . . . someone who never knew the Wilder family back then. I'm not saying this well. It's more than that. You feel like a sanctuary to me, a safe place I've been able to go with my past. And it takes a real friend to do that. I'm so glad you came over tonight to let me talk. Thank you."

Meredith smiled. "You're welcome."

"So, please, go ahead . . . ask me anything."

"Well, before the wedding happens between Sam and Audrey, don't you think you and Sam deserve to have a talk? Since you both went through so much? When you think of all you'd been cheated. Maybe you two could just chat to clear the air. You know, in case it would make a difference now. In case it would change everything."

Charlotte's sad expression took on a hint of joy. "I have something I want to show you. Something I've never shown to anyone." She went over to a small writing desk, pulled out a drawer, and lifted out a piece of paper.

"What is that?"

Charlotte handed the paper to Meredith.

"Looks like an invitation." Meredith read it out loud. "Mr. and Mrs. Alfred Edwin Hill would be honored by your attendance at the joining in holy matrimony of their daughter,

Charlotte Rose Hill, with Mr. Samuel Lee Wilder . . . " She shook her head. "It's your wedding invitation with Sam? I don't understand."

"Before Mr. Wilder had his infamous talk with me, I knew in my heart that Sam would propose, and that I'd say yes. While I waited for Sam to pop the question I just thought it would be wonderful to see what our invitation would look like. I wanted to see the words in print, so when I was eighteen I made this on my computer and printed it out. That's why it may not look very professional. It was just dreaming."

Meredith looked into the eyes of her new friend and searched for bitterness but there was none. "I gotta be honest with you. It is heartrending to see this." She handed the invitation back to Charlotte.

"I would be lying if I didn't admit . . . well, I still love Sam. I love him dearly, even after all these years. But I know Sam wouldn't have proposed to Audrey if he didn't love her. He's not the type of person to go into marriage lightly. And Audrey seems like a fine woman. I think they'll be happy. Raise a beautiful family. I know that means a lot to Sam. How could I stop something so good and holy?" Charlotte turned the invitation around in her hand. "Maybe this is one more thing that's keeping me from letting go of the past. I should have gotten rid of this a long time ago. I feel childish that I've held onto it for so long." Charlotte crumpled the invitation and tossed it into the wastebasket by the desk.

"Do you feel better?" Meredith asked.

"No."

They both laughed.

"Look," Charlotte said, "I've given it to God, which is some of what I was doing in the broom closet. If for some reason Sam and Audrey are not meant to be . . . only he can intervene now."

Well, yes, God can intervene—but sometimes he sends a messenger—in this case, a woman named Meredith Steinberg. Meredith knew she might have to ask God to forgive her for what she was about to do, so she sought him right then, breathing a quick prayer for clemency. However, she also knew that if she sat still and did nothing, she might regret it for the rest of her life. Meredith knew how to tear up on command. Not that she had to work too hard at it. All she had to do was to think of her friend's plight again, and the tears would come on their own. Meredith thought of Charlotte sitting by herself in the back of the chapel, very much alone in the pew during Sam and Audrey's wedding. Right away the mist formed. Meredith sniffled. "Do you have a tissue? Sorry."

"I'll get some out of the bathroom." Charlotte stepped away for a moment and disappeared down the hallway.

Meredith rose from her chair and wasted no time in implementing her plan. Feeling a bit like an undercover agent, she reached down into the wastebasket and dug out the invitation. She rubbed the heavy paper against her leg, smoothing out the wrinkles, and then stealthily slipped it into her purse. She arched an eyebrow and smiled. In the background somewhere she could almost hear the theme music playing from *Mission Impossible*.

26

*A*udrey couldn't remember such a lovely spring day. My, she was in a good mood. No, she was in a *great* mood, and she had no idea why. Oh, yeah, it was because she was planning a beautiful wedding with a great guy. Yes, that was it.

Audrey flitted around the greenhouse on the Wilder estate with childlike glee, gazing at the hanging baskets full of flowers, touching the flaming pink petals of the bougainvillea, breathing deeply of various aromatic plants, and marveling at the vivid leaves of the jewel orchid. The transformation of the greenhouse continued to amaze her. With each passing day Justin had transformed the dilapidated and disorganized greenhouse into a showplace. The moment she thought of Justin he was there, standing by the door.

"Good morning, Audrey."

"Hi." She grinned. "I can't get over it. This place is like a candy store for anyone who loves plants and flowers."

"I'm glad you feel that way." Justin walked toward her steadily, his limp almost gone now.

Audrey warmed from head to toe, mostly because the shock of his new identity hadn't worn off yet—the difference in his appearance, the change in his confidence, and well, his celebrity persona. The whole package of who Justin was as compared to how he was perceived before could not have been more opposite. Or more entrancing. Audrey hated herself for being affected, but either her willpower was weak, or she was facing something she'd never encountered before. Impossible to know which one—quite yet.

Justin reached near her shoulder, his soft flannel shirt brushing against her, and flipped a switch right behind her. The fountain, which was encircled by palm plants and bird-of-paradise, came to life. Water poured from a pail held by the figurine of a young woman, and it collected below in a crescent-shaped pool.

"You fixed it. How lovely." The expression on the girl's face was one of total serenity. What must that feel like? She stared into the pool, but it blurred her reflection.

"It was a little tricky bringing this to life again, but well worth it." Justin walked over to the worktable, and Audrey followed him.

She looked at his clean-shaven face, marveled again, and then looked away. "I hope I'm not bothering you out here."

"No, not at all. I don't generally give myself coffee breaks, so I have a few minutes to spare."

Justin busied himself, tending to some rows of herbal seedlings, which seemed to flourish robustly in the connected strips of plant pots.

"I've never seen containers like these."

"They're biodegradable. A friend of mine always says it's good to keep an open mind about trying new things. I tend to agree."

Audrey decided not to ask who the friend was, but merely said, "Yes, an open mind is good." She fingered one of the sweet basil leaves, squeezed it, and then brought her fingers under her nose. Oh, how she loved that smell. Well, she loved everything about this place. "Looks like you're going to start an herb garden."

"I am. Just behind the koi pond. I thought you and Sam would enjoy it as sort of my wedding present. Except that he's paying for it, not me." Justin sighed.

"What a perfect present, and there's plenty of room." Audrey leaned her weight against the wooden shelves, but the sudden jolt made one of the potted plants almost teeter over. She righted it and chuckled. "Maybe I'd better leave before I destroy something." Before Justin replied, she said, "I was sorry to hear about your wife and your baby. I mean, what you said on Easter Sunday. It was tragic, and I know comforting words aren't enough. Really they can't be enough, but I wanted to offer them anyway."

"Thank you, Audrey."

"And I noticed your limp is almost gone. You must be healing up well."

"I'm getting there."

Justin said no more on the subject, so she milled around for a bit. "I was wondering . . . do you mean for this greenhouse to be a place to provide flowers and plants for the house, a place to grow seedlings for gardens on the property, or is it supposed to be a haven?"

He paused from his work and looked at her. "All the above."

Their shared smile heated up the already warm greenhouse.

"So, which is your favorite?" Justin asked.

"Favorite? What do you mean?" Audrey felt a twinge of panic over the question.

"Your favorite flower."

"Oh, that." Audrey breathed again.

"What did you think I meant?" he asked.

Audrey fluttered her hand. "Oh, nothing."

"Let me guess. Your favorite is the orchid?"

"How did you know?"

Justin seemed to study her. "Something in the way you smile."

"Reminds me of a Beatles tune."

"It does. Come on, I have something else I want to show you."

Audrey followed Justin as he headed to the very back of the greenhouse and then to a small arched door, which was almost hidden by ivy. He pulled a key from his pocket and put it in the lock. "I didn't want you to see this until it was finished. Now it's ready for guests. For you." Justin opened the door, and lead Audrey into paradise.

"You made an orchid room." Many specimens of orchids, some of them rare, filled the space with fragrance and color and wild exotic beauty. "How wonderful." Audrey strolled through the room, touching and taking little sniffs here and there, and generally trying to absorb the jeweled splendor of the chamber. "This must have cost a fortune."

"It did. But when I told Sam what I wanted to do he was all for it. He said it would help to sell the house. But I think he also knew it meant a lot to me."

"Sam is generous as well as kind. But it's interesting that he wanted you to put in the orchid room to help sell the house and not for his own pleasure. He's not much of a plant guy."

Justin linked gazes with her. "Sam's a good man."

Ah, yes. Good reminder. I'm an engaged woman. We've got that straight again. "Yes, Sam is a good man," Audrey repeated back to him.

Justin led her around his orchid utopia, telling her a little about each variety. She tried to soak up all his knowledge, but her mind was not as attentive as she'd hoped. Her thoughts were on Justin's life and what he would do when the house sold. Where he would go.

When Justin came to the section with the largest orchids, he said, "These are the cattleya orchids. Some people call them corsage orchids, since that's been a popular use for them. But these flowers are so much more than a common fleeting prom ornament. If you look at them with care, you'll see just how achingly beautiful they are . . . so exquisite that even God would give them an extra sigh."

Justin was right. On closer inspection, the cattleya orchid was luminous and heady with perfume, and it seemed to be lit from some unknown source.

"One word." He held up his finger.

"I'd say this orchid is full of bravado. No, but it's more than that. It's unforgettable."

"Yes." Justin stared her a little longer than she'd expected, and then he walked on. He added, "They grow in the wild in Central and South America, but when man tried to take them from what they've always known, problems surfaced. They don't do so well. They struggle."

"Like people?"

"Very much like people. You take them out of whatever it is they're comfortable with, where they know they belong, and there's going to be some kind of struggle."

Just as the greenhouse was being renovated, Justin was being transformed back into the Plant Doctor right before her eyes. He talked about plants not just as objects of beauty but how they could be linked to our lives. He was making the connection with her as he did with countless viewers all those years on TV. "This is how I remember you, Justin."

"What do you mean?"

"The way you not only make people want to know more about flowers, but you make it all relatable and even magical. It's like you fed us little pieces of yourself and your world, and your great passion became ours."

Justin chuckled. "I couldn't have done all that."

"But you did." Audrey took two steps closer to him. "If you ever decided to go back, people would love you all over again. In fact, they've never forgotten you."

"The problem is . . . I may have shaved my face and cut my hair, but I still have a long journey ahead. There are just no guarantees."

It was obvious he meant something more but she would have none of it. "You just need someone by your side. That's all. You need—"

"Audrey, I appreciate what—"

"Look, I know several women who would kill to go out with the Plant Doctor." Audrey placed her folded hand to her mouth, to silence herself. Why had she said such a foolish thing? She really did need to think more before she just blurted things out.

"The last thing I need right now is a series of blind dates," Justin said. "But I know you're trying to help me, and I appreciate it. You and Sam and Nelly have been very good to me. But when it's time to date again . . . I wouldn't want any woman to go out with me because of who I was in the past. She would have to care about me for who I am now."

"Of course, she would like you for who you are."

Justin grinned.

Audrey looked up at him and winced. "Why are you grinning?"

"Because you have so much more confidence in me than I have in myself. I don't know where it comes from." He reached out to her face and then let his hand drop back down.

Audrey placed her hands behind her back, since they were quivering. "You are a gift to this world, and you can't even see it. Everything you touch seems to flourish under your care . . . your capable hands." She stared down at his hand, the one that had almost touched her face. "I want to help you in any way I can."

"Did you know your eyes are almost the color of the vanda orchid?"

"No."

"Not quite, but in this light, they look startlingly close." Justin reached behind Audrey and plucked a white orchid. He slid it into her hair just above her ear. "Now, let me see your hands."

Audrey shook her head, and then feeling like a schoolgirl, she presented her quaking hands before his eyes.

"Why are you trembling?"

She raised her chin, which also quivered. "I think you know why."

"Audrey." Justin's voice was just above a whisper. "I am searching to be whole again. It's not the right time in my life to be worried about a wife or even a girlfriend who might need to prop me up in some way. I don't want to be a burden to anyone."

"I do know what you mean. More than you know. I was deserted as a child. And you see, life abandoned you as an adult. I am very aware of what it's like to hope when there's none left. To dream when you know the rest of the world is laughing at you. I've needed propping up my whole life. I've always been in an obsessive search for the steadiest, most loyal people to surround myself with, praying that I'd never be deserted again. In the past, when I dated men who I found to be unreliable in any way, I would bolt. And when you ran off that day, it scared me in so many ways. But it didn't frighten me enough to make me stop thinking about you."

"I'm so sorry, Audrey, about your childhood. And I'm sorry I frightened you when I ran off—"

"Don't apologize. I understand. And I understand about the flowers too. Why this is so wonderful for you. Life can be such a bed of anguish. But flowers, well, they're the soft lining that makes it all bearable. I feel it too, Justin." She searched his eyes to see if he'd caught her meaning. "Don't you?"

"Please, Audrey, now listen. What we have here is impossible. You know that." Pearls of sweat formed on his forehead and trickled down his face. "And yet . . . "

"Didn't you say that it was always good to keep an open mind?" Audrey rose on her tippy-toes to draw closer to his face. "What if we're so close to happiness that . . . "

"Only for a moment." Justin closed his arms around her, and Audrey rested her head against his chest.

Yes, just for a moment.

"Your heartbeat is as crazy as my shaky hands." She grinned and eased away just enough to look into his eyes. She wanted to really see him.

"What are you thinking?"

"That I'm so deficient, so absent in my own life that I'm not even sure I know how to love a man . . . at least not very well. Maybe I only know how to play with him like a cat batting a mouse."

He took her by the shoulders. "Don't say that about yourself."

"But it's true."

Justin lifted her hand and placed his underneath hers, letting them mold together. "I see love between a man and a woman like the folded petals of a flower just before it blooms. They fit together like this . . . in their souls. You just know. Then the loving happens naturally without any help at all." He released her hand. "You *do* know how to love a man, Audrey."

They searched each other for a moment. Justin leaned down to her mouth, almost touching her lips. So close.

"Where did you come from Audrey Anderson?" he whispered.

She released the tiniest sound of delight and whispered back, "From a distant star, Justin Yule."

He smiled. "As I've said, some of the best things in life are in this place." And then he kissed her.

A soaring sensation took Audrey by surprise. It was like the ride she'd taken on a Ferris wheel—when she'd drop down from the highest point and her body was overcome with a rush of pleasure. The kiss was anything but peaceful or steady or reassuring. It felt disturbing and wonderful. Not at all like Sam. *Oh, Sam. What am I doing?* She pulled away. "Justin, what have I done?"

"If I'm not mistaken . . . I've kissed you, and you've kissed me back."

Audrey frowned. "That's not what I meant. I'm engaged to be married." She shook her head. "I've committed adultery, haven't I?"

"Uhh . . . not quite." Justin grinned.

"You have lipstick all over you."

A little more somber now, Justin took a handkerchief out of his pocket and handed it to her.

"You carry a handkerchief now," she said absently. As she wiped the evidence from Justin's face, guilt came down on her like a muddy rain. "I'm so ashamed of myself. This was my fault."

"I'm pretty sure I participated as well, so there's no need to take on all the guilt."

Audrey handed Justin his handkerchief.

He backed away. "Actually, it was irresponsible of me, and it wasn't a kind way to pay back my employer for his generosity. Even if you hadn't been engaged, though, it wouldn't have been right considering my circumstances. But I confess to a moment of selfishness. A man could live a long time on that kiss."

"I don't get it. You mean you used me? Never mind. I already know the answer. I'm the one who begged you to kiss me." Audrey took the orchid from her hair and gazed at its loveliness. "So . . . do you regret it . . . our kiss?"

"Maybe I should say it this way. I don't regret how I feel about you, but Sam trusted me to be a gentleman, and I've severed that trust. I will have to resign soon."

"But please let me speak to Sam first. Would that be okay?"

"All right," Justin said. "I'll wait until you find the right time to speak to him. But then I'll want to make my apology and go."

"I've cost you your job." Audrey pressed the fragrant orchid to her face and for a moment she was lost in its softness and its heady perfume, and the beauty of the kiss came back to her. "I don't want you to go. Please."

"It would be wrong to do anything else."

Audrey turned away from him, so she could look out through the windows, so she could speak without looking into those eyes of his. "You know when Sam came along in my life, I thought he was perfect for me. Someone I could trust to keep me safe in every way. I could finally end my frantic search. His arms were the warmest and safest I'd ever found. And he had money. Lots of it. That always makes life safer. It helps to smooth out all my cracks and rough surfaces. But lately I've been scared that I'm becoming weaker inside Sam's strength. That I'm only a breath away from total collapse. I've confused security with love. And I've only now come to know the difference . . . since I've met you."

"Audrey." Justin took her by the arms and turned her around. "Please don't make any declarations you might regret. It'll make it even harder for us."

"I won't deny my feelings . . . these first stirrings of—"

"Don't say it." Justin removed his hands from her arms. "Don't you see? These romantic notions are blinding you. It's like you're leaping from a well-lit pier into the depths of the ocean. Except for a little savings and the clothes on my back, I'm not too far from penniless, and after today, I won't even have a job. Sam has inherited a fortune. You'll never want for anything. He's a good man, and he has a generous spirit. That counts for a lot. And he loves you. He can take good care of you all your life. Maybe sometimes in such a dangerous world where everything imaginable can go wrong . . . searching and finding safety isn't such a terrible thing."

"I don't believe you." Her spirit ached with loss, but after Justin said no more, anger suddenly replaced the grief. "That doesn't sound anything like the illustrious Justin Yule would say."

"I'm not him anymore. Don't you see? This is me!" Justin's clawed fingers struck his chest.

"You know, sometimes you can be so disarming that I let my guard down," Audrey said. "More than I do with anyone, even Sam. And then you're like this, and I feel my heart getting trampled, and there's nothing I want to do more than to slap you!"

"You're right. You *do* need to go." He took his gloves from his back pocket and slipped them on. "I've got work to do."

Audrey's stomach churned. She was going to be sick. What were all those irrational feelings? It was awful and glorious all at the same time like the blackest night and the most golden morning all at once. Even in her confusion she wanted to be clear before it was too late. "I'm sorry. I've made you feel like the old Justin is all I care about. That's not true. I did admire who he was. I admit it. But I've gotten to know the new Justin, and he is equally wonderful. I care about him, even if he never returns to his old life. Even if he never makes his fortune back or any of his celebrity. Even if I make a fool of myself declaring my feelings when he doesn't care at all . . ." Audrey lost her voice, but tears replaced her words. She covered her face with her hands and wept.

Without hesitation, Justin turned back to her and drew her into his arms. "It's all right. Shh," he murmured these words over and over while he rubbed her back. "I do care for you, Audrey. Very, very much."

"You do?" Once again, calm replaced the turmoil, and she relaxed in his arms.

"Maybe what you need to do over the next couple of days is to think . . . and pray. And I will do the same. We both need direction. And if you still choose Sam."

"But—"

"*If* you do, I will tell you what a good choice you've made."

Audrey sniffled. "I don't know how I can—."

"But just in case . . . if you do marry Sam . . . I will move away from Middlebury. It would be the right thing to do for all of us."

"I couldn't bear it." She looked up at him. "So, you'd move back to Houston?"

"I don't know." He touched his lips. "But wherever I go, I will always have that kiss."

Audrey touched his cheek. "But that's not enough for—"

A woman cleared her throat at the door. Audrey startled and looked toward the doorway. "Nelly?"

Justin and Audrey disengaged and turned to face Nelly. The orchid, which had been wedged between them, fell to the floor crushed. Audrey left it there.

Nelly did not look amused with their intimate embrace. "Lunch has been ready for a while," she said, "but I couldn't find anyone to eat it. Now, I'm afraid it's gone as cold as the grave."

"Nelly?" Audrey said. "You know, in the movies when people like us say, 'This is not what you think it is'?"

"Yes," Nelly said. "Is that what you're about to say?"

"No, this *is* what you think it is. I'll be confessing to Sam. You have my word." Audrey took in a deep breath. "But I need you to do something for us."

"What's that?" Nelly asked, now looking more concerned than shocked.

"Pray."

27

Meredith stared at Charlotte's creased wedding invitation on the display case as if it were a ticking bomb. She knew what she might do with the invitation, so her heartbeat raced as if she were sprinting through the streets of Middlebury. If she didn't follow through soon with her plan she'd end up in the hospital. The doctors would ask what brought her into the emergency room, and with a fevered brow, she would have to reply, "Doctor, I went into the convulsions of uncertainty."

She almost chuckled over that last thought, but then went sober again. After hovering in a mode of vacillation for an undeterminable length of time, Meredith stuffed the invitation into an envelope, addressed it to Audrey at the Wilder house, and marched out of her shop toward the US postal box on the street corner. On arriving she pulled the handle and stared into the black hole of the receptacle—a place where things fell in, but no amateur hand—no common man or woman—had ever been allowed to take anything out. In other words, a person had better be certain when she . . . Let. It. Go.

Her hand juddered a bit, and in that tiny tremor, the envelope slid out of her hand and into the abyss.

She laughed at herself, and then she broke out in a brutal sweat. "It had to be done . . . this deed. Right, God?" She asked in a whisper. She heard no answer.

Meredith daubed at her forehead with a tissue, stopped in the middle of the sidewalk, and looked up to the heavens. Not caring who saw her, she said to God out loud, "Lord, I know about the fleeces in the Old Testament, so please, may I have some kind of thumbs-up sign from you so I can eat again? Breathe again? Live again? And in that order? Of course, I guess the fleece was supposed to come before the deed. Oh dear." Perspiration now trickled into tickly crevices.

"Lord, I'm not trying to be disrespectful when I say you are powerful enough to work retrospectively. I'm counting on that attribute for your followers who are earnest but who might also be a little too spontaneous."

No word. No sign. People began to make furtive glances at her. They murmured to each other, surely discussing the status of her sanity. "Oh, Lord, I'm dying here."

Meredith gave up and trudged back to her antique shop. Maybe she could bribe the postal employee with an antique lamp in exchange for the invitation.

28

Charlotte paused at the tearoom window, puzzled at the sight that had just passed by. Meredith had been standing on the sidewalk looking so distressed she seemed to be talking to the air, and then she walked back toward her antique shop. Hmm. There was plenty of staff to take care of the customers, so she opened the door to head next door to check on her friend.

"Miss Hill?"

Charlotte turned toward a dainty voice behind her. "Annabelle?"

"Hello."

"Hi. What's up?" Annabelle, a young girl she'd known from the library, sat behind a lemonade stand not far from the tearoom. "Selling lemonade, I see."

"Yes. Is it okay to be here?" Her expression fluttered with anxiety.

"Well, yes, I guess so. Where's your mom?"

"The hair salon across the street. She said I could set up shop here while she's there, if it's okay with you. Just for today. I'm trying out a new kind of lemonade. Want to try a free sample?"

"Sure. So, how's business?"

"Not so good." Annabelle poured a small amount of the liquid into a paper cup, dropped in a thin slice of lemon, and then handed it to her.

Charlotte took a sip. The imitation taste tingled her tongue, but not in a good way. She wanted to spit it out, but she swallowed and smiled instead. "You know what? I used to run a lemonade stand when I was a kid."

"Really?" Annabelle fussed around her tiny counter, lining up all the cups. "Maybe you can help me, 'cause I think I'm doing something wrong." Her small face lit up with hope and irresistible charm.

"Tell you what, if your mom will bring you by the tearoom after school on a Thursday I'll teach you how to make homemade lemonade from scratch."

"Really? Okay. Thanks." Annabelle grinned. "You know, the real reason I'm here is because I want to be like you when I grow up. I want to make food and make people happy like you do." She bounced on her toes.

"I think that's a wonderful thing." Charlotte gave her hand a pat.

"My mother says it's okay for me to want to be like you, except for one thing."

"What's that?"

"She says she hopes I'll get married someday," Annabelle said.

Charlotte squeezed out a smile. "Well, I can understand why she'd say that. Every mom hopes her daughter will not only pursue her dreams but that she'll one day marry and have a family."

"My mom says you've had a tragic life. You were Cinderella, but you never married your Prince Charming when you had the chance." Annabelle clutched a tea towel dramatically.

"She said that too, huh?" Charlotte set the cup down as her smile lost the last of its glow.

"My mom also says she hopes I won't make the same mistake."

"Hmm. Yeah." Charlotte hadn't thought of that angle in a long time. That maybe some of the people in Middlebury who remembered her break-up with Sam still thought her decision was foolhardy or worse. They would have been right. But then none of them knew the rest of the story. Except for Meredith. Someone honked his horn in the street, and Charlotte jumped.

Annabelle chewed on her lip and said, "I wasn't supposed to say any of that stuff, was I? My mom is going to be sooo mad when she hears what I did." She twirled one of her red curls around her finger. "I guess I don't have to tell her, though, if you don't." Her eyes grew as big as her lemon slices. "Do you think you'll tell? Or not?"

"I won't squeal on you. I promise."

Annabelle tilted her head and sighed. "Thanks. You know, some lady came over here, and she almost stopped to buy my lemonade. But she was sort of talking to herself. Kind of scary."

"That's probably Miss Steinberg. She owns the antique shop. I think I might need to go and check on her."

"Okay. Bye." Annabelle gave her a petite wave.

"See you later." Charlotte had almost made it to the antique shop when Roberta rushed up to her out of breath, her dark hair flying out of its bun and her black eyes flashing. "What is it? Are you okay?"

Roberta took hold of Charlotte's hands. "It's Obie. Have you seen him? He's vanished. I can't find him anywhere."

"No, I haven't seen him."

Roberta placed her hand to her forehead. "Oh, I just really thought he'd be here with you."

"What happened?"

"He came home from school just like always. We went over his homework, and then he said he'd take a nap. But when I went back to his room later, he was gone."

Charlotte tried to remain calm, but her mind raced with an array of scary possibilities. "I can help you look for him."

"I thought you might know of a favorite place of his. A spot where he might be hiding."

"Yes, I do know a place," Charlotte said. "The old outhouse."

"An outhouse?" Roberta frowned. "That sounds dangerous."

"It's not as bad as it sounds. It's in my garden out back. Let's take the side path around my shop. It'll be faster." She should have nailed that outhouse shut. Why had she forgotten?

Charlotte and Roberta speed-walked around the corner. Then she remembered Obie saying that the outhouse might be a time-travel machine. For some reason the memory made her break out into a jog. Roberta ran too. When they got to the outhouse it was obvious someone had lifted the wooden latch. She tapped on the door. "Obie? This is Charlotte. Are you in there? Miss Roberta's out here too, and we're both worried about you."

Little sniffling noises came out of the outhouse, and then a tiny voice said, "Drat, we've been discovered." It was Obie.

Roberta clasped her hands together and mouthed the words, "Thank you, Lord."

Charlotte smiled at her. Obie. That dear, sweet boy. What could she say to make him come out? Hmm. Maybe he needed his outhouse like she needed her broom closet. "The reason we're concerned," she began, "is because you didn't tell anyone where you were going." Charlotte kept her tone gentle, but considering the way he'd scared Roberta half to death, she was tempted to raise her voice a couple of notches. She took a big breath instead. "We worry about the people we love. I'm not going to come in until you tell us it's okay. Or you may come out. What would you like to do? It's your call." While she waited for Obie's deliberation she traced the ivy and violets she'd painted on the door. *Come on, Obie.*

After what seemed like forever, her favorite little buddy said in a tiny voice, "I'll come out."

Charlotte and Roberta smiled at each other. Okay. Making headway.

After another long wait, the door moved and then swung open.

Obie stumbled out, squinting in the light. Then he turned around and picked up a box in the outhouse and set it outside. Two kittens gazed up at them and mewed.

Hmm. Two kitties. Charlotte smiled. *Obie must have already found a home for one of them.*

"Honey," Roberta said, "why did you bring the cats with you to the outhouse?"

"I didn't want to leave them behind." Obie looked at them both. "In case the outhouse really was a time-travel machine I wanted us to go somewhere else."

Charlotte knelt down in front of Obie. "And where did you want to go?"

"I don't know." Obie stared down at the kitties.

Charlotte took hold of his arms. "Obie, I know you must miss your mother. So, did you think a time machine would let you go back? Give you the chance to see her?"

Obie picked at the hole in his jeans. "I knew it wasn't really a time machine, but I could pretend. I'm very good at pretending stuff. I wanted to ask Momma why she left me."

What could she say? What an impossible situation. Charlotte tried to compose her words. "Your mother was depressed. And when people get that way they sometimes do things that aren't right, and it hurts the ones they love. Sometimes they don't even know what they're doing. I know she loved you. Her note says so. But she was afraid, I guess."

Obie petted the kittens. "What was she afraid of?"

"Of life." Charlotte wasn't sure where that answer had come from, but once it was out, she realized how true it must have been.

"Oh." Obie sat down on the concrete step, and Charlotte and Roberta sat on either side of him.

They were quiet for a minute and then he said, "Momma going away like that was my fault."

Charlotte wanted Roberta to have a chance to speak, to mother him, so she went quiet for a moment.

"What do you mean, Obie?" Roberta asked.

"Sometimes I'd make a mess in the kitchen and she'd holler at me. When things got bad . . . sometimes I would wish her dead. And then it happened. She was dead." Obie's face wrinkled and then tears streamed down his cheeks. "Does that mean I did it?"

Roberta wrapped her arms around the boy. "Of course you didn't. It wasn't your fault."

"But how do you know for sure?" Obie looked up at Roberta.

"Because God doesn't work that way. You can't just wish someone dead, and then they die." Roberta wiped away the tears running down his cheeks.

"Really?"

"Yes, really. Do you believe us? What Miss Charlotte and I tell you?"

"I guess so. Sort of. You wouldn't lie to me. Would you?" Obie hugged his knees. "My mother lied to me . . . sometimes."

"No, we would not lie to you," Roberta said. "It's not the way we do things."

Obie scrubbed his boots against the concrete. "I'm not very good at taking care of my kittens."

"What do you mean? You've been very attentive. I'm proud of you." Roberta patted his back.

"I was supposed to find homes for them." Obie set the box on his lap. "I had to beg a friend to take one because Mr. Justin didn't want it. Mr. Justin said he wasn't settled enough to have a pet, but when the time was right, he'd go to the pound to get a pooch. What did that mean . . . settled?"

Roberta looked at her as if asking for input, so Charlotte said, "Well, I guess Justin just wants to find his way again. You know, what he's going to do with his life now. Where he's going to live."

"I want that settled thing too," Obie said.

Roberta looked at her over the top of Obie's head and gave Charlotte a silent sigh.

It felt heartbreaking to know that even though Roberta had done a great job taking care of Obie he still felt displaced. But then his whole world had been decimated. It would take time to feel safe again. In all the years Roberta had cared for children, she'd never taken them under her wing permanently. Perhaps there was still a chance to adopt Obie, even though it meant he would be raised by a single mother.

Obie suddenly slapped his leg and yelped, making her vault out of her reverie.

"I have an idea," he said. "Maybe I could ask that Mr. LaGrange if he wants one of my kittens. Maybe he wouldn't be so mean if he had a pet to love. Maybe he wouldn't be so scared of life . . . like Momma."

"Maybe you're right. That's an interesting idea," Charlotte said, grinning at Roberta. Kids were so intuitive.

Obie picked up the calico kitten and held her up, gazing at her. "But this one is mine."

The kitten mewed loudly.

"But what if this one dies?" he asked.

"Well, Obie, you used to be little, and you're growing up big and strong," Roberta said. "I don't know for sure what will happen to kitty, but I'm hoping she'll be just fine, and you two will be good friends."

"I'll name her Biggs. You're gonna be okay, Biggs." The kitten snuggled into the curve of Obie's arm.

Roberta gave the kitty a few strokes. "How about we take Biggs home for a bowl of milk?"

"First may we stop in the tearoom for some strawberry cake? Please, please?"

"Under one condition. That you never run away again." Roberta shook her finger at him. "Ever."

He nodded. "I promise. I guess I really scared you, 'cause even your hair looks spooked." Obie laughed.

"I'm sure it does." Roberta shot him a wry smile and smoothed her hair back into its bun.

Eliza came jogging toward them from the tearoom at an alarming pace.

Charlotte groaned. Oh, no. Eliza. As sure as thunder followed lightning it was bound to be bad news. When Eliza got within hearing range, Charlotte asked her, "What's up, and where are your shoes?" What was it with younger women and no shoes? They couldn't seem to find them or keep them on.

"No time for flip-flops," Eliza said. "You'd better come. Cordelia Murdock insists there are bugs in her pumpkin soup . . . again."

Obie whispered, "Coool."

Charlotte refrained from rolling her eyes. "It's fennel seeds, Eliza. They just look like bugs. Did you tell her?"

"Affirmative, and now Cordelia claims she saw one of the fennel seeds swimming in her bowl."

Charlotte felt herself aging. "Is that all?"

"Well, you know how Mr. LaGrange puts a little something in his tea when we're not looking? Well, this time he slipped the hooch into Edith's tea. She was aghast . . . that's her word." Eliza made a comedic, spastic kind of gesture. "Anyway, Edith took her cup of tea and poured it all over Mr. LaGrange's head. Last I heard she stormed out the door, threatening to call the sheriff."

29

Sam sat on a stool, working through another pile of his father's possessions. The more he dug into his father's closets and drawers and attics, the more rubbish he found. And the more valuables he uncovered. He'd hoped to clean and sort and move on with life, but the task grew bigger by the day. He might be working on the house and sorting through boxes for many more months to come. Was that how his father had wanted it? He massaged his aching neck and head.

"Mr. Sam?" Nelly yoo-hooed from the other side of the stacked boxes.

"I'm in here. Enter at your own risk."

Nelly chuckled.

"You still want to call me Mr. Sam?" He grinned.

"Old habits die hard. Or is it old dogs? Well, this old dog is coming through."

"You're far from old, Nelly."

"Well, my gout is acting up today, and I'm feeling old." She squeezed through a pile of boxes, which made them teeter for a moment.

Sam grabbed the pile until it settled down.

"Thanks. Here, I brought you some backup." She handed him a bottle of aspirin and a cup of water.

"Thanks. Stooping over for weeks has made my back feel like I'm a bug pinned to a specimen board. Only still alive."

"Mmm. You need my chiropractor. She'll set you straight." Nelly glanced around at the mess. "I wish you'd let me help you with this."

"Thanks, but you do such a great job feeding me I don't want to take you away from such an important task." Sam glanced over at Nelly as she peeked inside a box. He still thought of what she'd said that day at the pond—that he wasn't acting like a man who'd been given a second chance at love. But he wasn't sure if she meant he'd better start being more thankful, or if he needed to reflect on the reason for his lack of enthusiasm over the upcoming wedding. He dumped a couple of aspirin in his hand and washed them down with the water.

Nelly pulled up a chair and sat down. "So, you making any headway in here at all?"

"A little. Amazingly, in all this junk, I'm still finding more valuables . . . gemstones and stocks, and well, you name it. I knew my father was well-off, but this goes far beyond anything I imagined. Which grieves me all the more that he didn't mention you in his will."

"Now, now." Nelly waved him off.

"As I promised, I've taken care of his lack of loyalty. Funny about using the word *lack* to describe my father. He lacked for nothing materially and yet in every other way he was so needy. Anyway, I've set up an account for you, to thank you for all you did for my father." Sam lifted a checkbook off the table and held it out to her.

Nelly accepted the checkbook but not without some hesitancy. Before she opened it, she said, "Are you sure about this? You're gonna have children someday. And until you're in the thick of it you don't know how much diapers are and play clothes, and orthodontia, and techno gadgets that all the kids can't seem to live without these days. And if you have a girl you'll be out at least thirty thousand on clothes and doodads and such."

Sam chuckled. "I've put a lot of thought into it, and the decision has been made. Audrey approves of it too. I asked her this morning at breakfast."

Nelly looked at him funny. "You say you talked to Audrey this morning?"

"That's right."

She paused and then asked, "Did you two talk about anything else?"

"No. Mostly the weather. Are you trying to tell me something, Nelly?"

"No. Can't say that I am." She held her hand out like she was checking her nails.

"You've got that funny look like you're about to explode with something."

Nelly frowned. "Do you trust me?"

"Seems to me, you've earned it."

"Then trust me for a little while."

"All right." Sam held up his hands in surrender. "I won't question you anymore about it." He pointed to the checkbook. "Aren't you going to open it? You'll be doing me a favor, taking the money. I'm finding the immensity of my father's belongings to be more oppressive than freeing. And besides I'm just giving you pocket change from the Wilder fortune. Maybe that will make you feel better."

Nelly slowly opened the checkbook and looked down. Her hand slid over her mouth. "This isn't pocket change. I done robbed the whole bank. It's too much." She fanned herself with the checkbook. "You think I was loyal and loving all these years. But there were times I wanted to take a mallet to your father."

"And I'm sure my father would have benefited from it as you've told me before."

"And when I talk about a mallet, I don't mean the soft foam kind like the kids use."

Sam laughed. "Everyone felt that way about my father. The point is you stayed when no one else would have. When I think about the verbal abuse you endured at—"

"But it's so much, Sam. What am I going to do with a hundred thousand dollars?"

"Live a little of your dream, whatever that is." Sam stood up, leaned over backward to give his aching spine a stretch, and then sat down. "What is your dream anyway? I'm sure you don't want to work for me the rest of your life."

Nelly chuckled. "That wouldn't be a terrible proposition, but I do have a dream or two folded away in my heart. My momma's the only person who's ever asked me about my dream." She patted the checkbook on her lap. "Well, instead of doing my cooking on such a small scale, I wanted to open a café in Middlebury. But I held back 'cause I didn't want to compete with Charlotte and her tearoom."

"You mean you thought your café might struggle because of all her devoted customers?"

"No, I thought my cooking might put Charlotte out of business." Nelly winked.

Sam threw his head back laughing.

"I'm just messing with you."

"You two would work well together. Too bad you couldn't partner with her at the tearoom. You could buy out half of her business. It would give her more time. I heard she's going to do a cookbook, and I'll bet she'll need more hours in the day. If you went in with Charlotte you wouldn't have to start a place from scratch. Win/win. You've certainly got the money now. Wouldn't hurt to ask anyway."

Nelly frowned at him through her enormous grin. "I might talk to Charlotte about it. I just might. And thank you for this." She took a long whiff of the leather cover. "Dreams coming true smell mighty sweet."

Sam grinned. "Well, that felt good." *So few things in life did.* Hmm. Good thing he hadn't let those last words slip out, since Nelly would have given him another lecture on gratitude.

"So, what's *your* dream? I noticed you don't talk about geology anymore. Are you not going to work for that big city company after all? I thought they were going to let you work from here."

"That was my original plan when I moved out here. But I don't think so now." Sam put his feet on the box in front of him. "They let me take a leave of absence for the funeral and the wedding, but now that I've been away, I don't see anything that makes me want to go back, even if I can work at home. I'm going to say good-bye to all of it. I guess it's a season of good-byes, isn't it?"

Sam stared at the bottle of aspirin on the end table. "Anyway, my father was the one who insisted I make geology my life, but it was never what I wanted to do. I mean, if I loved geology, I'd always be talking about it. Wouldn't I? Like how those beautiful crystals form, and the motion of the plates, and the rise and fall of the oceans. Yeah, I'd talk about it, think about it, dream about it . . . wouldn't be able to get it out of my head. Yeah, that's how you can tell when you love something."

"Uh-huh." Nelly looked at him cockeyed. "You kind of wandered off there for a sec. Well, your father isn't holding you to anything now. So, tell me, what does Sam Wilder want to do?"

Sam laced his fingers together behind his head and looked upward. "I like people. They feel at ease with me. I guess I'd like to run a small business. Maybe like a B&B."

"Goodness me. You mean a bed and breakfast?"

"That's the one."

Nelly sat quietly for a while as if mulling it over. "I can see you doing that. I can. We only have two B&Bs in Middlebury, and I've heard they're doing quite a business."

Sam opened another dusty box, looked inside at all the jumbled mess of old rubbish and groaned. "I can talk to you so easily, Nelly. Wish it could have been that way with my father. I wonder what happened along the way."

"I think most parents want kids, but after they're born sometimes they lose sight of the miracle. They get so wrapped up in earth stuff they can't see from the clouds anymore . . . not like on that very first day, not when holding their baby was as sweet as a cherub's kiss."

"I'm sure that was some of my father's problem." He gestured around him. "But I would have given up all this to have had one really great conversation with him."

"Yeah, I wish it could have happened for you too," Nelly said. "But just like a runner, if you're always looking back, well, you're just going to stumble."

Sam leaned forward and looked at her. "But my life isn't a race."

"Maybe not. But you craved some good one-on-one time with your daddy, and yet here you are, just a few short weeks away from your wedding day and you're barely talking to your fiancée . You shouldn't be in here chewing the fat with me. You should be out in that greenhouse talking to Audrey. Telling her about your plans. Did you even ask her about how she feels about running a B&B? That business is usually considered something the husband and wife do together. Something they'd better both have a passion for, since it's not only the people business, but it's a round-the-clock kind of job."

"No, I never mentioned it." Sam leaned down and dug his fingers into his scalp. "I'm being a jerk here, aren't I?"

"Not a jerk. You're just losing sight of the miracle." Nelly rose from her chair and smoothed her dress. "I've got baking to do before dinner tonight, but before I go I'll say this. I know why it's taking you so long to go through these boxes. You aren't really sorting as much as searching. And I think I might be able to help you with that now. The piece of the mystery you talked about."

Sam studied her face. "Why didn't you tell me that day at the pond?"

Nelly slapped the checkbook against her hand. "Because it makes me feel like I'm sticking my nose in other people's business. That's why I've been holding back. What I'm talking about isn't just another box of gems and junk. This information is dangerous, like one of those defibrillators at the hospital. It has the power to restart somebody's heart. Or hurt somebody badly. But I've decided to tell you anyway."

Sam rose off the chair, his heart racing. "What is it? Where is it?"

"It's a clump of old letters. You were closer to the mystery than you thought. It's behind you in his smaller closet. The cedar room, the one you haven't been tearing around in yet. It's in the middle bottom drawer . . . in a secret compartment. There's a false bottom in it. Some of the letters, well, you're not going to want to read them. But they're important. I'm going to stand on the promise that the truth will set us free." Nelly waved her hand to the heavens. "I hope you're hearing me, Lord, because this could go south mighty fast." She backed away.

"Nelly, don't leave just yet. I do trust your motivation in waiting to show me these, even though I'm curious as to why you suddenly think I should see them now. But whatever is behind it all, thank you for finally telling me."

"You're welcome." Nelly smiled. "But I'd still rather go to the kitchen now just the same."

Sam opened the door to the cedar closet and gestured for her to go inside first.

"Now you know this isn't fair. I thought it was more than generous of me to tell you, but . . . " Nelly kept up her protests as she marched right inside the closet.

Sam walked in behind Nelly. The smell of cedar engulfed him immediately along with a memory from his youth. When he was a junior in high school he'd wanted to borrow one of his father's ties for a special occasion, but when he was discovered snooping around in the cedar closet, his father angrily banned him from ever entering it again. Perhaps his father was scared he'd discover something—a secret. It was another recollection he wished he could toss into the giveaway pile.

Sam hesitated, but then he knelt down in front of the built-in cedar chest. He looked at the middle bottom drawer, gave the handle a pull, and maneuvered the false bottom until it loosened. He lifted the panel out and saw the little pile of letters bound in a rubber band. Sam looked up at her. "I'd love to know the story of how you knew about this hidden compartment."

Nelly sat down on a bench next to the drawers. "When your father became confined to his bed, he knew he was dying and he wanted these letters destroyed. You'll see why when you read them. He didn't want anyone to find them, especially you." She took in a deep breath and let it out slowly. "You're going to want your checkbook back when you hear what I did. Anyway, he sent me in here to take these letters out and burn them. I agreed to do it, but instead, I took the letters in the kitchen and read some of them."

"You did what?" Sam placed his hand over his heart in mock horror. "You lied, Nelly?"

"Yes, I lied." Nelly scowled at him. "Mm, mm, mm. Horrible sin as it is. It's one of the Ten Commandments. Do not bear false witness against your neighbor. Well, I did one worse. I lied to a dying man. Your father asked me if I'd burned those letters. And I looked him straight in the eye and said yes. And I took it one more sinful step further. The reason Mr. Wilder didn't ask any more questions was because I did burn something in the kitchen fireplace so it would smell up the house a bit. Just some old newspapers, but when I closed the flue, it was enough to set off the kitchen smoke alarm. Then when your father was sound asleep I put the letters back."

Sam rested back against the wall. "Well, you are one impressive liar, Nelly. You would put the criminal mind to shame."

Nelly slapped the wall near his arm. "Now, I just opened my vein for you, and this is how you thank me?" A grin teased the corner of her lips. "I am sorry for my sin, though. I've begged the Lord to pardon me so many times, I can tell even He is weary hearing about it."

Sam set the letters down, stood up, and put his arm around Nelly. "All is well." When she started to get up off the bench he helped her.

"Honestly, after I did that thing with the fire alarm," Nelly said, "I thought I might throw those letters in the trash later, but something . . . something just kept me in check, making me not want to get rid of them."

"Maybe it was for such a time as this," Sam said.

"Maybe so. Maybe this explains a lot of things. . . . like why God seemed to keep me here even though it would have been easier to leave." Nelly moaned out a big breath of air. "Oh, it does feel good to tell somebody about this." She turned to go but added, "I don't want to be in here when you read the letters. Hope that's okay. I just think it needs to be a private moment between you and God."

"I understand."

Nelly walked out, but she didn't close the door.

Sam sat down on the bench and looked at the letter on top of the stack. It wasn't addressed, so apparently it hadn't gone through the mail service. Made sense if there was incriminating information in it. He slipped the letter out of the envelope. The stationery was a woman's, and the handwriting had a swirling, feminine touch. He sniffed the paper. It still had the faint smell of a women's perfume. He hesitated, wondering what Nelly meant about the letters being dangerous. But whatever it was, he felt the time was now. He unfolded the first letter and began to read . . .

30

$\mathcal{M}$eredith sat in her parked car at the end of the long tree-lined lane in front of the Wilder mansion. She tapped her fingernails on the steering wheel like the nervous little legs of a centipede as she waited for the mailman to deliver Charlotte and Sam's ancient wedding invitation to Audrey.

What monstrous folly! Her ploy had to have been born of sheer lunacy. Did she really think her plan would work? But who had appointed her the patron saint of lost loves? She was delusional. Certifiable. No, that wasn't it, but she knew what might have spurred her on. She, Meredith Alexandria Steinberg, was falling in love.

Meredith rested her head on her hands. That was it, wasn't it? She'd lost her heart to Wally, and now she couldn't stand for anyone else to miss what she had. Couldn't bear for any of them to live a lifetime without the bliss she'd been fortunate enough to have known twice in her life.

Yes, I love Wally. I love him. How had it happened so quickly? She was a lost cause, and all she'd done was gaze into those dancing brown eyes, listen to his small-town stories, and rest her hand over his as they played the organ together. Yes, she had gotten lost deeply in the enchanted woods of love, and she didn't care if she was ever found again.

Meredith wasn't sure how long she sat there succumbing to the joy of it all, dreaming about the future with Wally when she heard a noise. A car drove by, joggling her back to reality. Yes, back to the sobering matter at hand. She'd seen people massage their unsavory deeds so thoroughly that they could convince themselves they were not in the wrong. *Lord, am I guilty of that, blaming my impulsiveness on the giddy affections I have for Wally?* Even if she were to come out innocent, which she was not, her actions would be forever viewed as a cruel and unforgivable prank.

Meredith opened her purse and popped a couple of antacids. She had a bad feeling in her gut, and it wasn't the goulash she'd had for lunch. What a shame she'd missed the postal guy at the drop box. All of this running around could have been avoided. But there was no easy way out now; she'd have to pay for her sins by waiting for the delivery of the invitation. Her plan would go thusly; she would rummage through the Wilder mail before anyone picked it up, snatch the envelope back out of the pile, and no one but God would know what she'd done. And hopefully, he would forgive her for this miserable offense.

Of course, when she was growing up—and with the help of her rascally sisters egging her on—she'd been the instigator of a wide assortment of pranks. Meredith remembered how it used to drive her parents and neighbors nuts. They were mostly harmless shenanigans, like putting bubble bath in an outdoor hot tub or flying her mother's red underwear as a pirate flag on their tree in the front yard.

But all the misdeeds of her youth couldn't compare to the travesty of this one horrific act of misjudgment. And never was there so much at stake. In one foolhardy sweep she might have destroyed a couple's happiness forever and in the process she might have ruined her chances to be with her beloved. He would think she was a ninny. Or much worse. But she had a good heart. Didn't she? Meredith looked heavenward beseechingly. "I did mean well. I did, Lord. Doesn't that count for something?"

The afternoon sun beat down on her windows. She started the car's engine again and turned on the air conditioner. When the postal truck finally putted up the road toward her, she realized again just how volatile the situation was. Wouldn't he wonder why she was parked along the road, just sitting there? But the young man didn't seem to notice her. He stopped at the mailbox, dropped the mail in, and drove off, leaving a grey cloud of exhaust.

Hmm. Maybe it would be easier than she imagined. Of course, tampering with the mail was a federal offense. If anyone saw her and turned her in, it wouldn't look good for Wally. To have the pastor's girlfriend bailed out of jail just didn't have that "Sweet By and By" ring to it. And yet all she had to do was reach in and remove the offending invitation.

That's when she saw Audrey walking down the lane. She was going to pick up Sam's mail right on time. Her plan had been foiled! Before she could let Audrey get a good look at her through the trees Meredith panicked. She started the engine and drove away.

She turned on the radio to a happy tune. Then she snapped it off. She was a grown woman and usually acted as such, but right now sitting in a highchair would be too grown up for her.

You are many things, Meredith, but you are not a coward. She stopped, did a three-point turnabout in the road, and drove back toward Audrey, who now stood by the mailbox, staring at a piece of mail. She slapped her hand over her heart. It was obvious that Audrey had opened the envelope and was gaping at the contents—which was an invitation to Charlotte and Sam's wedding.

With mail in hand, Audrey took off running up the long lane, toward the house.

Meredith hadn't anticipated such a snag, but she met the challenge and slowly turned the corner and drove up the lane behind her.

Audrey glanced back at her and tripped. She stumbled, trying to right herself, but in the end, she plummeted down into the dirt alongside the road. The skirt on Audrey's pretty summer dress billowed up like a sail in the breeze and landed on her head.

Meredith drove up next to Audrey and stopped. She opened the car door to help her, but Audrey had already scrambled to her feet. Meredith shut the door and pushed a lever, letting the window roll down. This was not going to be a piece of cake.

Audrey looked at her through the open window. "Meredith? Is that you?" Tears already stained the woman's cheeks.

"Yes, it's me." *Unfortunately.* "That was quite a tumble. You okay?"

Audrey wiped off her mouth. "I might have bloodied my tooth a little when I fell, but I'm fine."

Goodness. Meredith gave herself another internal lashing.

Audrey gathered up the mail and stuffed it under her arm. "Would you like to come in for some coffee or something?"

Meredith thought for a second. No, maybe she'd like a double whiskey straight up. *Just kidding, Lord.* "That's very kind of you, Audrey, considering the circumstances."

"What do you mean?" Audrey walked up to her car.

Meredith sighed. "I know why you've been crying."

"You do?" Audrey shifted the wad of mail and held it to her chest. "But how could you know?"

"If you don't mind sitting for a few minutes in my car, I'll explain everything."

Audrey stood there for a moment saying nothing, and then she walked around to the passenger side and got in.

Meredith turned in the seat to face Audrey. "You got your pretty frock all dirty."

Audrey looked baffled. "Frock?"

"I mean dress. Sorry, I'm in the antique business."

"Oh. It'll dry-clean."

Audrey also had a dollop of dirt on her nose, but Meredith let it go for now. Instead she said, "I know you received an invitation today."

Audrey grimaced. "How did you know?"

"I just do. It was an odd thing to get, wasn't it?"

She nodded. "Yeah, really odd since it's wrinkled, and it didn't come in the right kind of envelope. But it was pretty cruel too, not to mention creepy, like somebody wanted to warn me or something. I know Charlotte isn't that way. I know she didn't send it. But who would do this?" Audrey took the invitation out from the pile of mail and set it on top. "Is that why you came? To tell me who would do such a terrible thing?"

"Yes. I'm here to tell you who sent the invitation." Meredith took in the deepest breath of her life and issued the most fervent prayer she could muster. But she still felt every bit the schmuck she really was. "It was me. I did it."

Audrey pulled back. Her face shadowed with a number of expressions, but to her credit she landed on confusion. "But why would you do this? It's so . . . wounding."

"Yes. On the surface it appears fiendish, but that was never my intention."

"Please explain." Audrey dug her teeth into her lower lip.

"I have always been a people watcher. Even as a child I saw things that other people missed." Audrey didn't look all that impressed, so she cut to the chase. "Look, I noticed you and Justin at the Easter dinner. You could open a lab with all the chemistry flowing between the two of you. Sorry to be so brusque."

Audrey picked at her puffy sleeve. "I won't lie to you. There is . . . something happening. Something neither one of us expected nor sought out. It's just now unfolding, and I don't know what to do about it."

I was right all along. "You don't know what to do about it?" Audrey's simple remedy stood in front of them as big as a wooly mammoth. Why couldn't she see it? "You should talk to Sam about it."

"I didn't know how to bring it up, but I will." Audrey held up the wedding invitation. "But why this, Meredith? Why not just talk to me like we're doing now? Why did you go to the trouble to print this up, wrinkle it, and then mail it? Just seems like a childish trick."

"I know. It was childish, and it was the coward's way out. I'll carry the burden of what I did to you for the rest of my life. Don't try to say anything to make me feel better, since the guilt will do me good."

"Frankly," Audrey said, "I don't feel like saying anything that will make you feel better. At least not right now."

"Good thinking. You're right." Meredith lowered Audrey's window to let the breeze blow through. "I need to wallow in the mire for a while to get it all over me. Remember the feeling, so I'm never tempted to do anything so impulsive again."

"Yeah, something like that." Audrey let a grin play at the corners of her lips.

Meredith smiled back at her, knowing full well it was time to say the rest. "By the way, the whole truth needs to be said. I didn't come up with this invitation. I just wanted you to see it."

"Who made it then?"

"Charlotte did . . . when she and Sam were eighteen. Sam never knew about it, and it's not a real invitation. It was just something Charlotte had dreamed of. So she made it on her computer and printed it out when she was in high school. Charlotte kept it all these years. When I talked to her recently she dug it out of her desk and showed it to me. She wanted to support you and Sam in your marriage, so she crumpled it up and threw it in the trash. That's why it's so wrinkled."

Audrey licked her lips. Then she shifted in her seat. "Let me get this straight. You mean you dug this invitation out of Charlotte's trash bin and mailed it to me, hoping I'd break up with Sam and marry Justin. And that Sam would marry Charlotte."

Meredith flinched. "It does sound pretty fantastical and presumptuous and manipulative when you string the whole scheme together like that, but yes."

"Wow, you've got more hut-spa than any woman I've ever known. Did I say that word right?"

"Actually, it's *chutzpah*, but I'll take it as a compliment. Right now, though, it feels like I deserve a straitjacket more than a compliment . . . but thank you."

Audrey chuckled. "Well, you're not out of the time-out chair quite yet. Some months ago Sam did tell me he'd dated Charlotte in high school, but he didn't say much more than that. The two of them must have been more serious if Charlotte was in love with Sam and if she was to the point of dreaming of a wedding. Unless it was only feelings on her end."

Meredith touched Audrey's hand. "There's more to the story, but this is the part that Sam needs to tell you. Not me."

"I don't know. I think we're so far down the road on this together, I think you'd just better tell me the rest."

"Yeah, I thought you might say that. But who can blame you?" Underneath Audrey's bottom lip were red teeth marks from her grinding. Maybe she'd better just put out all the laundry to dry. "All right. Sam and Charlotte fell in love in high school. Sam proposed, but Charlotte turned him down."

"What? Really?" Audrey shook her head. "Sam never told me he proposed to Charlotte. He never alluded to the fact that they had been serious. Marriage or the hope of it was never brought up. But I wonder, why did Charlotte turn him down if she loved him back then?" Audrey's hand went to her forehead. "Ohh."

"What is it?"

"If I'd known about their past I never would have had Charlotte do the food for our wedding reception. I can't believe Sam went along with it. How could he? Maybe he thought Charlotte no longer felt anything. That's why he never mentioned any of this." Audrey stared into space, looking like a sad pup.

Meredith wasn't sure how much more to say. She did know for a fact that Charlotte was still in love with Sam, and she had a strong sense that Sam still felt the same way about Charlotte. But she was exhausted from crawling out of the hole she'd dug, so perhaps she should let Audrey and Sam take the conversation from here. Or maybe Audrey already knew the truth in her heart. Oh, how complicated love could be! She had an unsteady and acid-prone stomach, and she didn't know if her guts could take much more.

Audrey played with the door handle. "But I have seen the way Sam and Charlotte look at each other. Such light. I've never once seen Sam look at me that way." She looked at Meredith. "I think it's the same way Justin and I look at each other." Her eyes went misty then, and she snuffled back the tears.

Good. Audrey figured it out on her own. "It's all right. No one is married . . . yet."

"I'll talk to Sam today about all of it." Audrey held up the invitation. "May I keep this?"

It didn't thrill Meredith to have Charlotte's private and tender musings out there circulating, but the lock on Pandora's Box had been jimmied and now the lid defied closing. "Yes. I guess it's all right. Although do remember that Charlotte thought the invitation was in the trash." While she divvied out acts of contrition maybe she should consider confessing to Charlotte as well, but after apologizing to Audrey she was pretty much dog-eared emotionally. Maybe she'd let it go, for now. Meredith pulled a tissue from her purse and handed it to Audrey. "You have a smudge of dirt on your nose."

Audrey looked in the car mirror. "You mean you let me talk the whole time looking like this?"

"It just didn't seem to matter as much as what we were saying. Besides, it's not nearly as bad as having egg all over your face, like me."

Something that was pretty close to a laugh sputtered out of Audrey's mouth. She licked the tissue and wiped the smudge of dirt off her nose.

"Listen, Audrey, I know I don't have any right to ask this of you, but as you talk about what I did . . . I'd be grateful if you'd tell people my reasoning. I sent the invitation because I thought it would be better to make a lot of people angry at me than to watch people getting married who still had things they needed to say."

Audrey handed Meredith the wadded-up tissue. "Wise words if ever I heard them."

"So, you're not going to hate me for all time and eternity?"

"I'm still shaken by it all. But I have this feeling when the dust settles . . . people will feel just the opposite." Audrey opened the car door. "By the way, I know how this sounds, but I don't know where Sam is. He left in a rush and didn't tell me where he was going. I know Middlebury is too big for you to keep up with him, but just wondered if you'd seen him around town today. Thought maybe you could use some of that sixth sense of yours to help me out." Audrey smiled.

Meredith chuckled. "Yeah, I deserved that." But better to have her teasing than crying. "No, I'm sorry. I haven't seen Sam."

"He didn't look well when I saw him. Maybe he went to the doctor." Audrey tapped her fingers against her lips. "Or, maybe I'll start my search for Sam by dropping by the tearoom."

"I guess that's a possibility."

It was a nervous smile Audrey wore, but it looked sincere. "I'll be honest, Meredith. I'm scared. I feel my whole world is collapsing right on top of me. But I also have to say, I've never been so excited in my life."

31

Charlotte closed the front blinds of the tearoom, even though a sprinkling of her customers remained sipping and chatting.

"Hey, we can take a hint, Char," Mindy said. "We're leaving." She sashayed to the front door with a young man in tow—Raymond Kolowsky, the nice young man who Mindy claimed was a pet or worse, a brain-freak.

"Sorry. I close early on Thursdays." Charlotte turned to Raymond. "Nice to see you again." She winked at Mindy.

Mindy narrowed her eyes at Charlotte. "Hey, don't get any ideas. Raymond and I are just good friends."

"Now, now." Raymond raised his finger in the air. "*With* the potential for something more," he said as he opened the door for Mindy.

Charlotte smiled at him. *Good for you, Raymond. You can sweetly dish it right back to Mindy.* Friendly sparring without trampling her was a good thing—not like that horrible ego-crushing meister named Brenner she only thought she was falling for.

"I hear you're going to have a photo shoot today for your cookbook. Word is all over town. My mom can't stop talking about it," Mindy said. "Congrats, Char."

"Thanks."

Mindy gave Charlotte a fist bump. "See ya."

"Later."

Mindy walked out with a grin and a parade wave. Guess she decided Raymond wasn't too much of a brain-freak after all.

Charlotte headed back to her last customer and Obie. She probably shouldn't have left Mr. LaGrange alone so long with Obie in case he decided to slip some schnapps in Obie's tea. She sat down at the big table with them. "So, how are the negotiations going concerning the kitty?"

Obie went down the checklist in his notebook, looking like a high-powered executive. "Well, Mr. LaGrange agreed to give the kitten a good name and not ever give her away unless he dies."

"I don't think Mr. LaGrange has any plans on dying right away." Charlotte smiled.

"Not if I can help it." Mr. LaGrange grinned. "I'd like to have a pet, though. I certainly have the time. Well, time is all I've got left anymore."

"That's good too. Lots of time to take care of your pet." Obie looked at an unchecked box on his list. "But we're stuck on point number five. The last one."

"What's number five on your list?" Charlotte leaned forward to look at Obie's list.

Mr. LaGrange mumbled something to himself and then said, "Obie wants me to pray for the cat every Sunday, and I told him there was no point."

Obie looked at him. "What do ya got against God?"

"Nothing." Mr. LaGrange shrugged. "I just don't believe he's there."

"But what if you're wrong?" Obie slapped the pencil down on the notebook. "I think you're just being mean about not wanting to pray for your cat."

Mr. LaGrange crossed his arms on the table and leaned toward Obie, looking ominous with his craggy wrinkles and bushy brows. "I'm not being mean," he hissed.

"Miss Eliza says you're mean," Obie said. "Only she says it's not your fault. She says it's gravity. I'm not sure what that means." He scratched his head.

"Eliza probably meant the word *depravity*," Mr. LaGrange corrected.

Charlotte felt like hiding in her broom closet might be a good option. The lesson at school lately had been on honesty, and Obie had tested the virtue to the outer limits. Charlotte touched the boy's shoulder. "Honesty is always a good thing, but sometimes we shouldn't just say whatever pops into our heads."

"Yeah, that's what Miss Roberta says too." Obie chewed on the end of his pencil.

Mr. LaGrange usually had a barbed comeback or two, but this time he looked fresh out. He looked exhausted and old, more so than usual, like a man carrying a heavy load and who'd paused on the road to catch his breath. In spite of all the grief Mr. LaGrange had caused her over the years, the sight of him in such a weary state tore at her heart. She'd always naively thought that tea could help soothe many of life's ills, but a whole lake of tea wouldn't wash away or even dilute the trouble that seemed to have permanently settled itself in the spirit of Mr. LaGrange.

"Maybe I *am* depraved," he said quietly. "But mostly, I'm just alone." After a moment or two, he slid his saucer over to Charlotte, which held three red petals from the carnation on his lapel. It was the same gesture he'd made every day he stopped in for tea.

"Oh, that reminds me." Charlotte pulled a delicate gossamer bag out of her pocket and held it out to Mr. LaGrange. "This is for you."

"For me? That's kind of purdy." The older gentleman dangled the silk strings from his fingers. "What is it?"

"It's a bag of potpourri." Charlotte smiled. "I made it from all the petals you've been leaving me in your saucer all these months. Just a gift."

He held it to his nose and breathed. "Mmm. You made something beautiful, although I don't know why." He set it down, but cradled it in his hands. "I'm not the best customer. I'm nothing but a cantankerous old man. And worse, I'm nearly an alcoholic. And this is what you give me in return for the trouble I've caused. This sweet-smelling offering." He stared off into space. Perhaps he was chasing a dream or two. Or facing a heart full of sad memories. Only God knew.

"What is it, Mr. LaGrange?" Even though the older man could be ill-tempered, Charlotte felt the moment called for some openness. So, she reached out and touched the older gentleman's shoulder. "What is it? Who's hurt you?"

The old man lighted his finger across the table. "I would only answer that question for you, Miss Charlotte. Only you." He lifted the bag to his face and breathed deeply again as if there were some answer, some sustenance in the bag. Then he set it down next to his teacup. "A long time ago I knew a little girl who was very ill. She attended my church."

Coming out of his silent cocoon, Obie suddenly exploded with, "You went to church?"

"Yes, that's right. I did, but it was a long time ago." He shook his finger at the boy. "Now listen quietly to my story . . . . please."

Obie hunkered down in his chair. "Yes, sir."

"And that little girl I'm talking about, well, her name was Emily," Mr. LaGrange went on to say. "I heard there was an operation that could fix her heart and save her life. But the family had very little money at the time. Anyway, Emily was the brightest little thing. So quick and funny and sweet. Everyone loved her." He paused, touching the back of his fingers to his lips. "I had some money, since I'd been working and saving for years. As an act of faith, I took almost all my savings and gave it to the family for their Emily. To help her heart, so she could grow up big and strong like you, Obie."

"What happened to her," Obie asked, "Sir?"

"Well, the doctors thought the operation had been successful, and everyone celebrated. They even had a little party for her at the hospital. Lots of bears and balloons and flowers. Her parents couldn't stop thanking me. Couldn't stop kissing their little girl. Couldn't stop praising God for the miracle."

"What happened?" Charlotte pulled some tissues out of her pocket and daubed at her eyes.

"Emily died a few days later of a massive infection, and no amount of antibiotics could help her. Nothing could save her. No one. Not even God Almighty."

"That's a real sad story," Obie said.

Mr. LaGrange fingered the silk bag. "There hasn't been a day go by that I haven't thought about Emily. What might have been. What might have . . . "

Charlotte couldn't think of a thing to say, and that was good, since words were never going to do. No amount of consoling or counsel would ever make things lovely again. So she reached out to Mr. LaGrange, took his hand, and wept.

Mr. LaGrange began to sob, and so it went around the table until the three of them wept together.

When the tears subsided and they'd cleaned themselves up with tissues and handkerchiefs, Mr. LaGrange rose from his chair. "I have two things to say, and then I'm going." He looked at Obie. "Remember this, little man. Kind deeds, even the small ones, may not seem like much at the time, but they can be like the tiniest tendril of a plant working the crack of a dam. They can be bigger than you ever imagine."

Mr. LaGrange picked up the silk bag of potpourri and took another whiff. Then he turned his attention to Charlotte. "Since I've moved to Middlebury, there have been two constants in my life. That I've known sorrow. And that when I come to The Rose Hill Cottage Tearoom, Charlotte will be there with a smile and a cup of tea. My dear, if there is a God . . . I see him in your face."

32

With the stack of old letters stuffed securely in his pocket Sam opened the door to the tearoom. The sign read, Closed, but the door was open, so he strode right in. He searched for Charlotte until he spotted her by the fireplace. Apparently she was in the middle of a photo shoot, but he'd wait the rest of the day if he had to. This day would not end until he'd had his say with Charlotte. He'd been living in ignorance for too long. He knew the truth now from their past, and he intended to make things right once and for all, even if only to plead for forgiveness for the abominable way his father had treated her.

When Charlotte spotted him, she smiled right away. "Hi."

He grinned. "You look busy."

"A little."

"I hate interrupting, but I need to talk to you, privately for a few minutes. Is that possible?"

Charlotte said to the photographer, "Do you mind if we take a short break?"

"No problem. I need to set up in the kitchen now anyway." The woman set her camera down on the table and folded up her tripod. "Besides I wanted a chance to sample some of the food you set out for me on that table over there. The smell is irresistible, and I never got a chance to eat lunch today."

"Then please take your time. Enjoy." Charlotte stepped over to Sam. "How about the gazebo in my garden out back?"

"All right."

Charlotte grabbed her sun hat, and then Sam followed her through the backdoor. They took a stone pathway to the open-air gazebo, one that was covered in some kind of wrinkly vine. Flowers hung in long purply clusters like grapes, but he had no idea what they were. He was certain Audrey and Justin would know, since they both shared a passion for plants. Before he had time to pursue that thought, he said, "I haven't seen this before." Sam gave the timbers a shake. "Good and solid. Did you do the work?"

"I hired someone, but I did the rest of the garden myself. When the weather is pretty we set up tables in here and have tea parties for little girls. They bring their dolls, and we all have sweets and savories and tea." Charlotte smiled.

Sam was clueless what a savory was, but he enjoyed seeing her so animated.

"They love it. Well, all except for the tomboys. They roll their eyes a lot."

Sam grinned. "It's a beautiful gazebo."

"Thanks." Charlotte sat down on the wooden bench.

A breeze blew a blossom off the vine near her hand. She picked it up, smelled it, and then placing it on her palm, Charlotte let the breeze take it on its way again. How willingly she could let go of things. It had never been so easy for him.

Sam motioned toward the tearoom. "I guess the photo shoot is for the cookbook?"

"Yes." She grasped the edge of the bench and gently swung her legs like she used to do when they were dating.

"I don't think I ever said congratulations . . . about the cookbook."

"Thanks."

"Are you excited about it?" Sam sat down on the bench next to her. "It's quite an honor."

"Yes, it'll be good for business. All the publicity. And it'll be fun. But I have this feeling you didn't drive into town to talk about my garden or my cookbook. Did you have some questions about the food for the reception? I promise my prices will be more than reasonable."

"Oh, no. It's nothing like that." Sam fell silent for a moment, not wanting to go on. He knew the faster he talked the sooner their discussion would be over, and he didn't want it to be over.

"What's on your mind, Sam?"

He looked into her eyes. There was something about the way she'd said his name—the smallest inflection—that brought all the memories back. All the joy of the past. The love they'd shared. Everything. But she seemed totally unaware that she'd done anything. "Now that I have you here, I'm struggling to find the words."

"Why? What is it?"

How could he tell her that being alone with her made the task so much harder? It brought back all the feelings as if no time had passed. "I'll just say it."

"I wish you would." She grinned.

"I found out recently what my father said to you on his deathbed. Nelly overheard the conversation."

"Oh." Her legs stopped their swinging.

"I know about your grandmother . . . on your father's side. Her half African American heritage. But I hope you didn't think that I would care one way or the other about it."

Charlotte smiled at him. "I knew your heart."

Sam wanted to hold her hand for his apology, but he placed his arm behind her on the bench instead. "I'm so sorry for the horrible things my father must have said to you before he passed away. How he must have made you feel tainted in some way, and yet it was his spirit that was corrupt. He remained blinded to his faults to the end."

"It wasn't an easy day for any of us. I will say this . . . until your father explained it to me recently, it was always a mystery. All those years I just thought your father hated me because he disapproved of me as a person. At least now I know."

"I wish you had told me more that day he died, but I understand why you didn't." Sam tugged on the button on his sleeve, almost tearing it off. "Now for the second part of my apology."

"The second part?"

"If I'd known about your grandmother, I could have guessed what my father might do. I might have been able to figure it out, that he would force you to say no to my proposal. But I know there's more to it than that."

"You do? You know the rest?" Charlotte leaned toward him slightly.

"Yes." Perhaps Charlotte felt relief now that he knew the truth. It must have been hard to carry such a burden for so many years. He pulled out the thin stack of letters from the pocket of his windbreaker. "These old love letters were in a secret compartment in one of my father's drawers. They're very revealing, but I'm sure most of it is information you've had all along. Now I understand the leverage my father used to threaten you with, to make you flee. Even though they never committed adultery, my father and your mother were sharing physical and emotional intimacies. This was going on during the years we dated. These letters are between my father and your mother."

"What?" Charlotte rose off the bench like she'd been shot. "Did I hear you right? *Your* father and *my* mother? But that can't be. All this time I thought it was the other way around. How—"

"Please, Charlotte." Sam held up his hand. "I know what you thought. But there is more, and the letters explain it. My father and your mother met clandestinely, but during that time they became fearful they would get caught. So, my father came up with the plan that they would accuse their spouses of adultery if they got caught. If anything happened, my father would tell people around town that my mother and your father were having an affair."

Charlotte took in a sudden lungful of air as if she'd been holding her breath. "I can't believe it. I mean, how awful considering that it was my mother and your father who were the guilty ones."

"That is true." Sam wanted so much to take her into his arms and comfort her, but it didn't feel appropriate. "I'm so sorry. I know this new information must be a shock. For myself, I feel relieved to know the truth, and yet I'm livid with my father for what he did to you, how he humiliated you and bullied you, swearing to spread that false gossip around town if you didn't say no to my proposal. And I'm angry that he was willing to manipulate our families with no thought of the aftermath. I'm not totally sure, but if you'd said yes, he might have followed through with his promise. And it would have been very hard on both our families."

Charlotte took off her hat and pressed the back of her hand against her forehead.

"Are you okay?" Sam asked.

"I'm all right. Just warm."

Her face looked flushed and damp. "But there's a cool breeze. Are you sure you're all right?"

"Well, I'm a little worked up right now, but I'll calm down in a minute." Charlotte pushed her hair away from her face. "I will tell you this, something else your father said to me when I was eighteen. He said that the scandal would destroy the close relationship you had with your mother. And it was that part of his speech that helped to solidify my decision . . . to walk away."

Sam shook his head. "I know why he would say something like that. He was envious of the close relationship I had with Mom."

Charlotte fanned herself with her hat. "I'm still trying to understand all this. If your father and my mother discussed these details, then my mother must have known everything. She must have been aware of the threat that drove us apart as well as the reasoning behind it. Maybe she even approved of it." She tossed her hat on the bench. "How could she do it? I was her daughter. Her only child. She loved me. At least I thought she did! Doesn't a mother want her daughter to be happy?" She tore at a cluster of leaves near the post and squeezed them inside her fingers.

"You're welcome to read the letters. Maybe it will help you understand."

Charlotte shook her head. "The long intimate version might be too painful. But I would like to know the answer." She looked at him then. "I'd like to know if my mother approved of the plan to break us apart."

It was true. How could he tell her? "I'm so sorry, but . . . " The words caught in his throat. "Your mother did approve of my father's plan. I'm convinced, though, that my father created a lot of fear in your mother about their future grandchildren and what could happen. I believe that without my father's controlling influence your mother never would have gone along with any of this. And I'm sure she would have loved her grand-children no matter their color."

"That's very kind, Sam, for you to give my mother the ben-efit of the doubt. I would like to believe it, but . . . " Charlotte threw the crushed leaves onto the ground. "To think this horrible scheme, all this pain sprang from one emotion . . . prejudice. God help us." She went quiet for a moment and then pointed to the letters in his hands. "Surely they didn't send those letters through the mail."

"No, I think they passed them to each other when they met."

Charlotte leaned against one of the posts. "All this time I thought my father was guilty, but it was my mother who was leading another life. They may not have slept together, but my mother was still unfaithful before God. You know, now that we're talking about it, I do remember that my mother would disappear sometimes, and Dad and I never knew where she was. Well, I guess now I know."

Sam gazed down at the letters in his hand, which had got-ten sweaty in his palms. "I always knew my father wasn't a good husband or dad, but I didn't know he was capable of such devious behavior and lies. It went on for so long I don't understand why people didn't find out."

"They must have been very cautious, since gossip flies pretty fast around Middlebury. Like hummingbirds on espresso. That's what my cook, Lil, always says."

Sam grinned. "I know you'll forgive them. That's what you do."

"But it will be one of the hardest things I've ever had to do."

"You have a tender heart, Charlotte."

"I don't know about that." She sat back down on the bench next to him.

"You do. Even though my father might have been ready to produce a scandal, he also knew you would bow out. He took advantage of your compassion, and that particular offense on his part will be hard for me to forgive."

"Had I been more mature or wiser or something . . . I don't know, I might have been able to stand up to him. But I was young. So afraid. Not for me, but for you."

Sam shifted on the bench. "Everyone feared my father, including me." It was so easy to remember all the glares and harsh words and deeds that had brought so many people so much pain. "My father left a deep and formidable wake everywhere he went. You are not at fault in any way. I only came to apologize for him since he refused to do the right thing the day he died."

Charlotte nodded, and then they went quiet, absorbing the sorrows of their past.

Sam wanted to reach out to her, but instead he stuffed the letters back into his pocket. Someday he would burn them.

She moved her hand closer to his but didn't touch him. "I want to say how sorry I am that I said no to your proposal. You weren't angry with me that day, but you could have been. I know I hurt you. I remember that day so well. We were on the bridge that crosses over Middlebury Creek, and after my final and unwavering answer to you, I told you to leave me alone. To not speak to me again. And then I turned and walked away. When I looked back at you one last time, I can never forget the look on your face. So bewildered. So desolate. Just the way I felt." She placed her hand on her heart.

Sam gripped the bench until his hand ached. "If my father had not done this terrible thing. If you had not been threatened, then you would have said yes to me that day on the bridge? You would have married me?"

Charlotte tilted her head and grinned. "In a heartbeat. Surely you know that. Yes, I would have married you."

He dropped his gaze. "We'd have kids by now. Two or three. They'd be teenagers, driving us crazy."

"Probably." Charlotte chuckled, but then it faded quickly. She rested against the railing and gazed up at the sky. There were no clouds to speak of. Only blue. And he knew she was running barefoot through the past the way they used to chase each other in the clover fields around Middlebury. But he also knew she might be thinking of the cookbook and what she still needed to do to prepare for it. And that was as it should be. He couldn't keep her trapped in the past. Now that the secrets were spoken and forgiveness had come, they would need to move forward.

Sam snuck another glance at her. Neither one of them seemed to mind the quiet that sat between them. He smiled to himself. She'd truly grown up while he was gone. She was still Charlotte, but she was a woman now, and he couldn't be more proud of her. She knew herself and what she was about. Beloved by all who knew her. Audrey was in many ways still a child, and she would have to find her way as an adult.

Not wanting to sit still any longer, Sam rose and leaned against the railing. Equal amounts of regret and shame pierced his spirit. Regret for all that was lost with Charlotte, and all he failed to fight for when it counted, and now the shame he felt for the judgments against Audrey. It was unfair to compare the two women. And who was he to preach on being a child anyway? Recently, he'd had little more than the professional insights of a preschooler, wanting to throw away a lucrative career in the geological industry for a business that would surely flop. What did he know about running a B&B? Not a thing. Without thinking, he said out loud, "Audrey is a vulnerable woman. Needy. She was abandoned as a child. Did I tell you that?"

Charlotte looked up at him. "Not that part. How tragic."

"The circumstances were pretty terrible. And now, I made a vow to her, you see, even before our marriage, that I would never leave her. So, even though the truth has finally been given to us, I don't see how it can change our situation. I can't—"

"I understand," Charlotte said. "It's very much who you are to be so honorable. I'm sure it's one of the things that made Audrey fall in love with you. I know it was one of the many reasons I fell in love with you."

"You still do then?" He caught her gaze. "You still have feelings for me after all this time?" His heart sped up just asking the question.

Charlotte winced and looked away.

It was an impossible question, one he shouldn't have asked. "I know it's not right to ask you. Not now."

"When I was little," Charlotte said, "I had one of those pretty snow globes that every little girl wants. When I'd shake it, bits of snow would swirl around this magical-looking castle. After I'd jiggled the thing for the hundredth time, I asked my mother if I could somehow get inside the toy and remove the castle. She said, 'yes, of course, but you'll have to destroy the globe to get to it.' Then, she said, 'And then you won't have a snow globe anymore . . . just the castle, which you might not think is so wonderful anymore.' "

"What are you saying?" Behind him, Sam held the railing in a viselike grip.

"It's just that sometimes it's not worth breaking the snow globe to get inside a dream. What if we forced it open now, broke it apart at the last hour, and the castle wasn't as glistening as you thought it would be?" Charlotte's voice faded, and her gaze seemed far away.

"Are you talking about love?" Sam felt a desperate need to understand her. "Are you saying that if we married now we'd be disappointed in the end?"

"No, I'm not talking about love. But when you mentioned about having children earlier, I should have told you something. It might make things easier for you to see how right it is for you to marry Audrey." Charlotte hugged her arms around her middle. "I've been to the doctor, and he says I'm experiencing early menopause. It's got a scary sounding name, but it's not dangerous. I doubt I'd be able to have children, though. Not now. I know how much you love kids. I'd never want to hold you back that way. I will be happy for you both. I promise."

"I've always thought adopting a child would be fulfilling," Sam said. "I think—"

"Sam." Charlotte picked up her hat, scooted off the bench, and walked to the edge of the gazebo. "We don't want to follow down the same path of my mother and your father. Although, I guess we don't know their whole story, do we? It makes me wonder about their past. You know, what led them astray? What made them so desperate?"

"We may never know what was lurking behind the affair." Except that they were being disloyal to their spouses and lying to their family and friends. That part was clear. But there might have been something more. Perhaps love had been snatched away from the couple in earlier years. Maybe that explained why his father was such an angry man. Maybe he thought he'd lost his one chance for love. Hmm. Given the right circumstances, Sam wondered if he could be guilty of the same thing someday. Since he was an engaged man, perhaps he was guilty even now—with Charlotte.

She gave the post a pat. "I need to get back inside. I will say one more thing, but then I won't speak of it again. Years later, after my parents passed away, both from cancer, and then your mother of diabetes, I realized the chance for a family scandal was over, so I did try to locate you. But someone told me you were settled and happy. That you'd moved to Dallas and you had a girlfriend there, so I just let you . . ." Charlotte's voice faded.

"I did live in Dallas for a few years, but then I came back to Houston. Closer to home, you see. And the girlfriend, Lily Gardener, well, we were . . . it just wasn't meant to be."

"Oh. I see." Charlotte nodded slowly and then reached out her hand to Sam. "Please, let's shake hands and wish each other well."

He took her hand in his and gave it a solid shake, almost too businesslike, but then he didn't let go. "What do you want, Lotty?"

Charlotte softened her expression when she heard the name he'd always given her.

"My eyes never could lie to you, Sam. You know what I want. You see it as clearly as that blue sky up there, but sometimes life moves on. Circumstances change. So now, I want to set aside my desires, and I want what's best for you . . . and for Audrey. As you've told me, Audrey's had a hard life, and I know for a fact that you're the one man who can make a difference. You can bring her the comfort and joy she's longing for. I release you. Go . . . and love her."

Sam let go of Charlotte's hand with great reluctance. She nodded as if releasing him to go out and live his separate life, but it was the loneliest feeling Sam had ever known. *Oh, Lord in heaven, what are we doing?* The chapel bells rang, but they brought no comfort. He reached into his pocket and pulled out a key. "I'd almost forgotten. I found this key in my room at the house. This is yours. I guess I need to give it back. It wouldn't be right to hold onto it any longer." He offered it to her.

Charlotte accepted the key and studied it. "I know what this is. I can't believe you kept it all this time."

"You gave it to me in high school. You said it was the key to your heart."

"It was just an old house key, and yet I gave it to you because. . . ." She grinned. "I was such a sentimentalist, wasn't I?"

A woman coughed, and they turned toward the sound.

"Audrey?" Sam said. "I didn't know you were coming into town."

"That photographer lady in the tearoom said I might find you out here." Audrey tucked one hand under her elbow while the other covered her mouth—a gesture she sometimes made right before she cried. "I think we need to talk."

"All right." Sam nodded. "You okay?"

33

*Y*eah, I'm okay." Audrey studied the flush all over Charlotte's face. There was no getting around it—Sam and Charlotte had been embroiled in an intimate talk. *Well, we're about to have one too.*

"Hi, Audrey," Charlotte said. She looked as though she might say more, but just smiled at her.

"Hello, Charlotte. By the way, congratulations on the cookbook. I heard."

"Thank you. Well, I need to get back inside." Charlotte headed to the tearoom cottage and left them alone.

"Why don't we walk," Sam said. "The gazebo is too confining."

"Good idea." They strolled down the rock path and out onto the street's main sidewalk. Audrey's breathing sped up so much she got a little lightheaded. She hated confrontation. "Let's go the residential way." The speech she'd memorized suddenly vanished in her head. Puffs of air cooled her face. That felt a little better. Even the smallest blessing was welcome, since what she had to say would not be easy.

Audrey glanced over at Sam's hands, which were just resting at his sides as they walked. It felt odd that they didn't automatically reach out to each other and hug or hold hands. They used to—before they'd moved to Middlebury. "I guess you had some things you felt you needed to say to Charlotte before the wedding?"

"I did. And now there are some things I need to say to you. Months ago, when we talked about people we'd dated in the past, I told you about Charlotte, but I didn't mention all of it. I want to clear the air . . . make things right, so we can get married without feeling like we're surrounded by secrets."

"This is a good time to share our stories." The path they took led them past homes and front yards, which all flaunted a profusion of spring color, of shrubs hanging heavily with blossoms. The green on the trees appeared so radiant that it almost hurt her eyes. They were in the throes of the new season, and yet she felt barren in her spirit.

When Sam finished telling her about the relationship he'd had with Charlotte in high school as well as his proposal, Audrey didn't expect to feel so much anger, but there it was just the same. "You should have told me at the beginning. You've never been devious about anything. But I can tell you this . . . I never would have hired Charlotte to do the food for our wedding had I known about this." Audrey pulled out the wedding invitation from her pocket and handed it to Sam.

He smoothed out the paper and gazed at it. "Where did this come from?"

Audrey explained how she'd come into possession of the invitation. By the time they were finished talking, they'd walked so far she thought they'd gotten lost. "Where are we?"

"We're fine. We're just on the east side of Middlebury." Sam reached out to Audrey and curled his hand around hers as they strolled along. "It was my responsibility to make sure you knew about what happened in the past. Without intending to,

I've hurt you, and I'm sorry." He stopped her and caught her gaze. "Will you forgive me?"

"Of course. Yes. It's impossible to refuse you when you say the words so genuinely."

Sam handed her the invitation back. "Well, I mean it, but you haven't heard the longest part of the story yet."

"Really? All right, but maybe we should head back."

They turned around, waited for a car to pull into a garage, and then headed back toward the center of town. As they walked, Sam told her about the secret affair between his father and Charlotte's mother. How his father disapproved of Charlotte's heritage, and how his father threatened her in hopes she would walk away from Sam's proposal of marriage. When he was finished with his extraordinary tale, he looked at her as if searching her thoughts.

"That's a really bleak story. I had no idea your father was so strange." Audrey stopped to pick up a pinecone on the sidewalk. "It must have been quite a blow for Charlotte. And I feel sorry for you too. With his dark way of looking at life, your father must have given you a perfectly awful childhood. And then when you grew up he destroyed a perfectly good love story. But it's a love story your father couldn't fully extinguish, no matter how hard he tried." Audrey reached up and touched Sam's cheek. "I've seen the light."

"The light?"

"In my chat with Meredith, she didn't go so far as to say that Charlotte was still in love with you, but she didn't need to. I see it in the light in her eyes every time she looks at you. And I can see the same light in your eyes too when you look at Charlotte."

"I'm sorry for that, but I intend to marry *you*, not Charlotte." Sam gently cradled his hands around hers as she held the pinecone.

"I know you are being sweet and gallant, and I'm moved by it. But if we go any more rounds, this is going to start having the tragic overtones of Romeo and Juliet, and it will be unnecessarily devastating."

"But I want to keep my—"

"I can't listen to any more of this. You don't love me, at least not the way you love Charlotte."

"But I love so many things about you, Audrey."

"That's not enough." Audrey pulled her hands away. "That's not really the definition of true love. I won't be reduced to a list of likeable qualities. I'm not a contestant in a beauty pageant. I'm supposed to be somebody's lover." How could she make him see? Perhaps the time had come for Sam to see other facets of Audrey Anderson. "I know why you won't leave me. It's because I made such a dramatic scene at the church that day in front of Pastor Wally during our marriage counseling. About the way I was abandoned as a child."

"What are you saying . . . that it wasn't true?" Sam looked at her with more intensity than she ever remembered.

"All of it is true, and I still carry the emotional scars to prove it. But over the years I discovered how to use my past to make my present a little easier. I learned how to manipulate a situation, using my history as leverage. I've always felt justified since it was true, and I believed I deserved to have what I wanted since no one cared a flying fig what I wanted growing up!"

Audrey realized she'd need to lower her voice or people might start looking out their windows at them. "I knew that my story coupled with your good character . . . well, let's just say that I knew you'd never break off our engagement. But that noble spirit of yours nearly cost us both a lifetime of happiness. Since you won't abandon me, I'm going to abandon you."

Her heart sped up again. Goodness, she'd need to calm herself. She hadn't necessarily planned to break off their engagement in one quick sweep. But now that she was headed down that road, it was too late to turn back. Audrey looked at the pinecone, noticed some missing and mangled scales, and dropped it back on the sidewalk.

"So, you're breaking off our engagement? But . . ." Sam's voice drifted away on the breeze. He was already gone from her. Perhaps in a moment or two he would already be thinking of Charlotte.

"Yes, that's what I'm doing." She should say the rest now—the truth about Justin—before she lost her courage. "I'm afraid you won't have such affectionate feelings toward me when you hear what I did."

"Did?" Sam asked. "What did you do?"

A little girl on a bicycle rode toward them on the sidewalk, and they separated to let her pass.

"Audrey, what did you do?" Sam asked again as he met her in the middle of the sidewalk.

"Over these last few weeks we've been spending less and less time together. Well, during some of those hours I wasn't always preparing for the wedding. I was in the greenhouse . . . with Justin. Oh, dear. This isn't as easy to talk about as I thought it would be."

"Justin? Yes, I knew you'd been spending time out there with him. Actually, I encouraged you to do it, since you enjoyed it so much. But it sounds like you mean something more. Let's walk. Maybe it will be easier for you to talk about it."

Audrey circled her arm though Sam's as they made their way back toward the center of town. "At first, we were just working in the greenhouse together, but then we shared walks around the pond. Somewhere in those days, it went beyond friendship."

"Really?" Sam asked. "You feel more for Justin than friendship?"

Audrey rested her head against him. "I was right about your character, Sam. You're so guileless you didn't even know what was happening. You didn't know that I was falling in love with Justin."

"I know you were fond of him, and you enjoyed some of the same things." Sam shook his head and said quietly, "But, no, I didn't see that coming."

"I know it seems kind of crazy, but there it is."

Sam stopped them both. "But does Justin have his act together? Would he be able to take care of you? Provide for you?" His brows furrowed.

"Still watching out for me. I will always love that about you." Audrey tugged on his sleeve. "But don't worry your brows too much. Well, you can a little . . . enough to pray for me . . . for us. Maybe what you're meant to be in my life is a brother. I certainly need one. I know I've always wanted a big brother." She turned away. "Let's stroll again, because I can't look into your eyes when I tell you this part."

They started up their walk and Audrey said, "Recently, when I was with Justin in the greenhouse, we kissed. Just once, but I knew instantly it was wrong and that I'd need to tell you about it."

"And here I thought you were in the greenhouse repotting the orchids." Sam coughed out a laugh. "Makes me feel pretty naive."

"I know it's shocking. It is to me too."

Sam rubbed his forehead. "It's just that I'm trying to imagine all this. Justin Yule was just a guy on the street a few days ago. He seems to be a decent man, and I'm very sorry for the tragedy in his past, but he admitted to us at Easter that he still had to find his way again. Are you sure you can handle that kind of instability? I wouldn't want to see you get hurt."

"That is so sweet of you. To be caring rather than angry. Frankly, I have no idea what kind of life Justin can give me. If he can provide for me at all. I only know how I feel." Audrey cringed at the simplistic sound of her words. "But I hope, and I pray it goes well for us . . . for all of us."

Audrey glanced down the street. The back of the tearoom was now in sight again. "I'm sorry I betrayed you. You didn't deserve that. Earlier when you were out in the garden chatting with Charlotte, I shouldn't have made you feel guilty. What you did was chaste. What I did was not. At least I assume you and Charlotte didn't kiss."

Sam stopped and tugged on her elbow to get her attention. "No, we didn't kiss. But the thought had crossed my mind." He brushed his finger across her chin, an affectionate gesture he'd done when they'd first started dating, which now seemed so long ago. "I'm sorry too."

Audrey latched onto Sam's arms and gave him a friendly shake. "Then we would have been fools to marry each other. I guess we convinced ourselves that we loved each other, and maybe we did a little. Who knows, we might have lived on it for a long time. We might have moved on from those torments of what could have been, and we would have found ourselves old and content. But maybe all the questioning and doubting would have driven us apart. Only God knows the answers. But now, there'll be no more need for wondering. The wait is over." Audrey slipped the engagement ring off her finger, placed it into Sam's palm, and closed his fingers around it. "We're free to follow our hearts now."

"Are you sure?"

"Yes."

"I'll accept the ring," Sam said, "but I want you to keep the Beemer. It was my gift to you, and it still is. No arguments."

"Really?" Audrey could hardly believe his generosity, but then again, she'd always known Sam had a heart as big as Texas. "Thank you. Truly. It's incredibly kind of you." She kissed him one last time on the cheek. Then she folded up the invitation and handed it to him. "But now you'd better get to it." She gestured toward The Rose Hill Cottage. "There's a woman in the tearoom who's been waiting for you . . . for a very long time."

34

It was one of the longest days of her life. Meredith had been avoiding Wally, but now she knew what she had to do—face the music. It was repentance time. So, with a sincere confession in her heart and on her lips, she drove to Middlebury Chapel.

Once parked and standing at the chapel door, though, her pinky finger, which had a long history of being skittish, trembled when she reached for the handle. She paused, released a tiny whimpering noise, and pulled on one of the big rustic doors.

Please, Lord, think forbearance. I love Wally, but now he might be tempted to loathe me instead of love me for what I did. I'd rather hide in a deep hole, one of biblical proportions, but I know you'd rather I didn't. So, here I am, Lord. I'm at your disposal. Which was a good place to be. Her grandmother once said, "Better to be slain by God than reign as queen on Satan's throne."

Meredith opened the door and walked inside. The smell of oiled wood and altar flowers welcomed her, and she could easily imagine the pipe organ swelling to its most stirring peaks. In this holy place anything seemed possible—even forgiveness.

Once back to reality, though, the organ sounds were replaced by her clogs as they clomped irreverently on the wooden floor like the heavy beat of pagan drums. Before desecrating the whole chapel she slipped off her shoes, walked up the aisle a few more rows, and then sat down in one of the middle pews. She would wait for Wally. *Mmm. What a pleasant thought—waiting for Wally.*

The chapel was empty, except for all the saints who watched from the stained-glass windows. Was it just her imagination, or did they seem to frown down on her today? Of course, she'd just learned from reading the Scriptures that even such a hallowed crowd of folks had known personal failure. Paul came to mind, a Bible character she'd recently discovered. He too wanted to do what was right, but he learned that carrying it out 24/7 was another matter entirely. Maybe she was in good company.

Meredith sat in an attitude of what her mother called quiet repose, which was something her fidgety mind and body had always had trouble with since the age of two. She tapped her fingers together, thinking it would be an excellent time to contemplate her recent peccadilloes, but her brain instead started a to-do list for the antique shop. When she realized her mind had dashed off again, she rolled her eyes and stopped toying with the list.

Birds warbled outside the window. Yes, those feathered friends were free to be themselves, and yet they were always in the perfect will of God. Maybe that was what she needed, to be confined to the limits of a bird's brain rather than live in the ever troubling open cage of free-will!

She pulled a bottle of antacids out of her purse, flipped the lid open on the container, and let several tablets spill into her mouth. Her tummy issues seemed to be getting worse. No surprise considering her recent delinquencies! She flicked off some nonexistent dust from her slacks and continued to ponder life as she waited for her appointment with Wally. But the wait got weightier as if she were receiving a spiritual audit—like the whole of her life was being examined—where she'd been, all that she'd done and said. *Goodness me.* If all the scenes of her life were laid out like belongings at a garage sale, it would surely look like a frightful heap of junk.

Did other people feel that way? Maybe the people of Middlebury went on their jolly way without concern for that dreaded ripple effect—the one that started the day a person was born. She knew the ripple effect very well since her own life left an undulating surge wherever she went. Perhaps along with love and marriage, what she really wanted was to have her passion for life funneled into a holy calling. And she wanted that purpose to be fulfilled with more wisdom than folly. "Amen."

Meredith heard footsteps and glanced toward the front of the church. She smiled. Wally.

He gave her a boyish wave. "Sorry if I interrupted you. Talking to God?"

"Or maybe he was talking to me."

"Good place for it." Wally strolled down the aisle. "Now, you've gotten my curiosity up as usual, wondering why you set up an appointment with me as if you're a member of the congregation."

"I am a member of your congregation."

"Yes, that's true." He grinned.

"Well, right now I need you to play the role of pastor for me."

"Now you've got me worried. You're not headed to prison, are you?" He chuckled.

"Not today." Meredith gave him an affectionate shoo when he approached her pew. "Don't sit next to me. I'll be so distracted I won't be able to make my confession. But don't you have a booth in the back or something like that, so I don't have to look right at you?"

"You're thinking of the Catholic church. They have confessionals. But we can go into my office if it'll make you feel more comfortable. It's so small it's almost the size of a confessional."

Meredith tucked her hands in her lap. "No, that's all right. I can do this. I've been practicing in the car."

"All right." After he sat down in front of her, he rested his arm on the back of his pew and turned to face her. "What's on your mind?"

"Well, it all started with Charlotte's baking. It was so intoxicating . . . the cake."

"Intoxicating?"

Meredith sighed. "No booze . . . much worse . . . pure butter. I think Charlotte needs a warning label on that stuff. Anyway, that's what started my moral decline."

Wally grinned.

She scooted closer to the edge of her pew. "You know how you told me to pray before I talked to Charlotte about the fact that Sam was about to marry the wrong woman?"

"Yes, I remember."

"Well, I did pray, and then I talked to her."

"Did it go well?"

Meredith looked at him. "I was right about everything."

"Really?"

"But Charlotte wasn't willing to talk to Sam, and so I decided to intervene."

"Oh?" Wally's fingers curled around the back of pew with a bit more fervor. "Do you want to tell me about it?"

"No, I don't want to, but I'm going to tell you because it's excellent penance for me." She ran her finger back and forth along the hymnal in front of her, wishing she didn't have to look at Wally while she told him her tale of woe, but there was no escape.

For Meredith the next few minutes played out like a car wreck in slow motion as she told her beloved pastor and friend and sweetheart about Charlotte's wedding invitation. She watched every nuance of his expression, searching for irritation or reprimand, but instead, he appeared to listen with care and compassion. When the dust settled from her verbal wreck, there had been no lightning bolts and no disparaging scowls. But still wanting to know his immediate thoughts, she gripped the pew in front of her and asked, "I have to know. Do you hate me for what I did?"

"No, of course not." Wally shifted in his pew. "It was a pretty bold gesture I admit, and I suppose from the outside it might look like a malicious prank, but I know your intention was good. And I did love the way you drove back to tell Audrey the truth and to apologize. There are so few people who can do that easily. Some don't do it at all."

Meredith groaned. "Don't give me too much credit. It wasn't easy."

"But you did it anyway. I mean, yes, what you did was pretty unorthodox. I usually recommend people just talk things through. But now that the information is out there, maybe all four of them will have some real discussion before the wedding. That's what they needed. I wish I'd noticed hints of these problems during Sam and Audrey's premarital counseling. Maybe I need to lengthen my session. Or make it several sessions." Wally smoothed his mustache with his finger. "But I believe some good might come from this."

"So, you don't hate me?" Meredith asked.

"No, of course not." Wally placed his hand over hers. "Why are you about to cry?"

"Because I'm so grateful." Meredith leaned over, took Wally's face into her hands, and kissed him full on the mouth.

When the kiss was over, he hovered close and whispered, "And what was that for?"

"For being such a good pastor."

Wally laughed. "Well, I've never gotten *that* reaction from anybody else in the congregation."

"I'm glad."

He grinned. "I'm glad for so many things. One being that a woman named Cricket decided to move to Middlebury and rent a shop."

"I hope you know, this is home now. Middlebury is. There's just no place else like it."

"I'm really happy to hear it." Wally rose from the pew. "By the way, how did you get such an adorable nickname?"

"I've had it most of my life. As you know, crickets are noisy and pesky, but in some parts of the world they're considered the most delightful creatures." Meredith batted her eyelashes.

"And *that* you are. I guess this means we're back to being sweethearts then?"

She gave him her most innocent look. "If you'll still have me after what I did."

"Of course I will." Wally walked around to her pew. "I need to know something, though. In the future, are you always going to be so crazy-impulsive and passionate and hopelessly wonderful?" He leaned toward her with the look of pretend rebuke.

Meredith couldn't think of anything else to do but scrunch up her shoulders and reply, "Maybe."

"Good. I wouldn't have you any other way." He sat down next to her and smiled. "But just to keep the deacons from having to up their heart medication, when you know you're about to go on another crime spree maybe we could chat about it first." He kissed the tip of her nose. "Would that be okay?"

"More than okay. I'm getting too old for this life of crime. I surrender. But I'm so glad you understand me. That blessing alone must be worth about a million bucks in antiques."

"I think it was Oscar Wilde who said that women are meant to be loved, not to be understood, but I think you can't love until you do understand."

Meredith reached up and smoothed a curl that draped over Wally's forehead. "So, will that go into Sunday's sermon?"

Wally gazed at her. "Sorry, I have no idea what you just said. I sort of get lost in those big brown eyes of yours, and then I'm left in this helpless state."

"Well, while you're not listening let me say that you have this swirl of hair that will not acquiesce to my touch. It's like this Superman curl, so I'm thinking maybe I'll leave it alone in case it would alter all those special powers of yours. At least I found out today that you're Superman to me." Meredith left his unruly tuft of hair and caressed his cheek with her palm instead. "By the way I have a gift for you."

"You do?"

Meredith opened her purse, pulled out a small decorative box, and nestled it in the palms of his hands. "To Wally."

"Thank you." He opened the lid. "It's a dreidel."

"You knew." *What a dear.* "You may also know then that it's a spinning top. It's a toy I played with during Hanukkah when I was a child. I wanted you to have it as a keepsake."

Wally looked at her, making her heat up and chill all at the same time.

"I will consider it a treasure." Wally leaned over and kissed her. "You are such a darling. What am I going to do with you?"

"Why don't you marry her?" came a gruff voice from behind them.

They both turned around. Surprise lit their faces as they rose to greet Mr. LaGrange.

35

Audrey packed her bags and then hurried straight to the greenhouse. She searched the aisles and the orchid room and then the koi pond and the outdoor gardens. She knocked on the door of Justin's apartment above the garage until her knuckles were raw. Justin had no car, but he appeared to have vanished. She ran back to the greenhouse and called out to him until her voice reached a feverish pitch.

Where had he gone? Justin loved the greenhouse in the evening. It was his favorite time of day to work. Surely he hadn't slipped back to his old ways or gone back to the streets. No, she was making hasty assumptions. Bad habit. He would never be so foolish as to return to a life that had no future. No hope. No love. But people did tend to seek out what they were comfortable with even when it wasn't the right thing. It was the same thing she'd done with Sam—over and over she'd run into his arms because it was the most comfortable place to be, even it wasn't the right place.

Audrey fingered an empty clay pot, which sat on the edge of the worktable. Her mistake about Sam had been an easy one to make. He would have been a good husband and father, though, and they both enjoyed each other's company. All in all, he was a good match, and yet now she could see that their relationship had taken on a tone of friendship rather than of lovers. She and Sam had wrapped up their marriage story with wedding bows, but then when she met Justin, all those pretty ribbons began to come undone and the paper was, well, only paper. The first stirrings of love with Justin had thrown out all her old notions of how love and marriage should be.

But where *was* Justin? She stared at the clay pot. Feeling desolate in his absence, she gave the pot just enough of a push to make it teeter on the edge of the table. After a brief hesitation, the pot fell and clattered into pieces.

Audrey lowered herself to the floor and put her head in her hands. What would she do now? To know that first blush of love felt like pure joy, and yet the idea that Justin might have fled was unbearable. Such a swing of emotions. If real love was part marvelous, it also had to be part insanity as well!

She let her misery flow into tears. Perhaps if Justin had gone he wasn't well enough to build a solid relationship with her. He had alluded to that possibility when they talked. More than alluded. He had warned her over and over. She was never too good at listening. But it was too late. What did she have now? Nothing and no one. She was like Sam's toy train when he was little—going round and round, hurrying nowhere. She had risked everything for Justin. But she couldn't go back to Sam. That part of her life was over. She absently checked her iPhone for messages. Nothing. Again. *That's because you have no friends, Audrey. Why would you?*

The word *selfish* came to mind. The definition was "to be devoted to one's own personal needs." Wasn't that just rich? It had become her whole philosophy of living. Coming from her background, no one would have known better than she how to care for the needs of others, and yet she had turned inward and bitter, grabbing anything and everything in sight that might ensure her own happiness. The next word that came to mind was *worthless*. And it too seemed as real as the building that surrounded her and the love she'd driven away. Did she even deserve to keep on living?

Oh, how lovely to be Alice in her wonderland, where you could drink a potion and make yourself smaller. So small that you could still see the world, but no one could see you.

The light in the greenhouse dimmed as a cloud passed over the sun. A shadowy memory, whether real or imagined, she didn't know for sure, suddenly eclipsed her thoughts. Flashes of dark places and hurried voices and the sensations of being trapped teased her and then tormented her. Would she never be free of the past?

Audrey picked up one of the shards of pottery that sat next to her on the floor and stared at it. The sharp edge and the needle-like point seemed to be waiting for her, as if it had broken that way for one reason. The shard had a wrathful look to it, and yet it was somehow inviting.

So many times in her youth, there had been that temptation of an early closure. Each time the desire came, the lure was always the same. Something seemed to whisper in her ear, telling her it was the only way out, it was inevitable, and that it was even noble. She grazed the shard of pottery across her wrist, but left no more than a faint mark on her skin. But the second time, Audrey pressed harder.

That is not the way.

Audrey startled. What was that? "Hello? Who's there?" Was it an audible voice or words spoken only in her mind? She had no idea, but the sound frightened her. She tossed the piece of pottery away, and it disappeared underneath the table. Audrey shivered, thinking about what could have happened so easily.

Then another voice came. "Audrey?"

Justin? "Justin, is that you?"

He appeared at the end of the aisle and quickened his pace. "Are you all right? What are you doing on the floor?"

"Where did you go? I called out to you earlier, but you didn't come." Audrey lifted her hands up to him, and in one sweep, Justin helped her to her feet. "I've been so worried about you."

Justin motioned outside. "I was just cleaning up one of the gardenia beds." He set the CD player and ear buds on the table. "Sometimes I listen to classical music when I'm working. I didn't hear you." He looked at the broken pot on the floor. "Did you hurt yourself?"

"No."

"You've been crying." He touched her face. "Please tell me why."

Audrey put her hands behind her and rested against the table. "Sam and I broke things off."

"Really?" Justin stepped closer to her. "Was it because of our kiss? Did—"

"No, it wasn't. Needless to say, Sam was shocked when I told him what we did, but you see, the news wasn't all that devastating, because Sam is in love with someone else."

"Charlotte?"

"You knew? How?"

"That day on the chapel steps," Justin said. "Before you arrived, we had a few minutes to visit. And he opened up. He shared a doubt or two. And he mentioned Charlotte."

"What did he say about her?" Audrey waved her hand. "No, no. I no longer want to know. But why didn't you tell me?"

"Because later I thought Sam might have just had a case of cold feet. Lots of couples have doubts before their wedding day, even couples who turn out to be happily married. I had doubts before I married my wife, and it was a good marriage. So, I wasn't going to ruin your chances with Sam."

"Oh." Her charm bracelet suddenly pinched her skin, so she rolled it off her wrist and set it on the table. "I don't know whether to be angry or relieved over your confession."

"Don't be angry . . . please."

"All right. I won't." It would have been tempting to be upset with Sam, but she knew too well why he hadn't wanted to call off the wedding that day with Pastor Wally. It was because of the ropes she'd tightened around his heart by telling him about her fears. "I'm the one who called off the wedding."

"You did?"

Audrey released a nervous laugh. "Just weeks ago I would have told you the chances of me doing something like that were impossible. I'm always so careful not to do anything that would cause me to be left behind. But I couldn't stop myself. That's how much I believed in you . . . in us."

"It was brave." Justin picked up her bracelet and smiled. "But why are you hiding your hands? Are you still trembling?"

Audrey lifted her hands up to show him.

"Steady as the cedar beams above us." He took her hands into his. "And the ring is gone." He kissed her left hand.

"I gave it back." Even though the ring had weighed very little, she felt much lighter and freer without it. "Now I'll tell you why I was crying. Even though I believed in what we can be together, I was afraid you'd decided to walk away. It's hard to forget your words. You said it wasn't the right time to be worried about a wife or even a girlfriend who might need to prop you up in some way. That you didn't want to be a burden to anyone."

Justin caught her gaze. "Well, I'm happy to say I've changed my mind. *You've* changed my mind . . . my whole life." He drew her into an embrace. "My darling," he said into her hair. "It's been hard to think of anything else since that day on the chapel steps. You're like the cattleya orchid . . . unforgettable."

"Really?"

"But all that joy didn't feel right, since I betrayed Sam. You were another man's wife-to-be. *His* wife-to-be."

"I understand. But I'm no longer attached. I'm free to be yours."

Justin lifted her off the ground, swung her around, and gently set her down.

She ran her hands along his arms. They were strong from hard work, but they weren't what she needed to be whole, to be safe. Only God could provide that. "We are so much alike. But I don't want to live in the shadow of my childhood anymore. It's so oppressive. I've let my past manipulate people and bathe my life in fear. I want to be free. We could be such an encouragement to each other."

Justin gave her shoulders a gentle squeeze. "It's intriguing you should mention this new direction, because as I was tending the gardenias . . . I had the thought that it's not right for me to squander the rest of my life, trying to pay back a life debt. It doesn't help anyone, and it can't bring my wife back or the baby. But as long as I'm still here, still breathing, I want to make a difference, and I see now that I have the ability to do that. It would be immoral, not righteous for me to throw away any opportunities to help people. To inspire people. And to give my heart away."

"And you got all of that out of being with the gardenias?"

"They were very inspiring gardenias." Justin grinned.

"It sounds like we've been given visions at the same time. Do you think it's a sign?"

"It very well could be."

Audrey gazed at him. Yes, he was still the same charismatic man she'd always seen on TV, but it wasn't the celebrity or the fine features or even the curious way she could connect to his past that attracted her. It was just Justin Yule.

He leaned down and kissed her, and the moment, sweet and impassioned, eclipsed all others. She wished it could go on forever, but she knew the end had already arrived. She no longer belonged here, not in the greenhouse or on the Wilder estate, and the earnest desire to leave, to start a new life, grew stronger by the minute.

Audrey drew away. "You've created paradise here, Justin, and I'd like to stay right here with you. Just like this. But we'll need to go. Sam didn't ask me when we'd be leaving, but it would be uncomfortable for us to stay any longer."

"It's all right," Justin said. "I've put a lot of thought into what I'll be doing now . . . where I'll be working. I might like to give the show another try. They did say if I ever wanted to come back, the door was always open to me. I also thought it'd be fun to teach some high school biology classes. I have a teaching degree."

"What a wonderful idea."

"I have very little to pack, but do you need any help?" Justin asked.

"No, I'm ready to go." Audrey glanced under the worktable and on a lower shelf sat Justin's sketchbook. She lifted it from its hiding place. "May I?"

Justin nodded.

Audrey slowly opened the book to the back. There were new drawings, and they were very different from his earlier work. "Ohh, my." A single white orchid, the same kind Justin had placed in her hair on the day they first kissed, was sketched in full bloom, but more than that, it was rendered with such effusive shapes and sumptuous textures, Audrey found herself wanting to breathe the orchid's perfume or pluck it from the page. "This is so . . . exquisite." Audrey closed the book and hugged it to her as if it were Justin.

He took a step closer to her. "This is how you inspire me."

"It is?"

"Have you ever seen a work of art that was so beautiful and stirring it made your heart ache?"

Audrey thought for a moment when she'd visited the art museums in Houston. "Yes, I have."

"Well, that is the way you make me feel." He slipped the book from her hands and set it on the table. Then he took her face into his palms and said, "Now I'm going to kiss you the way you inspire me." And he did.

When the velvet curtain of his kiss came to a luxuriant close, Audrey grinned.

"*Now* we can go." Justin took her by the hand and led her from the greenhouse and into a cloudless spring day.

The bright sun reminded her of a thousand mirrors reflecting and flashing all around her. Such a simple thing, sunlight, but such a thing of beauty.

On their way through a small meadow, Justin gathered a bouquet of dandelions and handed them to Audrey. She blew them into the breeze and stopped to watch the seeds as they drifted off like floating parasols. "Maybe that's what we need, little umbrellas to help us fly where we need to be."

"And where do you want to fly away to, my little love?" Justin asked, kissing her hand.

"It doesn't matter . . . as long as we're together."

As they walked hand in hand, their chatter echoed with hope and laughter—with plans for the future.

36

Charlotte waited on the bridge over Middlebury Creek—the same bridge where Sam had proposed nineteen years earlier. But now she waited with the hope that he was about to re-create the same event, only this time there would be no unhappy ending, no interference from Mr. Wilder. No more threats or disapproval. And if tears came, they would be from joy and not despair.

She leaned on the railing and breathed in the scent of euca-lyptus. It was the time of day that if one listened to the quiet long enough it came to life with earth sounds—like the chirp-ing of the night birds and the singing of the bugs. She gazed down into the water that burbled and flowed underneath the bridge. It would surely find its way to other nooks and crannies of her beloved town and far beyond. She grinned, thinking of Sam. So much had gone past, and yet there was so much more to come. When he'd nearly burst into the tearoom earlier that day, he'd taken her to the side and told her what had happened—that Audrey had called off the wedding, and that he had something important to ask her. Unfortunately it was all she could squeeze out of Sam at the time, but then it might have been because the lady photographer was standing so close by, listening in. The woman could have been sitting on their laps!

Charlotte chuckled and glanced at her watch. Five more minutes. Another five minutes seemed like an impossible amount of time to wait on Sam, but then it felt as though she'd already waited a lifetime for him.

She took the river stone from her pocket and rolled it around in her palm, looking at it one last time. It had been a pretty rock, one that Sam had found for her in this very creek just before he'd proposed. Over the years the stone had been a pleasant memento, reminding her of the smooth things in life that brought delight, but it had become a burden to her as well. Lately, it had become too heavy to carry. Charlotte pulled back and threw the rock into the rushing water. The moment would be remembered as a turning point, a letting go of the past. Of all the weight God had lifted from her life.

But what was that noise, that wailing sound she heard? Was it a show tune, of all things?

Sam, her Sam, strode up the path, belting out the song, "Some Enchanted Evening," so loudly and so off-tune it was as frightening as it was endearing. His grin beamed brighter than the streetlamp. "Charlotte. You're here."

"Of course I'm here."

He opened his arms, and she ran into them. He enfolded her like he had done so many years ago. She wasn't sure how long they stayed that way, but to Charlotte it would never be long enough.

"Everything about you is velvety," he whispered.

"It's the clothes. They're old."

Sam chuckled. "I love the way you dress. It's so soft. So you."

"Thanks." Well, maybe upgrading her look hadn't been as vital as she'd thought. When Charlotte eased out of his embrace, she said, "Earlier I was concerned that the wedding being called off so suddenly had caused some hurt, but I see your smile and the way you hold me, and I think I have my answer."

"Audrey and I are both relieved, and now we're both much happier."

"But it all happened so quickly." Charlotte shook her head. "I mean, one minute Audrey is talking about her wedding reception, and then she's called it off. What made her change her mind?"

"Well, she could sense something wasn't right, since we sort of lit up when we were in the same room together. And come to find out, that same thing was happening with Audrey . . . and Justin."

"Justin? My goodness. I didn't know." Charlotte remembered Easter Sunday and how ecstatic Audrey looked when she saw Justin. "Well, come to think of it, maybe I did see it coming."

"Well, I didn't. Guess that makes me as aware and as observant as pile of dirt. But then maybe I was so busy gazing at you I didn't even notice what was happening with Audrey. We humans are an appalling lot. Aren't we? The way we mishandle the gift of love."

"How true."

"You asked why Audrey changed her mind so quickly." Sam pulled out a piece of paper from his pocket and held it up in front of her. "Actually, it started with this crumpled piece of paper."

When Charlotte unfolded the paper and realized it was the wedding invitation she'd made in high school, she gasped. "How in the world did you—"

Sam held up two fingers. "Two words. Meredith Steinberg."

"What? But I wadded this up and threw it in the trash. When I knew you two would be married, it no longer seemed right to hold onto it. I felt the only healthy thing to do was to get rid of any reminders of the past. You know, so I could support you and Audrey in your decision. Or at least I could try." She held up the invitation. "But this means Meredith pulled it out of the trash while I was in the bathroom and then gave it to you."

"Not quite. I got this from Audrey. Apparently, Meredith put this in an envelope and mailed it to Audrey. That's how all of this got started."

"I had no idea Meredith was capable of such devious and divine behavior." Charlotte grinned, thinking of her friend that evening. "I don't know whether we should rail at her or hug her."

"I get the impression she feels terrible about what she did. It was pretty impulsive."

"To say the least." Charlotte leaned against the railing, trying to take it all in.

"It could have blown up in Meredith's face, but as it turned out it got everyone talking. That was just what we needed." Sam leaned against the railing next to Charlotte.

"Instead of razzing her about it, maybe I should throw her a party to thank her." Charlotte looked upward, and Sam followed her gaze. The gray clouds opened up like shutters on the evening sky and revealed a full moon in all its radiant glory. *Such a glimpse of heaven.*

Sam rested his hand over hers on the railing. "So, I guess it didn't work out with Doctor Lou Maverick, podiatrist extraordinaire?"

"Pediatrics." Charlotte gave him a droll look and chuckled. "No, it most certainly did not work out with Lou."

"Well, I for one am very thankful to hear it. Now may we talk about *us*?"

"Yes, please."

"Good." Sam slipped his arm around her waist. "Here's the thing, Miss Hill. I love you. I always have, and I always will."

"What a lovely rhyme."

"I worked on it all the way over here."

Charlotte grinned. "And I love you, Mr. Wilder."

"Okay, so there's a question I have to ask you, and it won't wait any longer. But it has to be on the bridge." Sam swept her up in his arms, which made Charlotte laugh merrily. He carried her to the middle of the arched bridge and set her down. Then he knelt on one knee and took her hand in his. "Are you ready?"

"I've never been more ready for anything in my life." Oh, how she'd dreamed of this moment. A hundred times. Perhaps a thousand times.

"Well then . . . Charlotte Rose Hill." Sam smiled. "Will you do me the honor of becoming my wife?"

Charlotte nodded. "Yes. Oh, yes. I will. I do. All the above."

Sam chuckled. He rose and pulled a ruby ring out of his pocket. "I didn't have time today to shop for just the right ring, so we'll use my grandmother's engagement ring until I can take you to Tiffany's tomorrow in Houston."

"Tiffany's?"

"Yes, Tiffany's all the way." He slipped the ruby ring on her finger.

"Oh, Sam, but this ring is perfect." She stared at it, admiring its loveliness. "It's so elegant. This is all I would ever need."

"I knew you'd say that, but I want more for you. This has been a long wait. A painful wait. There's been suffering on your part that never should have been. I want to make up for what my father did to you. And for my own failure in not fighting for you when I had the chance. It's like I'm not worthy to be the hero in anyone's story, especially not yours. So, I promise you that I'll spend the rest of my life trying to—"

Charlotte rested one finger on his lips to quiet his self-reproach. "My Sam. I love you for wanting to make up for the past. I will go with you to Tiffany's tomorrow. But I don't want you to think we have to spend our lives making up for what happened. There's no reason for guilt. And if there really was any guilt to be tossed around then some of it should be thrown my way for not putting up a struggle. But God is giving us the rest of our lives together. And what we will make of these years will be lovely."

"It most certainly will." Sam raised his hands in front of her, and instinctively she lifted her hands as well, just as they'd done when they were eighteen. They placed their outstretched hands together, palm to palm, and interlaced their fingers.

She smiled, knowing what was coming next. "I've dreamed of this countless times."

"And so have I . . . Lotty." Sam leaned down to kiss her. And what a kiss it was. It was an extravagant, marquee, diamond-on-black-velvet kiss. Tiffany's all the way.

When they finally came up to share the earth's air again, Charlotte rested her head on his shoulder. "That was pretty wonderful stuff."

"Even better than I remembered it."

She smiled at his words and snuggled into the spot just under his neck where she had always fit. "Sam?"

"Yes?"

Charlotte tugged on his shirt collar, knowing there was still a question troubling her. "I know we both want to have children, and I know trying will be a lot of fun . . . but if the doctor is right about my early menopause, are you sure you don't mind adopting?"

"I don't mind at all. As a matter of fact, I was thinking of Obie. I've seen the way he looks up to you like a mother. And I think he's a great kid."

Charlotte looked at Sam and smiled. "I'm so glad you've said that, and even though I know Obie loves Roberta, I know they're both hoping he can find a permanent home."

"Well, as soon as we come back from our honeymoon we'll look into it."

"And where are you taking me, Mr. Wilder?"

"Wherever you want to go, my love. How about Provence? I think it was made for honeymoons."

"To have tea in Provence with you isn't anything I could ever pass up."

"Then Provence it is." He looked across the street. "I see the bakery is still open. Do you want to have some espresso and stay up half the night talking like we used to?"

"Yes." Mist formed and a single tear tumbled down her face. "Oh, Sam, I missed you."

"And I you."

They leaned forward and rested their foreheads together as they had done in their youth, when their hearts were full of love, and when words were no longer enough.

"So, my love, we've broken that snow globe you talked about. We just have the castle. I hope you think it's just as wonderful. Just as glistening."

"It's so shimmery I may have to put on some sunglasses."

Sam chuckled.

In the midst of their sweet musings and laughter, Charlotte thought of the tearoom and all the gossip that would soon arise over Audrey's change of plans and Sam's switch in fiancées. "All over Middlebury, and especially in the tearoom, people will be asking us, 'Why did you and Audrey call off the wedding?' So, what do you think we should say to them?"

Sam grinned. "I guess we should say . . . that love got in the way of the wedding."

37

The day was overcast and muggy—not even the smallest sun-burst could to be seen—but it didn't matter. The little chapel near the town square overflowed with so many people and so much joy, to Charlotte, it was the loveliest, holiest, May morn-ing she'd ever lived inside.

Charlotte stood outside the arched oak doors with Mr. LaGrange by her side. He'd graciously agreed to give her away, a job he took on with sober determination, figuratively speak-ing as well as literally.

Charlotte smoothed her veil. "Almost time. You're doing great."

He swallowed loud enough to hear. "Well, thanks, but I haven't done anything yet." He daubed at his forehand with his handkerchief and then his eyes. "I'm as nervous as that kitten Obie gave me."

Charlotte smiled at him. "Neither one of us has hyperven-tilated from excitement, so I'd say you're holding me up well."

He chuckled, and his shoulders relaxed.

The pipe organ began to play, and the lofty music of Bach's "Jesu, Joy of Man's Desiring" greeted them at the door like a host of angels at the pearly gates.

"Here we go."

Mr. LaGrange offered his arm, and Charlotte grasped it. Then together, they started their holy march before God and man.

The moment they stepped foot inside the chapel, the crowd stood, which brought a pleasant swooshing thunder to the sanctuary, a sound that Charlotte loved. Now the thunder was for her.

Drenched in smiles, Charlotte glanced over the crowd, at the many friends she'd made over the years. They were all there to rejoice with her and with Sam. And she couldn't miss the beaming glow that radiated off Meredith. She would be impossible to live with now, of course, since her friend had been right about her matchmaking intuitions. She even overheard Meredith saying that Middlebury was in desperate need of a good yenta. *Lord, have mercy.* What was to come, she had no idea. She winked at her friend.

Charlotte took a deep breath. In minutes she would no longer be the bride-to-be, but Mrs. Sam Wilder. Goodness, gracious. Could anyone be as happy as she was today? Not likely.

She gave Mr. LaGrange's arm a squeeze. He was still breathing and walking. All was well. She wanted to close her eyes and then open them again to make certain it wasn't a dream. But she didn't dare, since she might trip in her beautiful Vera Wang gown.

The flicker of candles, the fragrance of roses, and the music of heaven made for a heady moment, but none of those trimmings could compare to the eagerness and rapture of gazing toward the front of the chapel and locking eyes with Sam Wilder. Oh, how she loved that man. There he stood, hands folded, dressed like a prince, and grinning from head to toe.

And as sure as scent on jasmine, Sam was there waiting for her. Just loving her.

Epilogue

In the end, Sam and Charlotte didn't sell the Wilder mansion, but opened it up as a B&B, and The Wilder Inn became the county's premiere Bed and Breakfast. Sam runs the books and the staff while Charlotte runs the kitchen. Since Charlotte wanted to devote more time to the B&B and give herself ample time to work on her cookbook, she sold two-thirds interest in the tearoom to Nelly and Lucy. The Rose Hill Cottage Tearoom became Three Friend's Tearoom, and even though customers were nervous about all the changes at first, the townspeople eventually came back in droves.

Sam and Charlotte adopted Obie, and now when he isn't in school or playing or being loved on, Charlotte gives him the important job of serving tea to the customers in the library, which he does with butler solemnity and only occasional giggles. Obie no longer feels the need to spend his spare time hiding in small places, so he funnels his energy and imagination into writing science fiction stories, using the patrons at the B&B as the characters in his ongoing adventures.

After a few short weeks of dating, Justin and Audrey eloped and moved to Houston where Justin returned to his job as the Plant Doctor on local television, and where Audrey took a job managing a flower shop. In her spare time, Audrey now offers a free class to disadvantaged kids, entitled, "All Things Growing, Including Me."

Pastor Wally and Meredith continue to frolic through the delight-laden fields of courtship, but a reliable rumor through Middlebury's grapevine confirms that an announcement of nuptials might come as early as Christmas.

Or sooner if Meredith has her way . . .

A Note to Readers

More than a decade ago I met a woman named Linda Becker who opened a tearoom in the Houston burbs called, Tea for Two. Her eatery and gift shop did so well, she opened a second shop. Over the years I've enjoyed her wonderful tearoom fare as well as the quaint ambiance. Linda's tearoom isn't just a café—it's a gathering place for friends, a place to eat home-cooked food, and a place so cozy you don't want to leave.

As a writer I thought it might be fun to create a heroine who owns a tearoom similar to Linda's and set her shop in a small town on the Gulf coast of Texas. So, that's how the novel, *A Marriage in Middlebury*, was born. Even though my story, the characters, and the town are fictional, Linda's tearooms are real places you can visit and enjoy. Thank you, Linda, for the great food, and the fellowship, and the inspiration.

Anita Higman

Discussion Questions

1. At the young and vulnerable age of eighteen, Charlotte Rose Hill found herself embroiled in a moral dilemma. Have you ever been caught inside an ethical impasse, one that made you feel as though there were no escape? How did you react, and how did the problem get resolved?

2. Meredith Steinberg believed that the people she cared about were going to make a tragic mistake in their lives because they weren't communicating well with each other. She chose a unique and comical way to get their attention. Would you have chosen a different way to handle the situation?

3. Have you ever had spiritual doubts like Mr. LaGrange? Did someone show up in your life like Charlotte as an encourager?

4. What were some of the ways that Justin Yule and Audrey Anderson grew as characters throughout the story? Do you think they still had a long way to go in their emotional and spiritual journeys?

5. Sam Wilder was also caught in a moral dilemma, since he struggled with his love for Charlotte while wanting to protect Audrey from rejection and abandonment. Do you think some of the impetus behind Sam's compassion came from his own feelings of abandonment from his father?

6. Because of what Audrey suffered growing up, sometimes she felt like she was just pretending at life, and these feelings of inadequacy made her become bitter and at times petty. How do you think God would want us to handle painful events from our past?

7. Did Justin think that the unhappy life he'd created for himself could somehow atone for the accident, an accident that he'd mistaken for an unforgivable sin? Do you think he was trying to play God by redeeming himself from the past?

8. Nelly Washington endured Percy Wilder's cruelty for many years. Have you known people who harbor this same kind of racial bigotry in their hearts? Why do you think people continue to cling to these prejudices concerning the color of a person's skin?

9. Do you think the story portrayed small-town life accurately? What are some of the upsides and downsides to living in a small town? to living in the city? Which place do you love the most and why?

10. Charlotte had a prayer closet. Have you ever had a special place like this where you could shut out the world and meet with God?

Want to learn more about author
Anita Higman and check out other great
fiction from Abingdon Press?

Sign up for our fiction newsletter at
www.AbingdonPress.com
to read interviews with your favorite authors, find tips
for starting a reading group, and stay posted on what
new titles are on the horizon. It's a place to connect
with other fiction readers or post a
comment about this book.

Be sure to visit Anita online!

www.AnitaHigman.com

Abingdon Press fiction
a novel approach to faith

Plan your escape.

What They're Saying About...

The Glory of Green, by Judy Christie
"Once again, Christie draws her readers into the town, the life, the humor, and the drama in Green. *The Glory of Green* is a wonderful narrative of small-town America, pulling together in tragedy. A great read!"
—Ane Mulligan, editor of *Novel Journey*

Always the Baker, Never the Bride, by Sandra Bricker
"[It] had just the right touch of humor, and I loved the characters. Emma Rae is a character who will stay with me. Highly recommended!"
—Colleen Coble, author of *The Lightkeeper's Daughter* and the *Rock Harbor* series

Diagnosis Death, by Richard Mabry
"Realistic medical flavor graces a story rich with characters I loved and with enough twists and turns to keep the sleuth in me off-center. Keep 'em coming!"—**Dr. Harry Krauss, author of *Salty Like Blood* and *The Six-Liter Club***

Sweet Baklava, by Debby Mayne
"A sweet romance, a feel-good ending, and a surprise cache of yummy Greek recipes at the book's end? I'm sold!"—**Trish Perry, author of *Unforgettable* and *Tea for Two***

The Dead Saint, by Marilyn Brown Oden
"An intriguing story of international espionage with just the right amount of inspirational seasoning."—***Fresh Fiction***

Shrouded in Silence, by Robert L. Wise
"It's a story fraught with death, danger, and deception—of never knowing whom to trust, and with a twist of an ending I didn't see coming. Great read!"—**Sharon Sala, author of *The Searcher's Trilogy: Blood Stains, Blood Ties,* and *Blood Trails*.**

Delivered with Love, by Sherry Kyle
"Sherry Kyle has created an engaging story of forgiveness, sweet romance, and faith reawakened—and I looked forward to every page. A fun and charming debut!"—**Julie Carobini, author of *A Shore Thing* and *Fade to Blue*.**

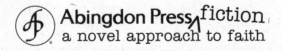 Abingdon Press fiction
a novel approach to faith

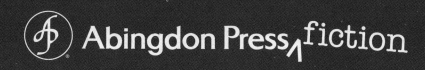

Discover Fiction from Abingdon Press

BOOKLIST 2010

Top 10 Inspirational Fiction award

ROMANTIC TIMES 2010

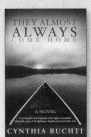

Reviewers Choice Awards
Book of the Year nominee

BLACK CHRISTIAN BOOK LIST

#1 for two consecutive months,
2010 Black Christian Book
national bestseller list;
ACFW Book of the Month, Nov/Dec 2010

CAROL AWARDS 2010

(ACFW) Contemporary
Fiction nominee

INSPY AWARD NOMINEES

Suspense

General Fiction

Contemporary Fiction

Abingdon Press fiction
a novel approach to faith
AbingdonPress.com | 800.251.3320

FBM112220001 PACP01002597-01